CHIRICAHUA

Other novels by Alfred Dennis

CHIRICAHUA

A Novel

by

Alfred Dennis

Walnut Creek Publishing
Tuskahoma, Oklahoma

CHIRICAHUA

This novel is a work of fiction. Names, characters, places, and incidents are either the product of the author's imagination or are used fictitiously. Any resemblance to actual events , locales, organizations, or persons, living or dead, is entirely coincidental and beyond the intent of either the author or the publisher.

ISBN: 978-0-9893241-8-2
Second Edition, Revised, Paperback
Published 2014 by Walnut Creek Publishing
Editing by KD Galbraith
10 9 8 7 6 5 4 3 2
1. Native American Fiction 2. Action/Adventure 3. Western

Books may be purchased in quantity and/or special sales by contacting the publisher;
Walnut Creek Publishing
PO Box 820
Talihina, OK 74571
www.wc-books.com

I would like to thank my dear wife, Jimmie, for all the support and encouragement. And my brother, Billy Tedreck, for making this book possible.

CHAPTER

ONE

The train rocks easily on its rails as it passes through the harsh Arizona landscape. The constant click-clacking of the steel wheels fill the cars, lulling the passengers into a trancelike stupor. Only one passenger is wide-eyed and alert. Escape is on his mind.

J. Mason Davis rests his manacled hands on the sill of the open window and let the hot sun and dry wind caress his young battered face. High in the distance, he can make out several large black birds. Buzzards, he guesses. No doubt circling something dead or dying.

"Hotter than hell, ain't it boy?" The fat man across from him asks. When Mason does not answer, the fat man scowls. "Don't bother answering then. You ain't said crap all the way from New York. Why open your mouth now?"

Mason turns slightly to face the man who addressed him, but remains silent. The bored contempt that leaps from his dark eyes speak louder than any words he can express.

"Peers to me you'd be a little grateful the way I've took care of you all this way." The fat man shifts his bulk, causing the seat under him to groan. In spite of the heat, he wears a long duster over his clothes. Frequently, he produces a stained handkerchief from its pocket and wipes his sweaty brow. "Course now, I know you'd like the irons off, but yer old pappy said leave 'em on all the way to Fort Apache if'n you give me any trouble. So that's what I aim to do."

The big man eyed Mason. The youth, with his brown skin, straight black hair and intelligent eyes, look back with blatant disgust and cool arrogance. It's a look the fat man hates, from the moment he first laid eyes on the boy in New York, and now he hates it even more. Young Mason looks harmless enough in his expensive cotton suit and linen shirt. However, his intense stare and constant clenching of his fists do not go unnoticed by his wary escort.

"Like to get them hands of yours around old Bosworth's throat, wouldn't ye now?" The fat man squirms in his seat and dabs at the sweat running down his neck. "Well, boy, it wasn't me that got his ass in trouble and got thrown out of New York City. Don't be giving me any of your high and mighty looks or I'll bust yer head again."

Mason's eyes flash at the mention of the beating he already endured at the hands of Bosworth. A beating he earned when he tried to escape at the first stop outside the city. Now he is in irons and sporting a bruised cheek and a deep gash on his forehead for his troubles.

Spitting into the brass spittoon at his feet, Bosworth wipes the dribble from his chin and turns his pig eyes back on Mason. "Just showing you who's boss, that's all. No hard feelings you need be a holding against me now."

"What did he do, officer?" Asks a nearby passenger who was listening to the one-sided conversation. His weathered face is full of curiosity.

Bosworth's eyes settle on the man and he smiles, happy to have an audience. "Well now, he's a bad 'un. Not yet eighteen years old and got his ass kicked clear out of New York City, he did. Now his rich ol' daddy is sending him to meet up with some kin down at Fort Apache."

"Looks Injun, half-breed, I reckon."

"You're pretty observant, mister." Bosworth nods. "What's your business?"

"Name's Luke Palmer. Run a spread down on the Gila, close to where old Geronimo was born." Palmer rubs his chin while he looks Mason over. "Yep, I know Injuns."

"Well now, like I was saying, Mister Palmer, you're an observant man." Bosworth hooks a meaty thumb in Mason's direction. "This boy here, he's half Apache."

Palmer glares at the youth and spits. "As if we don't have enough of them trouble making red sons already."

Bosworth grins, sensing he found a kindred spirit who dislikes the youth as much as he does. "Name's John Bosworth, Mr. Palmer, late of the Pinkerton Detective Agency."

"So, he's a rebel Apach, is he? Well, we know how to deal with his kind out here. We whipped ol' Geronimo and his ragtag bunch of braves some twenty years back. This one will get a dose of the same medicine, if he ain't careful."

Now Bosworth is curious. "You still havin' trouble with the Indians out there?"

The rancher glares at the youth while he speaks to Bosworth. "Yep, still a few young bucks running wild, thinking they're the next Geronimo." He spits again. Turning back around, he slouches down, pulls his hat over his eyes, and dozes off.

Silence falls inside the rocking coach as most of the passengers try to sleep despite the suffocating heat. Bosworth nods off and starts snoring.

Mason's sharp eyes take in everything around him. A man with beady eyes is sharpening his knife against the sole of his boot. A mother consoles her baby by rocking him in time with the swaying of the train. A whiskey peddler polishes the bottles in his sample case. Across the aisle, two men play cards. One man is slight but wiry. The other man is large and powerfully built. Money changes hands, mostly in the direction of the larger man. Poker is something Mason knows well. Well enough to know the bigger man is cheating.

Palming and dealing from the bottom of the deck, the muscular man handles the cards clumsily. In New York, his throat would have been slit from ear to ear, a payment befitting such a sloppy performance.

"Something amusing you, breed?" The bigger man said, noticing the smirk on Mason's face.

Mason looks calmly into the cold-gray eyes of the man, holds the look briefly and then returns his attention to the scenery outside the train.

"I'm talking to you, Injun."

The raised voice of the card player startles Bosworth out of his fitful sleep. "What the hell's the matter here?" He questions.

"Your Injun there has got a long nose," the big man sneers.

Bosworth looks at Mason, who is still staring out the window. "What'd you do, boy?"

Turning his head slowly, Mason settles his dark eyes easily on the big card player. "I was watching him cheat at cards," he said simply. His voice is cultured and educated; another thing Bosworth hates about him.

"You red son of a bitch!" The big man yells as he lunges to his feet. Cards fly everywhere. "The likes of you, calling me a cheat."

A colt revolver appears in his hand as if by magic. Its deadly mouth pointing toward the youth. Mason does not flinch. Other passengers in the railcar scatter as best they could in the cramped quarters. The woman with the baby stifles a scream.

"I wouldn't do that, stranger," Bosworth said, speaking calmly from his seat.

"No red son is gonna call me a cheat."

"He did, and there's nothing you're gonna do about it."

The gambler is enraged. "I'm gonna put another hole in his big mouth." The loud click of the hammer sounds in the tense silence as the big man cocks his pistol and steps forward.

"Sorry, mister," Bosworth said, getting to his feet. "Can't let you do that while he's in my custody."

"You the law?" The big man asks, the pistol wavering a little.

"Nope, just gonna make sure he gets where I was paid to take him."

"Then maybe I'll just take him out of your custody, fat man."

"Nope, you ain't gonna do that either."

"And who's gonna stop me?" The gambler straightens his shoulders, waiting for Bosworth to accept the challenge.

Bosworth pulls himself up a little taller at the question. "Me and my pardner," he tells the man.

Looking about the rocking car, the big man grins widely. "Well now, I don't see anyone but your fat ass to stop me."

"Look again," Bosworth tells him as a sawed-off, double-barrel shotgun appears from under his duster with both triggers eared back and ready.

The big man's eyes rivet on the twin barrels staring at his belly. Sweat beads on his face. A man can face a pistol at close range but not a shotgun. Death looks out of each barrel.

The big man returns his gun to its holster. "We'll settle this later," he said, looking Mason straight in the eye.

Mason said nothing. He is not cowed by the evil eyes that hold his.

"Sure," Bosworth said, keeping the shotgun trained on the big man. "Now why don't you be good lads and take your game to another car?"

The smaller man quickly gathers the cards. With a glance over their shoulders, the two men shuffle down the aisle and disappear through the wooden door into the next car.

Letting out a sigh of relief, Bosworth eases down the hammers. He sits once more across from Mason and rests the shotgun across his lap. He studies the boy. "You don't say shit all the way from New York, and when you finally do open your mouth, you almost get us killed."

"Too bad I didn't," Mason mutters under his breath. He heard stories about hotheaded cowboys itching to use their guns. Now, having seen one for himself, he is not impressed.

Mason stares back out the window, his thoughts turning to the events that put him on the train in the first place. It was an accident. The end result of his desire to do the right thing.

Although he lived uptown in luxury, he was hanging out in a poor neighborhood where few people took notice of his being a half-breed. One summer evening, a pimp named André snatched a girl named Mary for his stable. Mary was an innocent girl who lived alone with her widowed mother. When Mason heard about it, he went looking for them. He found André half drunk in a saloon, but when Mason approached him, André pulled a knife. The struggle was short but violent. When André lunged for Mason, Mason sidestepped, grabbed him by his coat, and flung him to the ground. Mason stood over him ready to fight but Andre never got up. Turning him over, Mason and a few bystanders discovered the drunken pimp fell on his own knife.

Mason rescued Mary at his own peril, but that did not matter to the authorities. The witnesses, mostly criminal types, disappeared when the lawmen arrived and no one vouched for the young Mason. Half-white or not, to the police he was an Indian, and a white man was dead. Mason was charged with murder. His wealthy white father was able to buy his freedom, but it came with the agreement that Mason would leave New York immediately.

Mason is lost in thought as he gazes out the open window. He is educated and brought up with the comforts of wealth. Now he is being exiled to the uncivilized West to live with some Indian relative he never met just because some drunken pimp fell on his own knife. He was a suspect because he is half Indian and judged a criminal by the white world just because of the color of his skin.

His attention is drawn to the sleeping Bosworth. His snoring is deep and ragged. Drool trickles from his meaty lips. Mason is disgusted. He looks around at the other passengers as they rest, waiting for their long boring journey to come to an end. Outside, the heat shimmers above the ground in visible ripples.

Mason vows that at the first opportunity, he will escape and return to New York.

CHAPTER

TWO

A buckskin clad figure slips quietly into the seat vacated by the gambler. Bosworth rouses and trains the shotgun on him. Mason turns from the window and watches with mild curiosity.

"Take it easy, hoss," the man said, raising his hands slightly. "I'm a right peaceable citizen." He smiles broadly. The man is slender but scrappy, with a few days growth of gray stubble on his chin. Scraggly white hair hung from beneath a worn leather hat. His face is as weathered as the buckskins he wears.

Bosworth eyed the man suspiciously, still holding the gun ready. "What do you want?" Bosworth asks without lowering the ten gauge.

"Seen the ruckus," the man said. "Being naturally curious, I was wondering what all the commotion was about."

Bosworth studies the man. He never trusts a man that smiles so easily. Being of a more serious nature, he seldom smiles himself and is suspicious of those who did without good reason. "Curiosity could get you killed, stranger," Bosworth finally said.

The sarcasm in Bosworth's voice is not lost on the stranger or on Mason. He has to admit, Bosworth is not a coward.

"Name's Zeb Macy," the buckskin man said. "Used to be a scout for the army."

"Used to be?" asks Bosworth, still wary.

"Yep, ain't no Apach left to fight, except maybe a few young bucks cutting up now and then. Army sure as hell ain't gonna keep me full time for the likes of them." The scout studies Mason openly, not sneaking a glance, but straight on.

Bosworth does not take kindly to the stranger's frankness and raises the shotgun a notch higher.

"I told you, I'm peaceable," Macy said.

"What exactly you after, Mr. Macy?"

Macy pointed at Mason. "Would our friend here be young Davis? J. Mason Davis?"

Instead of answering right off, Bosworth lowers the shotgun. He keeps it close at hand across his ample lap. After dragging the handkerchief across his sweaty forehead, he reaches into a pocket and produces a plug of tobacco. He bites off a chew and then offers the plug to Macy.

"News travels fast out here, Mr. Macy." Boswell said while he chewed. "Yep, this here's Master Davis for sure."

The scout takes the plug from Bosworth. "Don't mind if I do. Thank ye kindly." He studies Mason carefully, sizing him up. "Bigger than most Apache men."

"That a fact?" Bosworth spit a stream of tobacco juice. "Probably meaner too."

"I doubt that." Macy spits.

"He's a mean 'un alright. Don't let his young looks fool you. Done killed a man, I hear."

Macy studies the youth again, then starts to rise. "Well, I just wanted to see young Massai here. Me and him go back a long way."

"My name's Mason," the youth said.

"White part maybe," Macy said, grinning. "However, your Apache name is Massai. I knew you when you were knee high to a grasshopper."

Mason's eyes smolder. Never had he been called Massai. Macy does not know what he is talking about. Most whites do not. Although, he was raised among them and half white himself. He never trusted whites and never got along with them. James Davis, his father, sent him to the best schools, until none would admit him. His athletic ability was not enough to overcome his troublesome reputation and quick temper. One by one, the schools asked him not to return. He was called half-breed all his life and he hates the word. He heard it too many times and too many times a fight would break out over it. Mason does not know why, but trouble follows him around like a rotting stink.

How many times, he promised to stay out of trouble, dozens for sure. Maybe hundreds, but it always finds him. Every time he gets into trouble, he and his father grow further part. Now he is on his way to Fort Apache, sent away in disgrace. Now he is an outcast among the Indians, just as he was among the whites. He will arrive in irons like a common criminal. Mason's jaw clenches at the thought of his humiliation. He returns his attention to the discussion between the two white men.

"Do you know this uncle of his at Fort Apache, Alchi or something like that?" Bosworth asks Macy.

"Uncle?" Macy looks quickly at Mason, then turns and stares somberly into the seat across from him. "His... uncle... yep, I know him."

"Good, maybe you'll be kind enough to point him out to me when we reach this fort of yours?"

"Can't."

"Can't or won't?" Bosworth put a hand on the scattergun resting across his knees.

Macy notices the movement and grins. "You're a distrusting cuss, Mr. Bosworth." He spits a stream of tobacco juice and wipes his mouth on his sleeve. "What I mean is I can't. He won't be there."

"Won't?" Bosworth is surprised. "But he's supposed to meet us at Fort Apache and take the boy."

"I expect you'll be seeing him at the next watering stop. That's my guess anyway." Macy scratches his stubbled chin. "His name is Alchise. Toughest warrior Geronimo had. Chiricahua Apache. Got himself a rancheria down on the White River. Most likely he'll be waitin' for you over the next mountain."

"My orders are to take the boy to Fort Apache," Bosworth said. His forehead wrinkles into a frown.

Macy nods and let fly at the spittoon. "Your business, hoss, but if you want a little advice, let him have young Massai there when he meets the train at the watering stop. Save you a heap of trouble. 'Sides, you got all the trouble you need already."

"Trouble?"

"Them two fellers you ran out of here." Macy jerks his head in the direction of the next car. "Big one's Slade Bonham, gunfighter, killer, mean hombre. I'd be real careful gettin' off the train at Fort Apache. If I were you, that is."

"I see." Bosworth rubs his double-barrel peacemaker as he contemplates Macy's warning. "This Alchise, why ain't he in Florida with Geronimo?"

"Changed sides. Helped bring in the old bandit. Saved us a lot of horseflesh. He and James Davis were good friends. Davis was our Chief of Scouts back then. Word is he headed east with a few sacks of gold and young Massai here in tow."

Mason tries to ignore the old scout but he is curious to hear more about this Indian uncle and about his father, James Davis. He does not like Macy, but the man said he knew him when he was a baby, so he must know his mother, too. He is on the verge of asking Macy a question about his mother, but holds back, unsure whether he should or not. Maybe he will wait and ask his uncle.

"Would this Alchise feller know the boy is aboard this particular train?" Bosworth asks.

"He'll know." Macy chuckles. "This ain't the east, Mr. Bosworth. Trains don't come by real regular. Word is, young Massai's on his way." He looks Mason up and down. "Killed a man, you say?"

"Yep, that he did. Cut him open like a can of peaches."

"He was a pig," Mason blurts out. He leans out the window, resting his manacled hands on the sill once again. The air is hot but fresher than the air in the stuffy railcar.

"Weren't no pig," responds Bosworth. "If'n his old pappy wasn't rich, they'd of strung up our Master Davis here for sure."

"Do tell," Macy said with a whistle. He takes another look at the youth leaning out the window. "Do tell."

Out of the corner of his eye, a movement near the rear of the train catches Mason's attention. He turns to look toward the caboose. Thundering up out of nowhere, a wild looking group of young Indians are quickly gaining on the train. They break into high-pitched screams as they race their small mustang horses alongside the train. They seem to be playing some kind of game, trying to touch the train. The people in the car stir at the racket, rushing to the windows.

The locomotive's engine strains and losing speed on its way up the steep mountain slope, so the young riders have no trouble keeping pace. Caught up in the excitement, Mason takes in the sleek ponies, their manes whipping in the wind, their necks fully extended. Some froth at the mouth, but all of them have blazing eyes and flaring nostrils. The youths are dressed only in breechcloths and high Apache leggings. Hard muscled brown legs grip the horses' heaving sides as they race the train. The youths are riding bareback with only a braided piece of leather to rein in their mounts.

Mason can feel his blood run hot. He wants to join them, to race the wind on one of those magnificent animals. He aches to be free. Free of his chains, free of his troubles. Watching as one of the riders whip his tired horse for one last burst of speed, he finds himself looking straight into the face of a full-blooded Apache. A face much like his own, Mason has to catch his breath.

The wild-eyed young rider speaks, but Mason cannot understand him.

"Wants to know your name," a voice said. Mason turns to see Macy behind him, watching the riders.

"Massai," Macy calls to the rider.

Mason starts to correct him, but he is speechless. He is too caught up in the excitement of the moment.

Again, the youth shouts something he does not understand.

Macy translates. "He wants to know why the whites have the biting iron on you."

Looking down at his chained hands resting on the ledge of the window, Mason quickly jerks them inside, out of sight. Suddenly, he feels ashamed.

The Indian youth speaks again. This time, Mason hears the name "Massai" among his words.

"Says his name is Ponce," Macy continues. "Says he'll see you again, Massai."

Mason sits still as the young rider extends his bow and touches his shoulder through the window. Somehow, he knows it is a friendly gesture.

Mason wants to reach out and touch the bow, but he is embarrassed at being chained like a dog. Instead, he nods back at the Indian named Ponce. He watches as the young riders slow their heaving horses to a walk and disappear from sight.

Mason sits back in his seat, lost in thought. His heart races with excitement.

Bosworth studies Macy. "You seem to be well versed in the native tongue of these savages."

"Helps when you have them scouting for you. Need to know what they're up to."

"Yep, I can see where you might."

Macy gets up to leave. He stops as he looks at Mason. "Perhaps young Massai should learn some Apach. That is, if he wants to fit in on the reservation."

Mason's gaze follows the stooped shoulders of the old scout as he leaves the car. Reservation, hell! In spite of the exhilaration of watching the young riders and their horses and wanting to ride with them, Mason renews his vow to return to New York at the first opportunity.

CHAPTER

THREE

The shrill scream of the locomotive whistle jolts the passengers from their sleep. Here, high in the mountains above the canyon floor, the air is thinner and much cooler.

Mason feels the train lurch until it is barely moving. After a couple of hard jolts, it comes to a stop, sending a cloud of steam rushing through the open car windows.

A portly man in a black coat and hat yells from the doorway. Everyone has fifteen minutes to stretch their legs while the train takes on water. Mason is tempted to ask Bosworth to remove his manacles so he can stretch too, but he can see the fat man is on edge about something.

Macy pushes and shoves his way through the exiting passengers and comes to a stop in front of Bosworth. Squinting out the window, he bobs his head motioning for them to look.

A lone rider sits his horse fifty feet from the train. A rifle rests easily across the sorrel's withers. A slight breeze rustles both the mane of the horse and the man's long black hair. Other than that, he sits ramrod straight and as still as a statue.

"There's your man," the old scout said. "Old Alchise himself."

Mason studies the man as best he can from a distance. He is dressed identical to the younger Indians he saw earlier, except this man has on a buckskin vest. A broad leather belt containing cartridges circles his lean waist. A bow and quiver of arrows hang from his back and a skinning knife hangs at his side. Except for a breechcloth and leggings that cover him almost to his knees, his legs are bare.

The Indian holds himself erect and his face is set as if chiseled in granite. A broad forehead sits above dark, deep-set eyes. His nose is thick, adding character to his full wide mouth.

Mason never saw a more imposing figure, not even in New York City where the richest power brokers and the meanest cutthroats plied their trade. Mason guesses the Indian to be about average height, but his regal bearing makes him seem taller.

The sorrel horse steps forward and walks quietly to the end of the coach. Mason watches, mesmerized, as the warrior drops gracefully from the horse and bounds up the steps of the train with the rifle gripped in one hand. The few passengers who remain in the railcar back away.

Silent in his moccasins, the warrior Macy called Alchise now stands face to face with Bosworth. He is aware of everything—the other passengers, Mason, and even Bosworth's shotgun, which now hangs harmless and forgotten in the fat man's frozen hands. Recognition and contempt show plainly, as the Indian's eyes settle briefly on Macy, but fire leaps from them when he sees the youth in irons.

"I come for one you call Mason," the warrior said in a deep commanding voice. He speaks in broken English.

Extending a nervous hand, Bosworth tries to rise, but falls back in his seat with a grunt. "I'm John Bosworth, Mister Alchise, at your service."

Alchise ignores the offered hand and nods slightly toward the youth. "He Mason?"

"Yes," Bosworth said. His fat hand shakes as it points to Mason. "This here's J. Mason Davis." He turns to Mason. "Say something, boy. This here's your uncle."

Alchise's eyes move from the hated white man's irons to the boy's bruised cheek and the ugly gash. He turns glaring eyes on Bosworth.

"Remove chains," Alchise demands in words as sharp and cold as jagged ice.

Macy grins to himself when he sees Bosworth fumbling for the key. Despite the nearby shotgun, the fat man looks ready to wet his pants. Understandable, Macy thought, remembering his own reaction the first time he was confronted by the Chiricahua many years ago.

Mason watches with interest as Boswell removes the manacles with trembling hands. The big man shows no fear facing down the gambler and his drawn pistol, but here is a lone Indian scaring him half to death.

Once the irons were removed, Boswell reaches into an inside pocket of his duster. The Indian raises his rifle—not to take aim, but in warning. Boswell gets the message. Slowly, he puts one hand up and with the other reaches into his pocket.

"I have a letter for you from Mister Davis," he tells Alchise, pulling out a long envelope, he presents it to the Indian.

Without looking at his nephew, Alchise tells Mason, "Massai go stand by horse." When Mason does not move, his uncle looks at him. "Mason stand by horse, wait for Alchise." This time Mason obeys.

Alchise stares coldly into the bulging eyes of Bosworth as he takes the extended letter. Then he switches his attention to Macy.

"Long time no see," Macy said to Alchise in Apache.

"No long enough, Macy," the Indian replies in English.

"I pity you, old horse," Macy continues, this time in English. "You've got a wildcat on your hands." Macy nods to where the youth was standing near the sorrel.

Alchise looks toward the boy, then back at the lean scout. "White-eye make boy bad. No should go east with Davis."

"Well now, Davis is his Pa, ain't he?"

"Macy still talk too much." Alchise reaches for the scabbard at his side.

Macy takes a step back and grins. "Whoa, alright now, don't go gettin' your feathers ruffled."

With a final glare, first at Bosworth, then at Macy, Alchise turns and leaves the railcar. As the train pulls away, Macy and Bosworth watch the two Apaches, one a man, one nearly a man, fade in the distance.

Bosworth slumps back in his seat and retrieves his handkerchief. He mops up the perspiration that runs down his face and neck to a soaked shirt. "What the hell was that?"

"Walking death, my friend," Macy said, half lost in thought. "Walking death."

Alchise watches the train as it disappears in a fog of steam and smoke. He could never understand why a man would ride such a thing when one could ride a horse. His old friend, Massai, told him of his ride to the east. How his legs ached and the noise made his head hurt. Now his friend's namesake, young Massai, comes from the east on the iron horse.

Alchise looks at the youth. The boy was placed in chains and beaten, but he stands tall. He is straight of back and legs, and has the frame to carry the heavy muscles that come as he ages.

"Me Alchise, uncle to Massai."

Despite the daunting presence of the warrior, Mason speaks back in defiance. "Mason's my name. Don't call me Massai." He is not a fat old man like Bosworth. He will not let this so-called uncle intimidate him. Mason rubs his wrists. Now that he is free from his shackles, escape will be easier. He will take off as soon as he has a chance.

Alchise senses deep rebellion and anger in the boy, a fiery and unbroken spirit. If tempered properly, he will become a good man. A strong warrior and leader, but only if he learns to temper his demons. Similar to a horse, this one needs to be handled cautiously. Fighting will only make a rebel or worse, an outlaw.

"Now you are Apache. Need Apache name. You go back east then you be Mason. Now you are Massai, Chiricahua Apache."

"I will go back east."

"Maybe, maybe not. You no go today. Come." Alchise binds onto the sorrel's back and turns west toward the mountains, leaving Mason behind.

"What do I ride?" Mason calls after him.

Alchise calls back over his shoulder, "No more horse. You walk."

Massai studies the rough broken ground and the thorny thistles that grow along the tracks. "You've got to be joking."

"No joke. Massai walk."

"My name's Mason and I'm not walking anywhere!"

Alchise turns the sorrel around and stops, facing Mason. He weighs the situation before speaking. "Iron horse no come long time. Seven moons maybe. Maybe young Massai… maybe Mason… get hungry. Maybe mountain cat get hungry. Eat Mason. Better you come Alchise to rancheria."

The warrior turns the horse back again toward the mountains and kicks the sorrel into a slow trot without looking back.

Mason looks in the direction of the disappearing train. He can never catch up to it. Nor does he want to. All that waits for him on that train was fat old Bosworth and iron shackles. In the other direction is the backside of the Indian, also moving away from him. The rest is empty land, foreign, hot and harsh. He knows he cannot stay where he is. Reluctantly, he starts trotting behind the sorrel, wondering if his father instructed this wild Apache to make it rough on him. Mason soon stops, takes off his suit coat, and ties it around his waist. Then he starts after the horse again. He was a star runner in several of the schools he attended. The schools did not want him, only his ability to run and win, and win he did. He tightens his jaw as he catches up with the Indian. He will prove he can take anything the old warrior dishes out.

"Damn, slow down a little," Mason curses out loud after they travel a distance.

"No talk. Tongue swell. No water."

"No water?" Massai asks in disbelief. "It must be a hundred degrees out here. What fool would be out here with no water?"

"No fool. No water," the Indian said flatly and keeps moving.

Much to his surprise, at the same time he is cursing James Davis, Alchise, and even Bosworth, Mason feels alive and full of energy. The air is hot but fresh and clean, unlike the dinginess of the city. He is enjoying being out of the confines of the city, the iron, and the train. Here, in the desert, he feels free for the first time in a long time.

Not yet tired and feeling frisky, Mason reaches down and grabs several small pebbles from the desert floor. As he trots behind the horse, he starts flicking them at the sorrel's rump. With each direct hit, the horse lurches forward causing Alchise to have to rein him in.

"The cub wishes to play with the lion?" Alchise asks without turning around. He smiles slightly and kicks the horse into a slow lope.

"Damn it!" Massai scolds himself as he tries to keep pace. Several miles pass before Alchise pulls the sorrel up and waits for the exhausted Mason.

"Massai runs well," the warrior said when Mason catches up.

Mason does not reply. He is trying to conceal he is out of breath. Gulping in breaths quietly, Mason is determined not to let his uncle see his weakness.

"Why am I trying to impress this damn Indian," Mason berates himself under his breath. Never before did he care what anyone thought of him. Here in the middle of a desert, thirsty, hot and tired, he is almost running himself to death to impress a man he does not even know.

As he recovers his breath, the youth becomes aware of his surroundings. At first, the desert appears barren except for the cactus, sagebrush, and spindly trees that dot the valley floor. Observing closely as he follows Alchise, the surroundings come to life. Several times, they disturb an antelope, causing them to leap away gracefully. Jackrabbits, fast and surefooted, scamper out of their paths. Mason is so engrossed in watching a covey of quail sail safely out of harm's way, he barely hears Alchise speak.

"Take my foot. Hold on," Alchise tells him as Mason catches up.

"Why?"

"Just do. No question."

"Why?" Mason asks again. He cannot help himself. He has to say something.

"Because, young cub, it is Apache way. You half Apache."

"Only half," Mason reminds him.

"Maybe you right. Maybe white blood make you too weak to be Apache." Alchise kicks the sorrel and rides on.

Feeling Mason take hold of his foot, Alchise grins slyly and pushes the horse into a steady trot. Amazed, Mason finds the running much easier as the gelding pulls him along. Maybe, he thought, he can learn something from this old Indian. That is, he warns himself, if he can keep his mouth shut long enough.

The evening sun was beginning to slip behind the great mountains in front of them when Alchise pulls the sorrel up. A clear pool of water bubbled out of a spring near their feet.

Mason falls into the small pool face first, gulping down large mouthfuls of the cool water. When he looks up, Alchise is frowning at him.

"You soft," he scolds the boy. "Drink much water."

"Only the white part of me is soft," Mason smirks, his face dripping wet. "The red part didn't drink at all."

"Cub still talk back to lion."

Mason gets to his feet and wipes his face with the tail of his shirt. "Well, hell, you damn near run me to death across this desert, and then don't think I'm supposed to be thirsty?"

"Is not Apache way."

"You mean Apaches don't drink water?"

"Not like white man."

"Bullshit."

"Apache no drink bullshit either."

Mason cannot believe it. This stone statue of a man actually tried to make a joke.

"I'd like to see you run and not drink," he said to the Indian.

"Tomorrow, I run. Massai ride horse. You see."

Mason looks defiantly at Alchise. "My name's still Mason, old man. J. Mason Davis. Running across this dessert hasn't made me Massai or turned me into an Indian."

Alchise starts a small fire. Mason looks from the fire down at his soaked clothes in disbelief. Sweat is still pouring from him. "A fire? Are you crazy? It's hot as hell out here."

"No crazy. Soon get cold. Cub like 'em fire."

"I doubt it."

"You see," Alchise said as he hands the youth a greasy roll of paper. "Eat now."

"What is it?" Mason asks, looking at it with disgust.

"Jerky. Plenty good. You eat."

Warily, Mason examines his dinner. Popping a piece of the dark meat in his mouth, he hands the rest back to Alchise. The coarse meat is salty and tasty, but too hard to chew.

"Cub let jerky set in mouth," Alchise instructs. "Soon can chew."

Mason crouches beside the fire while allowing the jerky to soften in his mouth. From across the flickering flames, he closely watches the warrior.

"Are you really my uncle?" He asks.

Alchise studies the youth. "Davis not tell you?"

"No, Bosworth said you were."

"Davis no tell?" Alchise asks again.

Mason chews the meat in his mouth and swallows. "Look, this is how it is," he said in a tough voice. "My father refuses to tell me anything. Not even my mother's name. Until recently, I didn't even know I had an uncle, Indian or otherwise."

Alchise pulls out the letter Bosworth gave him. He holds it out to Mason. "What paper say?" He asks.

"I don't know."

"You want make paper talk?"

"Do you mean you want me to read the letter?"

"If cub want, I give letter."

Mason studies the wrinkled envelope and remembers the heated argument he and his father had the night before he left with Bosworth. "No, I don't care what's in it. I just know if it's from my father, it can't be good."

Turning the letter over several times in his hands, Alchise glances over at Mason. The boy's jaw is set in defiance, but his eyes are cloaked in sadness.

"Yes, you my blood," Alchise tells him. Then he drops the letter into the fire, unopened.

Mason watches the letter curl in the flame, then catch, and burn. Looking up, he stares into the dark pools of his uncle's eyes. "Maybe you should have read the letter. It probably was a warning about what a hellion I am."

"No matter. This new place for you."

Alchise hands the oilskin full of jerky back to Mason, who takes another piece of jerky and sticks it in his mouth. He stares into the fire while he lets it soften.

"Alchise?"

"Cub speak."

"My mother, was she pretty?"

Alchise hesitates and then replies simply. "Yes."

"What was her...?"

Mason starts to ask another question, but stops when Alchise rises abruptly and disappears into the darkness. Mason waits for him to return. He wants to know more about his mother. He is hoping his uncle will tell him something. When Alchise does not return, Mason is suspicious. What was so mysterious about his mother that both his father and uncle refuse to discuss her? He thinks long and hard, but still no answer by the time he falls into an exhausted sleep.

Mason awakes during the night, his body cold and shivering. His muscles aching from the long run and are now cramping from lying on the cold hard ground. Thoughts of his warm soft bed back in New York, with its clean sheets and soft pillows, fill his head. Sleeping on the ground is for savages. He turns over abruptly, trying to find a comfortable spot.

"Cub no sleep?" said a voice near him.

"You were right about the cold," Mason said. "It's freezing out here."

Alchise smiles at the shivering youth, but said nothing. He moves near the fire and sits down in front of it.

"Why are you awake?" Mason asks. He also moves closer to the fire and rubs his arms for warmth.

"Apache sleep light. You move. Wake up."

Looking up at the stars, Mason marvels. Never were the stars so bright or so close. The sky seems endless.

The small fire crackles and casts eerie shadows around them. Alchise adds some wood and soon the fire is giving off more heat. Mason moves yet closer and stretches his hands out close to the flames. Staring into the fire, he almost falls into a trance. Across from him, Alchise sits cross-legged, lost in thought himself.

"Were you really with Geronimo?" Mason asks.

Nodding slowly, Alchise answers, "Yes, we fight much. Kill many."

"People talk of him back east."

"Geronimo great war leader. Never quit fight."

"Why did you leave him and help the soldiers if he was so great?"

Alchise hesitates, considering his answer. "Him great warrior, but is time to fight. Time to not fight. Geronimo fight too much. All warriors dead or starving. Enemies many. White soldier, Nantan Lupan, Mexican soldier, white rancher—all our enemy. I want Chiricahua people to live. If Geronimo not stop, all be sent far away, no good place. They die."

"It sounds like you betrayed him." Mason squints across the fire, trying to make out the warrior's face.

"I speak Geronimo. Tell him no more fight."

"That's it? You just said you were quitting?"

"Apache different. Not like white soldier. Fight when fight is good. No fight when medicine bad."

Mason thinks about it. He is not sure what Alchise means by bad medicine.

"How come they didn't send you to Florida with Geronimo?" he asks. "I heard many scouts that helped the white soldiers were sent with him."

"When Geronimo surrender, Davis warn Alchise, go away. I do this thing. I never come in with others. I stay in mountain, never go Florida. Never." The warrior flattens his hands in a gesture and then makes a fist. "White eye General Miles, liar."

Mason watches the hard face of the man and knows what he said is true. This one would not lie. He wouldn't know how.

Staring into the fire, Mason listens as the small pieces of wood crackle and pop. A coyote howls somewhere in the distance and another answers. The silence is eerie. Raised in the city, he was accustomed to noise all the time. Here, one hears nothing but the sounds of nature. Occasionally, the wind gusts, sending its cold fingers up his spine. An owl hoots somewhere out on the valley floor, probably near the timberline. Mason leans back and gazes at the stars. He is tired and cold, but he feels something else, too. He is at peace, peace with himself and the world. It is a new feeling for him and his last thought before drifting off again.

The soft toe of the warrior's moccasin nudges Mason awake. Despite the cold, he fell into a deep sleep. Mason watches the old warrior. The cold does not seem to affect him in the slightest and if it does, he does not let it show.

Alchise shoves another piece of cold jerky into Mason's hand. "Eat. We go rancheria today."

Turning the hard, greasy meat in his hand, Mason frowns. This was both his dinner and breakfast. He thinks about the hot filling breakfasts his father's cook in New York made for him every morning. He shakes his head and then pulls his belt another notch tighter. He doubts there are any fat Indians in Arizona. If there are, they probably do not have any teeth left.

Handing Mason the reins of the sorrel gelding, Alchise steps back and waits for him to mount. Mason knows very little of horses, but he knows this horse is different from those the young men chasing the train were riding. Taller and straight legged, the sorrel has a refined head with large eyes and short ears. Where the smaller horses were rough haired and narrow through the chest, this horse is sleek and barrel-chested. There is no doubt the sorrel can easily outrun the smaller horses. As Mason approaches, the horse shies, eyes widen, and nostrils flare.

Alchise is the only one to ride the sorrel. He is use to no other hand. Backing up, the horse lunges to the end of the reins. Trained not to pull against a rope, he does not jerk away, but shies backwards as Mason comes near.

"Horse, him no like white smell, maybe," Alchise said.

"Maybe," Mason said, imitating Alchise's way of speaking.

"You walk, lead horse. Him get used to white smell."

For once Mason does not argue. Leading the horse, he follows Alchise toward the distant mountains. The mesa they are crossing climbs steadily and then winds back down into the valley.

The horse settles down enough to let the stranger rub his neck as they walk. Mason remembers how Alchise swung easily onto the horse's back. Taking a handful of mane, he makes a similar move.

"I did it!" He yells from atop the horse.

Alchise turns just in time to see Mason land on his backside in a cloud of dust.

"Why in the hell did he do that?" Mason sputters as he picks himself up off the ground.

"Cub scream like cougar, scare horse maybe."

Mason remounts the horse. This time he is careful to get a good grip and keep quiet. Again, the jittery animal dumps him. Three more times, Mason remounts and each time he finds himself on the ground. With each failure, Mason's anger and frustration rises, along with his cursing, until Alchise intervenes. The Indian takes the reins and swings easily onto the horse's back. The horse did not resist.

"Young one make horse mean soon, I think," he said to the youth, who was dusting himself off and nursing scrapes.

Mason shakes his head in disgust. "Whites in the east always mount from the left. You mounted from the right. The horse doesn't know how it's done properly."

"Alchise don't know which side whites get on in east," he tells Mason, "but Apache jump on horse any side. When enemy chase with rifle, no have time to run and look which side. Him be dead, maybe."

Alchise slides easily off the horse and holds out the reins to Mason. The youth takes the offered reins and swings upon the smooth back again. This time Alchise leads the horse and the horse remains calm.

As they walk, Alchise said, "We get to wickiup soon or maybe cub starve."

Mason looks down at Alchise, not sure if the warrior is making a joke or an observation. He is indeed hungry, hungrier than he has ever been before. He hopes the wickiup, whatever and wherever it was, is close by.

Holding onto the horse with a death grip, Mason frowns. He is being led like a baby. Thinking back on the young warriors racing the train on their wild mustangs, he feels embarrassed.

Seeing that the sorrel is behaving, Alchise drops the reins and starts to the west in a half trot. The horse follows along after him.

"I guess he's gonna let the Indian half of me ride for a while," Mason calls to Alchise.

"Good. If young cub can keep white half on, we go to rancheria."

Mason surprises himself by smiling at the remark. Despite himself, he has to admit he is beginning to like this uncle of his. His father and other adults back east order people around, like they own them. They have no patience or respect for others, especially young people like himself. Alchise is different. He tells Mason what he is going to do, then does it. He understands when you cannot do something. Instead of fussing at you, he shows you how to do it.

"I'll stay on," Mason said, rubbing his stomach. "I'm hungry enough to eat a horse." He chuckles. "I mean a steak."

"No eat horse. No starve." Alchise motions to the open landscape around him. "Many food here."

Mason looks around. All he sees is cactus, scrubby cedars, and pinion trees, as well as sagebrush, tumbleweeds, and bunchgrass. He sees everything but food. Alchise stops and begins shaking a pinion tree. Little round nuts rain down on them. He scoops up a few and hands them to Mason. He puts one between his teeth and shows Mason how to crack the nut and extract the sweet, white meat inside.

"You no starve now," he tells the boy and heads off again.

Mason finds the pinion nuts meaty and somewhat tasty. He studies the warrior trotting in front of him. A strange man, but a man he can learn from if he tries. Looking down at the nuts left in his hand, he knows he will have to learn for now. At least until he can find a way back east.

All morning they travel. Mason is astonished at how Alchise can trot at such a pace and not show a sign of fatigue or even break a sweat. After all, the man is old enough to be his father.

The gelding is in a trot, too. Mason bounced uncontrollably at first, but finally he is learning how to get in rhythm with the stride of the horse. He apparently was accepted. The sorrel made no further attempts to unload him for several miles.

Just when he is feeling confident about his riding skills, the gelding spooks and deposits Mason flat on his back. He lands face to face with a coiled rattlesnake.

The snake is near enough to strike and the vigorous shaking of its tail produces a rattling sound that freezes the youth in place. One move, a blink of the eye, can cause the angry rattler to strike. Surprisingly, Mason is calm. Not a muscle flinched. He may not have ever been this close to a poisonous snake before, but he knows death when he sees it.

The snake raises and lowers its head, trying with his poor eyesight to see what disturbed his nap in the warm midday sun. Mason is transfixed by the scaly body, broad head, probing tongue, and wide set eyes. Suddenly, the snake rolls his body into a ball as one of Alchise's arrows pierces its fat body, pinning it to the ground. Rolling away from the writhing snake, Mason looks up to see Alchise smiling at him, his bow in his hand.

"Cub must be hungry to try catch snake with bare hands."

"Funny," Mason mumbles.

He watches as Alchise deftly skins and guts the snake. Rolling the skin into a tight ball, he flips it to Mason. "Make cub good belt."

A fire is built and the rattler spitted over it in a short time.

"Massai no starve now. Mason no starve either," Alchise said, indicating the roasting snake.

"I'm not eating that damn thing!"

"Good, more for Alchise. I catch horse. Cub watch snake, no let run away."

Mason watches the warrior disappear quickly and quietly in the direction the horse went. He remembers his father walking around their big house as silent as a cat. It is the same with Alchise. He does not walk into the brush. Instead, it is as if he melts into it.

Watching the snake's body cooking over the fire, it is all he can do to turn the branch that holds it from the flames. Dead or not, the snake repulses him. He wonders if he can bring himself to handle one of the ugly monsters on his own. Perhaps, if he was hungry enough.

"You kill snake?" A voice behind him asks.

Mason whirls around, startled to find several young Apaches studying him. Like Alchise, they move silently and give no warning. Mason recognizes them as the young Indians who chased the train. The tall one in front is the same youth who spoke to him through the window. Embarrassed that they came upon him so easily, Massai curses himself for not being more diligent.

One of the youths speaks to the others in Apache. Mason understands nothing. A short stocky youth steps forward and pretends to sniff the wind. Then he, too, said something. All the young men laugh except the tall one in front. He alone keeps quiet.

"They say," the tall one said to Mason in decent English, "that you look like Apache, but dress like white-eye." He hesitates and then adds. "And you smell like white-eye."

The other Indians laugh again. Mason says nothing but he feels his face turn red with humiliation. They were clearly making fun of him.

"Where are the iron bracelets?" The tall youth asks.

"He does not speak the tongue of the Apache," a fat youth said, also in English.

Massai glances toward the fat young warrior. So, there are fat Indians, despite the hard deer jerky he has been eating. The thought strikes him as funny.

Finally, Mason finds his tongue. "You speak English?"

"Yes," the tall one responds. "We learn good English at reservation school. Quaker squaw teach good."

"My name is Mason," he tells them, addressing the tall one, who appears to be the leader.

"Mason?" The tall youth asks. "We hear you are called Massai."

Mason set his jaw. "No, my name is Mason. My uncle is Alchise." He said his uncle's name proudly, bragging, although he does not know why.

A dark, well-built youth speaks up from beside his horse. "Some call you breed. No one want breed," the muscular one taunts.

A scowl comes to the face of his tall companion. "Ignore this one," he said to Mason. "He is evil tempered."

"Sounds like he is smart-mouthed to me," Mason remarks. He notices the comment makes the tall one smile slightly.

"I am Ponce," the tall youth said, introducing himself. "The fat one there is Dosenay. The one with the bowlegs is Taglia. That one there is Wolf," Ponce said pointing to the one who sniffed the air. "This is Bonito, the one who smiles all the time. Chato is the one who calls you "breed" and the young one holding the horses is Loabreno."

Mason studies each of the young men as he is introduced, hoping to remember their names. He knows he will remember Ponce and Chato, but for different reasons.

"Where is the great Alchise?" The one called Chato said, contempt dripping from his words.

"This one does have an evil temper," Mason said, eyeing the one called Chato.

Mason can see that each of the young Indians was armed. He knows he is outnumbered and that they can take him easily. Still, he refuses to show fear or intimidation. Come what may, he will stand his ground and let them know he is not a coward.

Ponce grins again, pretending sadness. "Yes, we tried to teach him better, but he is a Mescalero. Bad tempered people, the Mescalero."

"I am sorry. I would have liked to have been friends with a Mescalero." Mason spit the words back at Chato. His meaning is not lost on the young ones.

"Maybe you become friends with my knife," Chato challenges, starting forward, only to be stopped by the strong arm of Ponce.

"Let him come," Mason said, setting himself in a boxer's stance.

"You have no knife, my friend," Ponce reminds him.

"Maybe Ponce will lend me his," Mason replies.

Again, the muscular Chato starts for Mason, only to have Ponce whirl upon him menacingly and speak in Apache. The two Indian youths lock eyes for a moment before Chato wheels around and heads back to the horses. Mounting easily, he rides a distance and sits staring back at them.

"Eat your snake, Massai," Ponce said with a slight grin. "We will meet again."

"You didn't have to stop him," Mason said, letting the mistake about his name go this time.

"Don't underestimate him. He is a bad one."

"So am I." Mason's voice went cold and hard.

Ponce and Mason look at each other for a moment before Mason extends his hand. The young Indian looks at it briefly before accepting it. The two youths exchange smiles.

Mounting his horse, Ponce whirls the little mustang in a circle then stops. "Come to the reservation, my friend."

"Maybe I will."

Mason watches as the young warriors race out of sight. Mesmerized, he imagines himself as one of them, flying across the desert on the back of one of the little mustangs. Thinking of it makes his blood race, and his heart beat wildly. He is so engrossed in his fantasy, he does not hear Alchise walk up behind him.

Alchise was listening to the confrontation between Mason and Chato. He heard the threats and challenges. There was no fear in the young cub's voice. Alchise is pleased. "I see cub meet Wild Ones," Alchise said.

Mason turns quickly to find his uncle just a few feet away. "Wild Ones?"

"Wild Ones try follow ways of Geronimo. Cause trouble on reservation, with white ranchers. Try to live in old days."

"You do not approve?" Mason asks.

"Big change. We no longer masters of this land. Must learn ways of the whites or no survive."

"Ponce does not seem so bad."

"Him leader. They follow. Geronimo. Cochise. Victorio and Old Nana, all leaders. Now all dead. Same happen to Ponce, maybe."

"But who will kill him?"

"Me. Maybe. Hope no need. Alchise ride with Ponce's father. He my friend. Was great warrior." Alchise pokes at the cooking snake.

"What was his name?"

"He dead. Forbidden to speak name of dead." Alchise removes the snake from the spit and begins cutting it up.

"Is that why you didn't tell me about my mother last night? Because she's dead?"

"We speak Ponce father now. He dead."

Mason realizes Alchise is going to be as stubborn as his father on the subject of his mother. He wants to confront Alchise. There are things he needs to know. He does not understand why Alchise will not speak of his own sister. He will let it go for now.

"Did the white soldiers kill Ponce's father?" Mason asks instead.

"Alchise kill him," the warrior said quietly.

Massai is shocked at the words. Looking into the older man's face, he can see sorrow. Saying nothing more, he accepts the piece of meat offered by Alchise without any objections.

"Him wounded bad, soon die. Mexican soldiers near. If they catch him alive they torture, take scalp. Very bad. I kill and hide body. He would do same for Alchise.

Mason understands what the warrior said. He wonders if he could kill his own friend. Biting into the soft meat of the snake, he hardly tastes it. His mind is on what Alchise told him. No wonder the Apache was so hard to defeat.

Looking up at the warrior, Mason speaks with his mouth full. "This is good." He waves the piece of meat in his fingers.

"Better you eat snake, than snake eat cub."

"I thought he might for a minute back there," Mason said. The two men lock eyes briefly and give each other a slight smile.

Laying his meat aside, Alchise looks at the younger man soberly. "Out here many things try to kill young cub. You have much to learn—gun, knife, trail, enemy, and many things."

"I know about knives," Mason said, his chin jutting out in defiance. He thought about the dead pimp and visualized the knife sticking out from the man's chest. He shakes the image off. "I know how to fight. I taught myself."

Alchise nods. "Maybe. Maybe not know enough."

"I know plenty," Mason said, again with a full mouth.

"Davis, him good with fight. Why he no teach young one?"

"I guess I gave him too much trouble."

"You no like Davis?"

Massai thought awhile before answering. "He is my father, but it was as though I didn't belong there. I always felt out of place."

"Where does cub belong?"

"I think maybe here. At least for now."

"Good. This home to all Apache for long time. It good, you like."

The day passes quickly. Alchise and Massai alternate riding and running. Sometimes both trot beside the horse to give him a breather. The sun was hot. Hotter than Massai ever remembers.

Somewhere along the trail, he discarded the suit coat, leaving only the cotton shirt and pants. The hard leather shoes were causing blisters on his feet. At one point, he stops and tears off his long shirttail and uses it to line his shoes to provide some padding.

It is almost sundown when the gelding pricks up his ears and strains forward. Coming to a small river that Alchise calls the White, they turn up a trail that leads into the mountains.

Alchise smiles and points at the stands of tall pines covering the mountainside high above. "Rancheria."

They are home.

Chapter

Four

Mason does not realize they traveled almost forty miles in a single day, but Alchise knows. For one not use to this country, and considering the extreme heat, the young cub's endurance is cause for pride. The warrior looks at his charge and nods, his eyes showing the satisfaction he feels.

A horse nickers from the corral as they enter a clearing. In the clearing sits a sturdy log cabin. Mason smiles in spite of his exhaustion. He imagined nothing like the beauty of this place. The picture in his mind was of a desert, barren with only a grass shack or something of the kind. This is magnificent. The clearing smells of pine needles and cedar, and of flowers and sweet grass. A cool breeze welcomes him.

Shadows from the tall ponderosa pines cast their long fingers across the horse sheds and corral, reaching almost to the small homestead. Smaller sycamore and oak trees line the banks of the river that flows below the corral.

Mason notices that Alchise built one corner of the corral out into the water. In flood season, the high water could wash the oak logs away. However, in the heat of summer, he does not have to worry about his horses having water when he is away.

Pulling the hackamore from the sorrel, Alchise turns him in with the grey horse already in the corral. Pouring some oats into a wooden trough, he steps back and watches as the horses feed greedily.

"Oat come from white trader at fort. Horse, he like 'em oat."

"I thought Apaches lived off the land," Mason chides.

"Horse no Apache. Oat no grow in corral."

Finishing with the horses, Alchise leads the way to the cabin. Homemade wooden chairs, covered with animal hides, line the front porch. Two windows, covered with bull hide shutters, frame a large oak door. Mason notices firewood stacked off to the side next to some kindling and a pile of shavings.

Against the outside wall, several skin boards stand empty, waiting for hides to stretch across them. Two coal oil lanterns hang from the eaves. At least he did use some of the white man's conveniences, Mason thought as he passes through the heavy door.

"Why do you cover the windows with hides and make such a strong door?" Mason studies the heavy oak barrier.

"Our brother, the bear, him come through door to lodge if not strong."

"Bear?"

Mason suddenly notices the deep scratches in the oak door planks.

"Was I supposed to sleep tonight?" He asks half joking.

"You sleep. Bear no hurt Apache, we clan brothers."

Mason studies the older warrior's face. He is serious. "I hope the bear knows that."

"Bear know."

Once inside, Alchise strikes a match and lights an oil lamp that is hanging from a ceiling beam. The light is dim but Mason's eyes slowly adjust. The cabin consists of one room, not large, but roomy enough. He can see two bunks against opposite walls.

Other than the bunks, a small wooden table, with cut logs for chairs, and a well-used wood cookstove are all that serve for furniture. Mason thought of his father's mansion in New York. The kitchen alone is larger than this cabin. There, ornate rugs cover polished marble floors. Here the floor is dirt. Alchise walks around the cabin and taps the log walls with the butt of his rifle.

Seeing Mason eyeing him with curiosity, he grins. "Me make sure young cub no try catch snake in cabin."

"Snakes, too?" Mason asks as he looks around anxiously. "Wonderful."

"You sleep here," Alchise said, pointing to one of the bunks.

The bed is piled high with clothes and gear.

"What do you want me to do with your things?"

"Not Alchise, all belong to cub."

"Mine? You're giving me all these things?"

"Not Alchise give, your blood on reservation give."

Mason fingers the leather leggings and moccasins, the cotton shirts, the cartridge belt, the knives, and a beaded leather vest. His hands stroke the new Winchester rifle and scabbard, then the bow and quiver of arrows. The painstaking work that went into each of them is obvious. They were beautifully crafted. He remembers the shavings near the chair out front and realizes that Alchise made the bow and arrows himself. The warrior put a lot of work into getting ready for Mason's arrival. The youth is grateful. He truly appreciates his uncle's kindness and generosity.

Mason thanks Alchise for the gifts and is eager to try them on. He is just about to slip a tired foot into a new moccasin when Alchise holds up a hand, stopping him.

"Tomorrow, we must purify you first with sweat bath then you wear new clothes. Be Apache."

Massai studies the room. There is no bath that he can see. He does not know what a sweat bath is, but he is certainly due for a bath of some sort.

After eating a hearty evening meal, Mason falls exhausted into his bunk and sleeps peacefully. It seems like only minutes after he closes his eyes when he wakes up from a loud screech. Jerking his head up toward the sound, he sees a small banty rooster perched on the open windowsill. Relieved, he grins as he watches the rooster strut back and forth. Throwing out his chest, the cocky little rooster sends forth his battle challenge to the bright new morning.

"Little warrior," Alchise said, indicating the rooster. "Him try impress squaws outside." Alchise is standing at the stove frying side meat and eggs for breakfast.

"Squaws?" Mason asks as he walks to the other window and peers out. Sure enough, outside several small hens peck and scratch the ground.

"Massai hungry?"

"Starved," Mason replies, not bothering to correct Alchise on his name. He walks across the dirt floor to the table. "Why don't you put a floor in here? Seems it would be easy enough."

"Floor no good. Snake, scorpion come live too. Dirt better floor."

"Makes sense, I guess." Mason sits at the wood slab table and makes short work of the eggs, bacon, and flatbread placed before him.

Mason grins to himself. If only Bosworth could see the warrior that had him shaking in his boots, now standing here cooking eggs. Apache are unpredictable. He remembers Macy saying you never know what they are going to do next.

"Little squaws give small egg, you eat many?"

"No, thanks, I've had plenty," Mason said.

Good, then you wash dish. Alchise feed horse then we go sweat lodge." Alchise disappears through the door.

"Wash dishes, damn!" Mason bristles. In New York, his father has staff that did all the cleaning, cooking, and washing.

"No cuss dish. Wash," the warrior said, sticking his head briefly back through the door. "Apache no cuss."

Mason is more surprised than embarrassed. "Apaches never cuss?"

"Only what white soldier speak." Alchise replies, disappearing again.

"Apache no cuss, but Apache warrior wash dishes?" Mason's question falls on deaf ears. Alchise is gone.

After washing the metal dishes, he walks out onto the porch and sees that Alchise is starting another fire. A small leather covered lodge of some kind stands within arm's reach of the fire.

Mason takes a moment to inhale the fragrance of the pines, then looks down to where the river flows. The only sounds he hears are the rushing water as it ripples over the rocks and the crackling fire. There seems to be an air of peaceful serenity over the little homestead. Without knowing why, Mason senses that he might belong here in this peaceful place and not in his father's big comfortable house in New York. For the first time in a long time, he does not feel alone.

His thoughts are interrupted when Alchise, dressed only in his breech cloth, calls to him.

"Now cub take sweat bath," he tells the youth. "You make body pure. Make peace with spirits. Become Apache again."

Following Alchise's instructions, Mason takes off the remains of his white man's clothing and stands naked before the lodge.

"This holy place. No cuss. No think bad thoughts. Maybe no have strong medicine. Spirits not smile on you. Cub understand?"

Mason nods. The last thing he wants is bad medicine and wonders if it is like having bad luck.

Ducking inside the lodge, Mason notices two blankets spread near a small circle of stones. The lodge itself has cedar pole stays covered with grass, and the hide covering that he saw from the cabin.

Sitting cross-legged on the blanket, Mason watches as Alchise pulls hot rocks inside the lodge. Placing them in the circle of small stones, he pours cold water on them causing steam and vapor to explode into the wickiup. Mason quickly realizes with the hide covering, little of the steam can escape.

Almost instantly, he becomes uncomfortable from the intense heat in the close confines. The steam from the hot rocks shrouds his body. Sweat escapes from every pore. Rich men in the east have their steam baths. His father took him to one once but they were not as hot as this.

The temperature continues to rise and Mason's breath grows heavy. Opening his mouth to gasp for breath, the hot air seems to sear his lungs. He can barely make out the form of Alchise across from him. The warrior shows no sign of discomfort. Mason is determined, he will not either.

Blinking to clear the sweat from his eyes, Mason is surprised to hear Alchise start singing. Quietly at first, then his voice rises to a crescendo and then back to a whisper.

The warrior is using some kind of rattle to keep time to his singing. It is not a song; it is like a prayer. Mason never thought of Apaches as being religious, yet the solemn beauty of Alchise's song is definitely spiritual. When as a child his father sent him to church, Mason did not take to religion. The harsh warnings and fear of damnation touted by the Baptist preachers did nothing to draw Mason to his creator. Davis finally gave up and let young Mason stay home. Thereafter, he was referred to in church circles as a heathen. "That heathen," the preachers called him whenever he became the object of their conversations. He was seen as an ungrateful half-breed heathen rescued by a loving father.

Yet here in the sweat lodge was a warrior, still a heathen according to the white standards, praying and singing chants to the spirits. Mason can feel the singing stir something within him as he tries to mimic Alchise. Suddenly, Alchise stops chanting. Looking across at Mason, he gets up and gestures for him to follow.

Two warriors, one naked and one nearly so, run for the river and fling themselves into the cold, deep water. The initial shock is breathtaking and Mason surfaces with a desperate gasp for air. After he catches his wind and his heart stops pounding, Mason notices Alchise observing him. Quickly, he lies back in the water and starts swimming with a slow lazy backstroke.

"Ah, this feels good, uncle," he said.

Alchise grins as he watches. After a few moments, Mason begins to swim circles around the older man.

"I see Davis teach you to swim. First, like otter, then like frog. Swim funny."

"I learned to swim in the ocean. We swam there many times," Mason tells him.

"What mean ocean?"

"Ocean? It's like a big lake, only bigger."

"Bigger than river?"

"Bigger than your desert."

Disbelief floods Alchise's face as he disappears under the water. Bobbing back to the surface, his long black hair mats around his face. He pushes it back and looks at Mason a long time. Maybe the cub is again toying with the lion, he thought.

"Bigger than valley we cross?" He asks the youth.

"Oh, much bigger."

Alchise grins again and starts for the bank. "Maybe we swim across this ocean one day."

Mason follows his uncle's lead and heads for the bank. Youthful muscles rippled in his long arms as he pulls himself from the river. The youth's back is straight and heavy, showing promise of great strength in maturity. His stomach is hard and flat except for the muscles that flow across it.

Alchise shakes his head. Many young squaws on the reservation will be after this one. Young Massai is indeed a splendid figure of emerging manhood.

"Young cub purified body with sacred sweat lodge. Now spirit Apache. Now wear Apache clothes. Be Apache."

The moccasins and deerskin shirt fit as though tailored for him. The soft leather deerskin leggings encase his legs comfortably. Stepping proudly out of the cabin, Mason looks to where Alchise is standing by the corral. Alchise sees him and nods in approval.

Taller than most Apache men, Mason possesses a broad intelligent forehead framed by thick black hair. Wide set black eyes separated by a straight thick nose look back from a ruggedly handsome face. Straight and true as a tall pine, Mason is the picture of a Chiricahua warrior.

Alchise stares at him briefly. "You look same as old Massai. When he young warrior."

"I thought you were not allowed to speak a dead warrior's name?"

"I not know he dead," Alchise responds.

"Macy spoke like he was."

Alchise grunts. "Macy white-eye. Know nothing. Come, time for cub learn be Apache."

Alchise catches his sorrel and then the grey gelding that nickered when they arrived. Except for the color, the grey was a match for the sorrel in size and conformation.

"He's a beauty!" Mason exclaims.

"He yours."

"Mine?" Mason's mouth hangs open in disbelief. "Thank... thank you, uncle!"

"Not thank Alchise. He gift to you from someone else."

"Who?"

"In time you know."

"But who would..." Mason starts.

Alchise holds up his hand to cut him off. "No talk. Cub talk too much. Learn now."

The days pass quickly. Each night Mason falls exhausted into his bunk disgruntled with himself. He is younger, but still no match for the tireless Alchise. From sunrise to sunset, they journey from the cabin. Every day Mason gains in stamina but it is a struggle. Things every Apache boy learns from childhood, Mason now learns in a short time.

Alchise is a patient and willing teacher and Mason is an enthusiastic student. Longing to return to New York is pushed aside in his eagerness to learn the Apache way of life.

Day after day they run, crossing the mountains, up and down the heavily timbered slopes, then out onto the valley floor. Running through the sagebrush and prickly cactus in the heat of the day is grueling. Before long, however, riding and running become almost second nature to Mason. However, he still has much to learn.

Alchise can make learning a game, but Mason never loses sight of the seriousness of it. Alchise hides and Mason tries to track him. The warrior is pleased when the hunter finds the hunted. Mason's eyes are quick and sharp. Alchise only teaches him what to look for and his natural ability takes over.

The two Chiricahua are free as the wind and they race that wind across the mountains and valleys. Soon, Mason's legs become like a vise, holding onto the grey as he thunders after the sorrel. Shell after shell fires from the charging horses as the two warriors pepper the cactus lying in their path. At first, Mason aims only at the body of the huge Saguaro cactus. Then he turns his improving aim on the small yucca plants.

A month passes and the rifle is put away. Now is the time for the bow, the arrow, and the skinning knife.

"Young one has learned the white man's weapons well, now it is time for Apache weapons," Alchise said. "And Apache tongue."

Turning the bow over in his hands, Mason groans. "You know I can't hit the side of a mountain with this thing."

"Then we no eat. Kill meat with bow or catch 'em in snare, or we no eat."

Mason glances at the warrior. "Aren't you hunting?"

"Alchise old, tired. Young one hunt for us now."

"Uh huh, and if I don't kill, we don't eat?"

"Maybe."

For a solid week, Mason hunted and the two Apaches existed on rabbits caught in the small snares that he set. In spite of hours of practice, the arrows fly harmlessly over or under their intended targets.

Mason's mouth waters just thinking of the thick deer steaks Alchise prepares so well. It makes him determined to go after bigger game.

Rising before Alchise, he slips out of the cabin early one morning before dawn. Armed only with the bow and a quiver of arrows, he trots off toward the valley. Today, he promises himself, he will bring down a deer or an antelope. Rabbit for every meal is getting old. He is not going back without a decent meal over his shoulders.

Alchise grins to himself as Mason slips out of the cabin thinking he is undetected. The young one is learning. He is even starting to pick up the Apache tongue. Alchise often speaks only in the Apache language to Mason, ignoring him when he fails to comprehend or when he responds in English. This way the boy will learn quickly.

"Cub quiet as hungry bear," Alchise murmurs to himself before drifting back to sleep.

Mason is a natural and skilled runner. He loves the feeling of his legs carrying him tirelessly across the flat valleys and over the crested mesas.

He heads due north to a spring seeped along a canyon wall where many deer and antelope watered. He feels confident. Today he will not fail.

He learns to approach quietly as he stalks his prey. Getting within bow range is not too difficult. Hitting his intended target is the problem.

Slipping in close to the spring, Mason crouches behind a grove of cedar trees and waits. Patience. Many times Alchise spoke to him of patience. A hunter's most prized possession is patience. It is the difference between success and failure.

Red clay and limestone outcroppings make up the bulk of the small cliff that shelter the little spring. It is no more than ten feet high but its wall is nearly vertical. Game will have to come past him from either side. They cannot navigate the steep embankment. He will have a broadside shot at anything that approaches. A movement caught his eye. He tenses and then relaxes. It is only a roadrunner making its way to water.

He smiles. If the skittish little bird cannot detect his presence, then he is well concealed. Only a breeze betrays him, and so far, the morning is still.

A desert fox slips quietly along the bank. He hunts hard through the night but finds nothing. He too will have to try harder. A blue jay scolds him from the safety of a nearby pinion tree. Mason's intense eyes take in everything.

Fascinated, he watches as the jay dives after the fox driving him away. Then Mason sees what he came for—a fat little buck. The animal approaches the water. It tests the air and hangs back in the shadows, always leery of an enemy's presence. Cautiously, the majestic animal makes his way toward the water.

Mason's fingers tense on the bowstring. His arrow is notched and ready. Only a few more feet. The buck's tail twitches, his ears prick back and forth, listening. Finally, he is at the water's edge. Massai pulls the heavy bow back silently. Then all hell breaks loose as a large tan blur springs on top of the deer.

With one swipe of his mighty paw, a big mountain cat breaks the buck's neck. Mason gasps in surprise but quickly regains his composure. He redirects his aim and let the arrow fly. It hit its new target, penetrating just behind the cat's left shoulder. Screaming in rage and pain, the big cat bit at the arrow. Throwing himself sideways and flipping over, he claws the air and let loose with an earsplitting scream that makes Mason's hair stand on end.

He saw these cats from a distance but never this close. Nervously, he notches another arrow and sights on the thrashing mass of teeth and claws. The big cat hears the bow twang and spin, looking directly into Mason's eyes as the arrow drives deep into his chest. Rising to his full height, he spins around and then collapses.

Approaching the cat cautiously, Mason prods it with his bow. Satisfied it is indeed dead, he pulls out his skinning knife.

Alchise is leaning on the corral fence watching the horses eat when the sorrel's ears prick up. Pawing nervously, the horses back up, their ears pointing toward the river and the trail. A slight breeze blows toward them, bringing the fearful smell of their worst enemy.

Alchise strains his eyes until he catches sight of Mason coming up the trail, a deer slung over his shoulders. Alchise is puzzled. He knows a dead deer does not startle the horses. They carried deer over their backs many times. After stamping in their corral, the two horses race to the far edge of the enclosure, away from the deadly scent. Finally, as Mason nears, Alchise discovers why the horses are so worked up.

"The young cub made a kill. Uh… two kills."

Mason grins with pride. "Yes, uncle. I figured how to kill the big buck the easy way."

Alchise grunts but he is eager to hear the story. "How you do this?"

"It was easy. I let the cougar kill the deer and then I killed the cougar."

Examining the hides of both animals, Alchise knows Mason speaks the truth. He knows that it happened but does not ask for further details. Apache warriors do not boast, and Mason needs no encouragement. Besides that, he reasons, the boy will only tell him another ocean story.

"You're not going to ask me what happened." Mason coaxes.

"No."

"But it's a good story."

"Cub always tell good story. Ocean story, good story." Mason seems genuinely disappointed, but manages a smile. No matter how hard he tries, he cannot convince the old warrior that he is not joking with him about the big water.

Seeing the boy's frustration and succumbing to his own curiosity, Alchise relents. "Cub tell Alchise good story while we skin deer."

Mason knows his uncle will ask eventually. He is learning that Alchise is naturally curious. Every night after supper, he questions Mason until they go to bed about the east and the big cities found there. About the railroad and big ships that cross the ocean. His eyes widen as he tries to imagine these wonders, but he is not certain he believes them. Hardest to believe was the story of the new talking machine, which is a new invention. Not only is there no reason for such a thing, he has to see it before believing the story from this cub.

The old warrior nods with satisfaction as Mason finishes telling of killing the big cat. "Cub do well, make Alchise proud."

"Aw, it was just luck," Mason said, but inside he is pleased with his uncle's praise. "At least we have venison now."

Alchise studies the youth. "Many men have luck, young one, but some need help from Great Spirit. Alchise think cub have more than luck. Maybe cub have good medicine."

No more was said of the kill. Both hides are stretched against the side of the cabin where they can dry before curing. Alchise fixes Mason something to eat and then they embark on the day's training.

"Mason need no horse today," the warrior tells him. Alchise mounts the sorrel and, with Mason trotting along behind him, they start toward the low valley to the west.

Mason is curious. No horse, no bow, no weapons at all except his skinning knife. What does his uncle have planned today? Never before did they carry a water skin, but Alchise has one slung across his shoulders this morning.

Pulling the sorrel to a stop, Alchise surveys the vast valley below them. He looks to the sky. White clouds drift slowly overhead thick as sheep's wool. The light blue sky has a red cast to it as the sun reaches its zenith.

Normally, they were in the countryside early, but Mason's hunt and the skinning of the slain animals delay them. Already the heat waves hover above the ground, dancing in the bright sunlight. Most of the desert animals return to their various burrows and nests to lie and wait out the midday heat.

As far as Mason can see, nothing stirs, not even a tumbleweed. A hawk circles high overhead, his sharp eyes missing nothing.

Alchise hands Mason the water skin, then dismounts. No longer did Mason require the water he needed on his first day in the desert. His body became accustomed to going all day in the heat with little or nothing to drink. Alchise knows this, so why did he bring the water?

"Today you do something different," Alchise said in the Apache tongue. "It is a difficult thing to do. We will see if you are ready." Alchise's words flow easily, not at all broken like his English.

Mason learns enough Apache to understand most of what his uncle says. Sometimes he forgets and asks something in English, only to be ignored. Then Mason searches his memory for the correct words, trying out different ones until he has it right. Often he makes his mentor laugh with his choices.

Many of the words are difficult to pronounce properly. One has to roll the tongue to get the proper sound to come forth. It reminds Mason of the thick brogues of the bully boys back in New York.

"You will take water in mouth. Do not swallow or let fall out. Hold water until Alchise ask for."

This is a new one, Mason thought, as he takes a mouthful of river water. Alchise is always coming up with something new for him to try. The challenges always excite him. He has confidence in his body and in its ability to cope with any new test. Fear is unknown to him now. Here in the desert and in the forest, Mason feels like the steel wheels that carry the steam engines of the railroad. He feels indestructible. His body tenses as he holds the water in his mouth. He is ready for this new trial, whatever it might be.

Alchise looks back at him, then nods and kicks the sorrel into a slow lope. Mason can feel the water sloshing inside his mouth as he runs after the horse. The natural desire to swallow is tremendous and it forces him to concentrate. His mind begins to play tricks on him. Did he still hold the water or did it run down his throat? Trying to feel it with his tongue is no good. It is already the same temperature as his mouth. Mason curses to himself. No, the water is still there. He cannot and will not fail.

The only real fear Mason has is that of failure. To fail at something in front of Alchise is the one thing he dreads. He knows his uncle will only smile and have him try again, as with the bow. Mason does not understand why he feels such a need to succeed before Alchise. In the past few weeks, his respect for the warrior has grown tremendously. He never really knew such respect before he came west to live with Alchise. In New York, Mason watched the great boxer John L. Sullivan win several fights on the barges, but he did not respect the man. He respects his fighting ability but nothing more.

He respects his father's status and his ability to make money, but he did not respect James Davis the man. Alchise, he respects. The warrior does not have money and knows nothing of boxing, but his presence demands respect.

Watching Alchise astride the sorrel, Mason cannot think of the right word. Nobility, maybe? He read about the great kings and knights of Europe. He supposes Alchise is like these men in some ways. His bearing, his pride, but mostly the genuine kindness and generosity along with his sense of fairness. Each day, Mason wants to become more like his uncle.

Where John L. Sullivan is loud and boisterous, Alchise is quiet, almost humble. Where his father, James Davis, was greedy and materialistic, Alchise is content with what the land provides. He has no need to show off or try to impress people. His every presence is impressive enough.

Mason ran far. He can no longer feel the water. They crossed the valley and were high into the mountains when Alchise pulls the sorrel to a stop.

Mason's heart beat fast as he breathes deeply through flared nostrils. His tightly pressed lips feel numb.

"Put water there," Alchise commands, pointing to the ground.

Mason opens his mouth and the water spills forth onto the dirt at his feet.

"Cub do good."

Mason tries to speak but his jaws are stiff from being held shut so long. For the first time, he is at loss for words, even to ask why.

"Come, we go to rancheria," Alchise said, extending his arm to Mason.

The old warrior's arm is strong and unwavering as Mason grasps it and swings up behind him.

No words are spoken on the ride back, but Mason feels proud. He did not fail. There is nothing else to say.

CHAPTER

FIVE

Someone unfamiliar with Mason might assume he was raised on the reservation. He looks and acts like an Apache. Only his uneven Apache speech gives him away as not being from the reservation. The Apache tongue is difficult, but even in that he is making rapid progress.

Coming in from a successful early morning hunt, Alchise reins the sorrel in hard causing Mason's grey to bump into him.

"We have visitor," Alchise announces in a flat voice.

A bay horse stands tied to the hitching post in front of the cabin. Mason knows immediately whoever it is, they are white. Very few Indians can afford the expensive saddle that sits on the horse.

After Alchise dismounts, Mason leads the horses over to the corral. Flipping their morning kill onto the ground, he drags the gutted deer into the shade, and then watches as Alchise enters the cabin. Whoever it is, it is apparent Alchise knows him.

"Tawano," Alchise said, greeting the visitor softly.

"You make good coffee," the middle-aged white woman said, lifting the metal cup in her hand. She smiles broadly at the warrior.

"Long time since you taste my coffee."

The woman looks toward the door, then back at Alchise. Her eyes search the strong face of the Indian.

"Tell me about him," she said.

"He makes old man proud," Alchise replies.

Again she smiles, her straight white teeth showing between shapely lips. "You are not old by any means and you have always been proud."

"He like my old friend. Like old Massai."

"Not as bloodthirsty, I hope." The woman raises the cup to her lips and takes another sip.

"Time different now, Tawano. Boy is strong. No afraid."

"Is he handsome?" She asks, again casting a look at the door in expectation.

"The young maidens will like much," Alchise said smiling. Then, quickly, the smile vanishes. "Why have you come?"

She grips the cup with both hands. "I had to see him, Alchise. It's been so long." She hesitates. "His birthday was last week. He turned eighteen."

Alchise nods with understanding. "Tawano be careful. Cub smart, learn quick."

"Did the clothes fit him?"

"Yes, but boy grow fast. Big. Strong. Need bigger shirt now." Alchise's voice fills with pride.

"I will make sure he has them." She moves closer to Alchise. "I'm sorry, but I couldn't wait."

Alchise moves away. "What of your man?"

I told Frasier I was riding today."

"Dangerous you come here."

Defiance fills her face. "I have done nothing wrong."

"True, but your man, Frasier, hate Apache."

"I don't care, Alchise. I had to see the boy."

Alchise smiles slightly at the woman. "You always a stubborn one, Tawano."

She smiles back. "Mrs. Frasier," she corrects. "To the boy, I am Jean Frasier."

Alchise nods again in understanding. "Come, he at corral."

"Wait," she said, stopping Alchise from opening the door. She raises her hand gently and touches his firm weathered cheek. Alchise draws in a sharp breath. "Have you been well?" She asks him.

"Yes, I well," he replies. "The boy make me young buck again."

"Your English is much improved."

"I teach boy Apache. He teach me English." Alchise removes her hand from his face, holding it briefly before letting it go. "Come, see boy."

Mason is surprised to see a woman, especially a beautiful white woman, walking from the cabin behind Alchise. Two inches taller than the warrior, she is slender and graceful. A few streaks of gray in her auburn hair compliment her lovely mature face. She has the largest blue eyes Mason had ever seen, and a small, elegant nose. She seems comfortable and completely at ease around Alchise. A familiarity that is unspoken but obvious.

The woman approaches Mason. "You are Mason." It is more of a statement than a question.

Her voice is rich but gentle and stirs something in the youth. He hesitates before answering, then straightens his shoulders and lifts his head.

"I am no longer called Mason," he tells her in proper eastern English. "Please call me Massai."

It is the first time he uses the name Massai in reference to himself. He quickly glances at Alchise and sees the warrior's eyes shine bright with approval.

"Of course," she said. "Massai." She studies him briefly. "You look like your father."

"No one has ever said that to me before," he replies. "Do you know my father?"

Taking his hand, the woman gazes into Massai's eyes. "I am Mrs. Frasier, a dear friend of your father's."

Confused, Massai wants to release her hand but she holds on with a powerful grip. It seems an eternity before she finally releases him and steps back. Her face flushes when she does.

"Forgive me for staring," she tells him. "But I haven't seen you since you were very little."

"Then you knew my mother?"

The tall woman lowers her eyes for a moment and then blinks once as she returns her gaze to Massai's face. "Yes, I knew her well."

Massai fells a surge of joy. "Would you tell me about her?"

Alchise was standing back to let them talk. Suddenly, he steps forward and glares furiously at the woman. "No! It is forbidden. I will not allow it."

The warrior's crisp words are in Apache, yet Massai can tell the woman understands. The way she drops her eyes to the ground and steps back, the sudden blush of her cheeks as she reacts. Yes, he is sure she understood.

"No, Massai, I'm sorry," she stammers, regaining her composure. "I... I do not know what your uncle said just now but I do know that it is forbidden to speak of the dead."

Massai feels confused and frustrated. The white woman lied. She understood Alchise but said she did not. Why would she lie?

"But you are white," he protests. "It is not forbidden for you."

The woman shakes her head and raises her eyes to his. "Yes, but this is your uncle's home, Mason… Massai. You are his responsibility. I cannot disrespect his wishes."

Alchise steps toward Mrs. Frasier. "It gets late. Dark come soon. You go, maybe."

With that, Massai knows the conversation is over.

"Well, yes," Mrs. Frasier stammers. "Time does get away, doesn't it?"

To Massai, she seems reluctant to leave, yet she gathers her skirts as if to run from them, from him. She turns away and starts toward her horse.

"Good-bye," Massai calls out to her in Apache.

Mrs. Frasier did not turn around but Massai notices she hesitated for a second. Then she mounts her horse as well as any man.

Before leaving, she glances at Alchise and then turns to Massai. "Come to the ranch and see me, Massai," she tells him. "You are always welcome."

"Thank you," replies Massai.

The two men watch as she disappears down the river trail. Alchise is the first to move. He turns and heads to the corral.

"Who was she, uncle?" Massai asks, following him.

"Only a white-eye woman who once knew your father," Alchise said somberly.

"I got the feeling she didn't want to leave. You know…"

Alchise cuts the youth off. "Come, we must skin deer before sun falls."

"She also understands Apache, but pretended she didn't," Massai continues. "Probably understands it better than I do."

He waits for a comment from his uncle but gets none. Massai knows when Alchise stops a discussion, it is over. He will learn no more about the white woman until Alchise allows it.

With the visit by Mrs. Frasier, Massai almost forgot his joy in killing his first deer with a bow. Working together, he and Alchise skin and boned out the meat in short order. Little is said and Massai notices that Alchise seems to be preoccupied.

"My first deer with a bow, uncle and a large one."

"If deer no chase arrow, you miss maybe," Alchise comments.

"True, I was lucky but I still got him."

Alchise, hearing the joy in the youth's voice, softens. "Spirit with cub today, this good sign. Young Massai medicine strong maybe."

Massai nods but remains silent. His uncle believes in the spirits and the power of their medicine. Perhaps it is more than luck after all.

The next day, both teacher and pupil are back to their normal routine. Dirt and dust flies everywhere as Massai springs from his hiding place beneath a blanket on the ground. Yelling defiantly, he sends an arrow flying harmlessly over Alchise's head.

Turning, Alchise smiles broadly. Before him stands not a half-breed, but a true Chiricahua. Today, he did not let Massai win. Today, the cub outfoxed the old lion.

CHAPTER

SIX

Many months passed since Massai's arrival. No longer was he a spoiled city boy from the east. Massai became an Apache brave. Naked, except for a breechcloth and moccasins, Massai crouches like a cougar over his kill. Alchise looks deeply into the eyes of his student. For a moment, he feels as though he is looking into the eyes of the old Massai.

Countless hours of hunting, running, and tracking across the harsh desert and mountains hones his magnificent body into solid muscle. Never has Alchise seen anyone like him. Pride swells his heart when he looks at the young man. Massai's hair grew past the headband and he took on the wild rugged look of the bronco Apaches of old. As promised, Jean Frasier provided larger clothing. Alchise simply tells the boy the items again come from relatives on the reservation. If Massai was curious about the relatives, he kept it to himself.

"Aiyee," Alchise said to Massai, who trots beside the sorrel on the grey. "You are now ready."

"Ready for what, uncle?"

"Young Massai know soon. Tomorrow we go reservation."

The next morning finds them at full gallop. The wind tears at their hair and faces as they push the horses hard, asking the animals for more speed. Then even more. Massai is exhilarated. He loves racing the horses against the wind. It makes him feel so alive and free. Running stride for stride, the sorrel and the grey are perfectly matched. Desert critters scurry to safety as the thundering hooves speed through their territory.

Pulling their winded horses to a stop on top of a mesa, Massai looks down on a small village. Since his arrival from the East, Alchise kept him close to the rancheria in the White Mountains. This is his first look at a real Indian village.

Alchise nods toward the village. "No Apache. These people Yaqui," he explains.

By the cluttered unkept look of the village, Massai knows it cannot be Apache. Cur dogs run out to meet them as they descend into the small village. Ragged, big-eyed children follow the two riders through the maze of brush hovels.

Massai hears Alchise's name whispered several times as they pass. The warrior looks straight ahead, ignoring any greetings called out. Massai learns that an Apache warrior never talks to or even acknowledges a Yaqui. They pass through in peace, but without stopping.

After they traveled almost three full days from the rancheria, Massai knows they are near the village of the Chiricahua on the San Carlos Reservation. He wonders if he will see Ponce again, and hopes he will. He is hungry for the company of those his own age.

Later that afternoon, Massai spots the round tops of more wickiups in the distance. The wickiups are larger and sturdier, and the villagers do not appear to be as in awe of Alchise as the first village had been. Here, some of the people wave and speak to Alchise as he passes. Others walk away without acknowledging him. Massai can feel the electricity in the air as they pass through the village. Stopping in front of a large wickiup, Alchise calls out a greeting and then they both dismount.

A white-haired elderly man hobbles slowly into sight. Deep lines crisscross his weathered face like ravines in a rocky mountainside.

"Alchise, my son," the old warrior said, shaking hands. "Welcome home."

Massai is puzzled. The two shake hands like white men.

"Thank you, my father," Alchise replies. He holds out a hand to where Massai stands. "I bring another with me."

The elderly Indian tries to focus on Massai, but his eyes are weak with age. "Come closer," he tells Massai.

Massai drops the reins to the grey and walks to where the old man stands on thin bowed legs. The closer he draws to him, the older he looks, but in spite of his age, the man stands proud.

"My father," Alchise said, addressing the old man, "this is Massai. He has returned to us from the East."

The old man turns to Massai and studies him thoughtfully. "Massai," he said in a shaky voice, "the great spirit returns you to your people." He reaches out and grasps Massai's forearms in a powerful grip that surprises the youth.

"He has grown to be a powerful young man!" The old warrior exclaims, smiling. He squeezes Massai's forearms one last time before letting him go. "Come," he tells them both, "sit and rest. You have traveled far."

Alchise turns to Massai. "This is my father, Nachita," he explains. He speaks the old warrior's name with reverence.

Massai is surprised. Alchise never mentioned his father. Then he realizes that Nachita must be his grandfather.

Massai takes a seat to the left side of Nachita, leaving the most important place, the right side, for Alchise, as was befitting his age and rank. An old woman brings them bowls of steaming meat and some kind of dark brown bread. Nachita and Alchise speak as they eat. Massai understands most of what they are saying but not everything. He finishes eating and places the wooden bowl beside him on the blanket.

Nachita turns his weak eyes to Massai. "Maybe Massai would like to walk through the village," he said. "Meet the people. They hear about you coming from the East."

Massai looks at Alchise, who nods. Eager to see the village and perhaps meet Ponce again, Massai leaves quickly.

Alchise smiles to himself. In time, the youth will be content to sit with his elders, but he is not yet accustomed to all Apache ways or the honor of being included. Alchise remembers when he was young. He wanted to listen and be near the older warriors when they talked about raiding or fighting with the Mexicans. He learned much from their tales. As a young man, he had not yet seen a white-eye. For the cub, it is different. He already knows about the outside world. It is the Apache's world he has to learn.

Massai makes his way through the village. It is a large reservation and there are many wickiups. Sycamore trees, along with cottonwood, oak and cedar, grow along the river and throughout the village. Pinion and smaller trees hide some of the dwellings.

Dogs and cattle freely roam the wide-open village. Pole corrals hold the horses. The afternoon cook fires are blazing as the squaws prepare meals. Earthen jars and cooking pots are stacked on the ground near the fires.

As he walks through the village, several greet him, curiosity plain on their faces. Young maidens smile then duck their heads shyly and scurry off. Children hug their mothers as the stranger walks by and then cautiously follow him at a distance.

Passing a wickiup, Massai hears a voice from inside call to him. "So young Massai visits us, the tame Indians."

Massai stops before the wickiup. "I see you know me, but I do not know you," he said.

Ponce steps from the darkness of the wickiup. "I see you also learned to speak the tongue of our people."

"Ponce!" Massai said with surprise. He smiles at the young man, showing his happiness in seeing him again.

Ponce takes a long look at the muscular youth dressed in a blue tunic and cartridge belt. A blue headband circled the black hair.

"Alchise has made a Chiricahua out of you," he said with some satisfaction.

"He tried."

"He has done well."

Massai laughs slightly. "You really think so?"

Ponce smiles. "Come, let us walk to the river then you shall see if I lie."

"What's at the river?"

"Women," Ponce said with mischief in his voice.

"What do you want with women?" Massai asks.

It is Ponce's turn to laugh. "Did you not have women in the East? What did you do with them there?"

"Yes, but I am wary of them," Massai replies. "Women are trouble."

Massai does not have to try hard to recall his last encounter with a girl his own age. Her father tried to shoot him with an old flintlock rifle. Luckily, it misfired. Then there was Mary. Trying to rescue her from André landed him in jail and finally on a train to Arizona.

Ponce's laughter interrupts his thoughts. "Ah, true, but they are the only enjoyment left to us tame Apaches now."

In spite of his attempt to be light, Massai notices that Ponce said the words "tame Apaches" with contempt. Although he looks and acts Apache, Massai does not fully understand the significance of the reservation. To him, the land the Indians live on is vast and beautiful. He does not grasp Ponce's meaning of the words "tame Apaches."

"Why did you wear the biting iron?" Ponce asks Massai as they start walking toward the river.

At first, Massai does not understand what Ponce means, and then he remembers. The first time Ponce saw him, on the train, he was shackled. It seems like a lifetime ago.

"I have seen the biting iron on many of our braves," Ponce continues. "When they get drunk on tiswin or the white man's whiskey, the soldiers come and take them away."

"I tried to escape Bosworth, the man who brought me here," Massai explains. "He chained me until we met up with Alchise." Massai purposely left out the fact that he left a dead man lying on a New York City street, which made both his father and Bosworth wary of him.

"In the midst of all this beauty and you have only a dark scowl to offer?" Ponce chides.

Massai shakes off the bad memory. It happened to Mason, not to Massai. He turns his attention back to the present and gazes about him.

True to Ponce's predictions, several young women laze about in the late afternoon sun on the sandy banks of the river. More swim and bathe in the shallow water unaware of the approaching young men. Massai blushes when he sees they are naked. He swallows hard as his eyes follow two girls emerging from the water. Ponce watches, too. Spying Ponce and Massai standing near their clothes, the women let out a screech and duck back into the water.

With a hearty laugh, Ponce calmly sits down and starts talking to Massai while the girls fling insults at them. Some of the young girls are screaming in protest, but Massai can tell it is mostly for show. Most of the girls seem indifferent to their presence, except one. She stays out in the deep water. Only her head is exposed. Her long black hair floats on the surface behind her. She does not feign embarrassment, nor does she look pleased to see the young men. Her gaze is steady and unwavering.

Massai boldly returns her stare, unaware for the moment of any other girl. Their eyes meet and lock onto each other. She is not teasing as the other girls were. All Massai can see of her is her face and hair. Her beauty strikes him. Her large soft brown eyes bore into his. It is the look of a woman who likes and appreciates what she sees.

Massai is captivated. Never has he seen a woman so beautiful or so forthright. Breaking the spell, he forces his eyes from hers then abruptly turns back toward the village.

"Where do you go so fast?" Ponce asks, once he catches up to Massai.

"Alchise will be ready to leave soon," Massai said bluntly, hoping his racing heart will not betray his emotions.

Ponce grins. "Oh, I see. It couldn't' be that you are scared of the women, could it?"

Massai stops and turns to Ponce. "Why should I fear her? I don't even know her."

"Her?" Ponce's eyes sparkle with mirth. "You have found one to favor already?"

Massai throws a look of disbelief at his new friend and starts once more for the village. Ponce walks at his side, keeping up, stride for stride.

"Well, it is good to be scared of them," Ponce tells him, trying to sound serious. "Angry buffalo are easier for a man to manage. Not as pretty, but easier to handle."

"She is beautiful," Massai murmurs as they walk.

Next to him, Ponce sighs. "Ah, yes. I thought that was who you were staring at. Her name is Alchuni."

"Alchuni," Massai repeats, rolling the name around on his tongue, tasting it for the first time.

"Yes, Alchuni is beautiful. She is also the daughter of Salto, and that means trouble for you, my friend."

Massai stops and looks at Ponce. "Trouble? What do you mean, trouble for me?"

"Much trouble, I'm afraid," Ponce tells him. "Salto and Alchise are enemies, so neither will approve. Then there is Chato."

Massai thought a moment. "Chato? The one who rides with you? The angry one?"

"Yes, the Mescalero. He has already killed one man over her." Ponce looks directly into Massai's eyes. "He would think nothing of killing you, too."

"Alchuni, she is Chato's?"

"No, but he intends for her to be."

Massai shakes his head and starts walking. "Doesn't matter. I do not look for a woman." After a few steps, he stops again. His curiosity about the girl was getting the better of him. "But tell me, Ponce, why did Chato kill someone over Alchuni if she does not belong to him?"

"A warrior asked for her. Chato went crazy when he heard and killed him." Ponce places a hand on Massai's shoulder. "Do not misunderstand, Massai. Alchuni is a good woman. She does not desire Chato, but he wants her and will kill again over her."

Massai does not understand. "A warrior asked for her?"

"Alchise taught you to speak our tongue, to ride, to track, but has he not taught you about women? About our ways between men and women?"

"No, he has not."

"When an Apache warrior wants a woman for his squaw, to marry, to take to his bed, he must ask for her," Ponce explains. "He must pay whatever her family wants for her."

Massai's mouth falls open. "Pay? You mean he buys her?"

Ponce shrugs. "Of course. How else could he have her?"

"The woman herself has nothing to say about whom she marries?"

Ponce gives a little laugh. "She can say all she wants. In the end, she will do as her father says or get a whip to her back. It is the Apache way."

Massai feels sick. This is barbaric. How can they permit such a practice? In the East the selling and buying of a woman is illegal. Taking one more glance at Ponce, he knows from his friend's expression that it will do little good to question him further.

They follow the foot path back to Ponce's wickiup. Motioning for Massai to sit down, Ponce pulls out an earthen jar and offers it to his guest. Massai sips the tart liquid from the jar, makes a face, and hands it back to Ponce.

"I see Alchise hasn't taught you about tiswin either," Ponce said, as he takes a big swig from the jar.

"Just to stay away from it," Massai said, politely refusing more.

Ponce studies his friend's face. "I can see that you have you have grown to like your uncle."

"Yes," Massai said honestly. "He is like a father to me. More so than my real father ever was."

Ponce takes another drink of the corn liquor. "Alchise has big medicine," he said after wiping his mouth with the back of his hand. "No other warrior in the Apache Nation can match him. Even now. When he quit Geronimo, it took the heart out of the old chief and he surrendered." Ponce's voice is almost reverent as he speaks.

"What about Massai?" Massai asks. "Old Massai?"

Ponce thought a moment. "Yes, he is also a great warrior, but I think he lacks one thing Alchise has."

"What?" Massai is curious about the man he was named after.

"Vision. He lacks vision." Ponce takes one last drink of the tiswin and puts the jar down. "We were a beaten people and only Alchise could see it.

Was willing to see it. We had to change or be slaughtered."

"But you lead the Wild Ones?"

Ponce shrugs.

Massai laughs. "Then Ponce must not have any vision."

"Oh, I have vision, Massai," Ponce said, half laughing. "I just don't have any sense."

It was getting dark. Massai stands and holds out his hand to Ponce. "It is your turn," he said. "Come to the rancheria and we will hunt together."

Ponce looks down at the outstretched hand of Massai. "I see," he said with a slight smile, "that Alchise hasn't removed all of your white man ways." He locks his eyes on Massai. Accepting Massai's hand, he shakes in the white man's fashion. "I would like to be your friend, young Massai. I would like us to ride and hunt together."

CHAPTER

SEVEN

S mall, well-beaten paths lead from one wickiup to another all across the village. Tumbleweeds and small rocks are always ready to catch an unwary traveler's foot and send him crashing to the ground. Massai has been watching his footing, deep in thought. He does not notice the girl until he nearly bumps into her.

"Alchuni," Massai blurts out in surprise. They are so near to each other he can smell the yucca soap she washed with. Her jet-black hair still drips water, causing her soft, doeskin dress to cling to her breasts.

"You know my name?" She asks, equally surprised. Once composed, she said, "You are Massai. Nephew of Alchise."

"Yes, I am Massai." He can feel himself blushing and is thankful for the falling darkness.

"We heard you were coming."

Two of the other girls pass. Giggling, they look back several times before passing from sight. Massai feels awkward. Alchuni is even more beautiful up close and he is becoming aroused by her nearness.

"Talk travels fast out here."

"Yes," she said with a coy smile. "Now I must go before talk travels about us."

Impulsively, Massai reaches out and gently takes her arm as she tries to pass. "Why? I would like to talk more with you."

Alchuni looks down. "I cannot. Maidens are not allowed to talk to young men." She starts to move away.

Confused, Massai releases her arm. "Then why did you seek me out?" He asks.

"I did not seek you out. You blundered into me." She laughs. It is a delicate and musical sound. "But, yes, I wanted to meet you."

"Can I see you again?" He asks.

She said nothing, but smiles. Her snow-white teeth gleam. He has his answer. As she walks away, Massai turns to watch. Her brown legs are bare almost to her knees and are slender and shapely. His eyes move upward and he watches the gentle sway of her hips until he can see her no more.

When he finally finds his way back to the wickiup of Nachita, Alchise and another warrior were sitting outside. Massai stayed longer with Ponce than he intended. His preoccupation with Alchuni caused him to lose his way back in the fading light.

Alchise looks up as Massai comes into the light of the fire. "Massai gone long time."

"I went to the river with Ponce."

The two warriors look at each other and grin. They know why young men went to the river.

Alchise indicates the man next to him. "This is Loco, my brother. Another uncle for you."

"My brother told me of you," Loco said to Massai. "I see he tells the truth."

Massai greets his uncle and then takes a seat beside Alchise. He cannot get use to not shaking hands like the whites do. Indians are more aloof. They do not show feelings like the white men. After they come to know you, they are more jovial and fun loving, but until then, you rarely see any emotion from them.

Alchise looks at Massai. Something bothers Massai?" He asks.

Loco chuckles. "It is a woman. I can always tell. I remember you, Alchise, when you fell in love with the woman..."

Alchise glowers at Loco and the man stops in midsentence. Alchise looks at Massai again, but Massai took no notice.

"Is this one beautiful, nephew?" Loco asks.

Massai is embarrassed at their bantering but he knows it is all in fun. He found himself instantly liking Loco.

"Very," Massai answers in a sheepish tone.

"So, who is this beautiful maiden?" Asks Alchise.

"Her name is Alchuni."

The brothers stiffen then Loco laughs, breaking the stillness.

"Just like you, my brother," Loco said. "Remember the Membreno maiden? Our father was the sworn enemy of her father, too."

"I remember," Alchise answers, but his response is stiff, causing the atmosphere to change from teasing to serious. Alchise draws a deep breath and rises to his feet.

"Massai, Salto is my enemy. You will stay away from the girl," he commands in a stern voice.

Abruptly, he walks away into the night, leaving Loco and Massai alone. Alchise never spoke to Massai so harshly, not even when he first arrived and behaved so badly. Looking over at Loco, Massai waits for an explanation.

"Alchise and Salto have been enemies for many years," Loco explains. "In time, his anger will cool."

"I have never seen him so angry."

"He has no anger for you, nephew. He thinks of the old days. That is why his anger spills out."

Massai nods. His mind drifts back to the lovely Alchuni.

As if reading his mind, Loco said, "I know this maiden. She is very beautiful."

"She confuses me, uncle."

"How so?" Loco turns to Massai, giving him his full attention.

"She runs into me on purpose, near Ponce's lodge. Then says we must not be seen together and hurries off."

Loco smiles. "She wants you to know she is interested in you. It is not considered good behavior for a maiden like her to be seen talking to a young man unless she is accompanied by an older woman."

Massai is curious. "What do you mean when you say, a maiden like her?"

"Alchuni is a maiden," Loco said softly. "A virgin. She is highly prized and could bring many horses and hides to her family. This she is proud of. She also knows about Salto and Alchise."

"I see," Massai said. "How do I get around Alchise, and what about Salto?"

Loco smiles broadly. "Do not worry about Alchise, Massai. He will come around. He loves you like a son and will not deny you happiness."

"I do not want to disobey his wishes."

"Do you not want this girl?"

Massai has to think. He is young. Yesterday he wasn't even thinking of women.

"Yes, uncle," he finally said. "Yes, I do."

"Then pursue her, but I warn you, another wants her too."

"Chato?"

Loco looks at Massai closely. "You know of him?"

Massai nods his head slowly. "Yes, I know of him."

Again, the young warrior thinks of Alchise. He has no wish to disobey him. In New York, his disobedience caused him to be branded a rebel and troublemaker. Here, now, after everything Alchise did for him, he has no wish to disrespect his uncle. Still, he cannot get Alchuni off his mind. Just the thought of her stirs him deeply.

"Tell me, uncle. What happened between the Membreno girl and Alchise?

"Alchise married her."

Massai smiles. "Against their fathers' wishes?"

Loco chuckles softly. "Alchise gave so many gifts to her family, her father could not refuse. He was such a greedy man. Once they were married, the two families were bound to make peace."

Massai's eyes light up. If Alchise went against Nachita's wishes, then he cannot hold it against Massai for doing the same.

"What happened to the girl," he asks.

Loco hesitates then speaks quietly. "The Mexicans raided our camp. She was taken prisoner. Alchise looked for her many years, deep into Mexico. He killed many in his travels. They called him Siebodo Simpos—the crazy one. Finally, his thirst for blood was finished." Loco flattens his hands and Massai knows there will be no more talk about it tonight.

It is late. Massai and Alchise sleep the night in the wickiup of Nachita. It is roomier than Massai thought. Nachita has only one old squaw. Alchise's mother was also killed several years earlier by the Mexicans. Navajo blankets adorn the walls, along with Nachita's weapons of war. Now he is old, but at one time, he was a respected warrior.

When dawn broke, Massai wakes and silently walks out into the fresh morning air. Alchise is pulling his sorrel from the corral as he approaches. The village is already alive with fires and crowing roosters.

"You will stay with Loco," Alchise tells him, glancing at the sleepy-eyed Massai.

"But why?"

"You are of an age to become a warrior. Your novice time is near. Soon the medicine men of the tribe will give the trials of manhood. You must take them. Loco will be your sponsor. He will help and advise you. Listen to him. He is a great warrior. It is a great honor for him to accept you. If you fail, he, too, will bear the shame."

Massai studies Alchise's face. "This is what you wish?"

Alchise smiles. He forgot the anger of the night before. "No, young cub, it is what you want. If you do not pass these tests, Salto will not let you court the one called Alchuni. This is why Chato has not already taken her for his wife. He is not yet considered a warrior."

"Then you approve, uncle?" Massai asks. "I can see this maiden?"

Alchise places a strong hand on Massai's shoulder. "It is not for me to approve of a man's heart. You have much to overcome before she can be yours."

Massai nods. "Do not worry, uncle. I will pass these trials no matter how difficult they are."

"Alchise already knows this," Loco said, joining them.

Alchise mounts his horse. "I will come for you when the trials are over," he said to Massai.

Together, they watch Alchise ride off into the morning mist. Massai then follows Loco to his wickiup where he is introduced to Loco's family. Seeing the face of one of the young women, Massai blushes. He recognizes her as one of the girls at the river. She recognizes him as well and whispers something to her father.

Loco whispers back and then turns to Massai. "You do not know all Apache ways. For this reason, your mistakes are forgiven... once. Do not let Ponce lead you astray, nephew. The result will be painful next time."

"I will not tell you of the punishment," Loco adds, "for I do not believe it will happen again. A young man preparing for the rites of manhood should not take foolish risks that could ruin it."

Massai swallows hard and nods. There would be no further trips to the river to watch the maidens bathe, of that he is certain. Looking around at the faces watching him, he smiles sheepishly. Here he is in the middle of an Apache village, dressed in buckskins, and about to take the rites of manhood. Already he is breaking rules and customs without even trying. Maybe he did not change that much.

"Trials start early tomorrow," Loco informs him. "Today Massai visit friends, rest body and mind. He escorts Massai out of the wickiup and walks away.

Alone and with nothing to do, Massai walks slowly through the village. Several boys play some kind of game with a hoop. He is unfamiliar with the game, but watches as the youngsters roll the hoop skillfully back and forth.

"The mighty warrior Massai has nothing to do but watch children play?"

Massai does not have to turn to know it is Chato speaking. Ignoring the Mescalero, Massai walks on toward the horse corrals along the river. Better to leave trouble in the dust.

"Breed!" Chato calls out.

The word cut into Massai like a knife. He turns around to face his tormentor. Chato stands several yards away but makes no move to advance.

"Alchuni is my woman, Breed," Chato tells him, his face twisted in anger. "Talk to her again and Ponce will not be able to help you." Chato sneers. "And neither will the mighty Alchise."

Chato swaggers off, confident he intimidated the half-breed. Now the woman will know. The entire village will know. As Massai watches the cocky Chato walk away, fury grabs him like a doubled fist, but he holds it in check. To fight over a woman would only cheapen her in the eyes of the village. There will be another time for Chato, he promises himself.

Massai continues walking until he comes upon Ponce sitting quietly in the shade of a large sycamore not far from the river. His friend seems lost in his thoughts. Massai joins him. Leaning back against the smooth bark, he studies the peaceful moving water. Noise from the village drifts on the wind to where they sit. Neither speaks. Occasionally, they can hear the laughter of children.

"So, you take the tests?" Ponce asks, breaking the peaceful silence.

Massai nods.

"You will do well," Ponce tells him. "I took them last year. They are nothing."

"Nothing?" Massai asks in surprise.

"Nothing, my friend. You will only have to stand in one place for two days, run fifty miles, and then live without food for ten days." He shrugs his shoulders. "It is nothing."

"Nothing?" Massai asks again. "It doesn't sound like nothing to me."

Ponce glances over and grins. "I make a joke, young Massai. I know you will do well. Alchise trained you. You are ready or you would not be here."

Massai frowns. "I hope you are right."

"Don't worry. Either way, you will win."

"What do you mean, Ponce? How will I win either way?"

"If you pass, Alchise and Loco will be proud. If you fail, you won't have to worry about Alchuni anymore." Ponce laughs. "See, either way, you will be relieved."

Massai half smiles. "Oh, that makes me feel better."

Both young men laugh.

"Come," Ponce said, standing up. "I'll race you to the river."

He takes off, his legs pumping furiously. Massai chases after him and overtakes Ponce before they reach the river's edge.

Stripping down to their breechcloths, both hit the water at the same time. The sun is hot, but along the banks of the river was shaded and comfortable. Two squirrels scold the intruders from branches high overhead. The youths float lazily in the river, enjoying each other's company. For the moment at least, Massai forgets about the upcoming trials and Alchuni, and time passes quickly as the day wears on.

When the sun starts dipping in the afternoon sky, Ponce calls out to Massai. "It gets late. You should rest for tomorrow."

Both young men swim to shore and pull their dripping bodies onto the sandy bank. Massai rolls over until he is on his back looking up at the sky.

"This is a very peaceful place."

"Yes," Ponce responds. "Too peaceful."

Massai can hear a note of hostility in his friend's voice. Ponce is the leader of the Wild Ones. To them, the peace is maddening. To Massai, it is salvation.

CHAPTER

EIGHT

It is early when Loco's big hand shakes Massai awake. It takes a moment for him to remember where he is. Outside, the village is alive. Cook fires are crackling and smoke hangs over the wickiups like a blanket. Loco's daughter, Tiana, brings steaming bowls of food for both men. With mischief in her eyes, she smiles sideways at Massai. After whispering something to her father, she disappears back inside. Two other women occupy the wickiup. At first, Massai thought the younger one was another daughter. He is shocked to find out she is Loco's youngest wife.

The Indian agent at the fort and the Quaker missionaries tried to stop the practice of polygamy, but failed. If a man is wealthy enough to afford two wives, then he is considered lucky. Massai shakes his head. One would be enough, sometimes maybe too much.

"Eat well, Massai," his uncle tells him. "Today the trials start. You must be strong." Loco then steps inside the wickiup.

Tiana pops back outside immediately and walks to where Massai is eating. "Would you like to know what Alchuni says of you?" She asks him.

Massai eyed the girl with suspicion. She is slender, smaller than Alchuni, and she is devilish. Dark shiny hair hangs far below her waist and waves gently as she moves her head. She is pretty, but Alchuni is beautiful.

"Well, would you?" She asks again.

"Does Tiana know Alchuni?" Massai asks without answering.

The girl smiles shyly then kneels beside Massai. "She's my best friend."

"What does she say about me?" He hopes his voice sounds indifferent and does not reveal the pounding in his chest. He takes another bite of his food to cover his nervousness.

"She says, she will marry you."

The words jump out at him, almost causing Massai to choke on his food. He puts the bowl down before he drops it.

Tiana giggles. "Did you not ask her?" She teases.

Massai's mouth moves but words do not come out. Leaping to his feet, he looks at the giggling girl then turns and strides to the corral where he keeps his grey.

Tiana follows him. "And..." she said as she catches up to him at the corral, "she said to give you this."

He turns to Tiana. She holds out her hand to him. In it is a small, carved figure of a thunderbird. Massai takes the offered trinket and turns it over several times.

"What's this for?" He asks.

"Alchuni said it's to bring you luck." Tiana studies Massai's handsome face. Her eyes dance. "Many tried to win her before Chato came here. She always walked away, but you are different. You she loves."

"Love?" Massai can barely get the word out. He only spoke to the girl briefly.

"Yes, Massai," Tiana said with soft giggle. "Love always comes before marriage or at least it should. Don't you agree?"

Tiana is talking about something Massai has little knowledge of and makes him uncomfortable. In spite of himself, he finds Tiana's words exciting and his heart races.

"Myself," she continues, "I like a man like Ponce."

Suddenly, Massai understands. Tiana wants Massai to speak to Ponce about her. He frowns. Ponce only wants to tease and play with the girls. As a Wild One, he surely will not take one serious enough to marry.

He turns the thunderbird over in his hand again then closes his fingers tightly around it. "Thank, Alchuni for me."

Tiana is not to be deterred. "Did you ask her to marry you?" Her eyes are serious now.

Massai hesitates. He didn't, did he? He could hardly remember what he said to Alchuni, he was so taken by her beauty. "No," he finally said. "No, I didn't, Tiana."

Tiana put her small hands on her slim hips. "You must have said or did something or she would not have given you her love charm."

Massai opens his hand and studies the little carved figurine. "I only asked if I could visit her lodge. That's all."

Tiana shakes her pretty head. "You have much to learn, cousin. To an Apache maiden that is the same as asking her to marry you."

Massai is confused. He also wants a way out of this conversation with Tiana, but does not want to hurt her feelings. Fortunately, Loco calls to him from the wickiup and Massai almost trips in his haste to leave Tiana.

"Clumsy buffalo," she calls after him then giggles.

The trials start, ten young men and their sponsors stand outside the sweat lodge as a medicine man sprinkles some kind of dust over them. Dressed only in breechcloths and moccasins, the youths stand quietly in a line. This is big medicine. Peponito, the great sachem of the Chiricahua, is overseeing the trials. Most of the youths are in awe of the legendary medicine man and some even fear him. His powers are great and so is his reputation.

Massai stares straight ahead at Loco. He notices most of the contestants are younger than Chato and himself. Only one other is the same age. Wolf, one of Ponce's Wild Ones, is also taking the tests.

None of the villagers watch. Children are not permitted near the sweat lodge. For the first time, Massai understands the seriousness of the trials. Peponito chants and shakes gourds filled with the seeds of the Yucca plant. Stopping suddenly, the wizened old medicine man throws a handful of dust into the fire. Flames shoot up and hot sparks fly as Peponito flings his arms out and chants to the spirits.

Massai thought some of the youths are going to flee in terror, so intimidated are they of Peponito's medicine. Massai himself does not flinch. He saw the fire trick many times at circuses and traveling magic shows in the East.

Filing into the sweat lodge, Massai finds himself seated next to Wolf. The steam seems even hotter than it did in Alchise's sweat lodge. To go into a place such as this without previous experience would be almost unbearable. He smiles inwardly and lets his body relax and enjoy the steam. He is confident he will pass the tests. Alchise prepared him for this without his knowledge or understanding of what was to come. His appreciation and respect for Alchise grows even more.

Finished with the sweat lodge, the candidates have to stand in the hot sun. An Apache warrior has to withstand many hardships to survive the harshness of their land. Deprivation and hunger are part of everyday life. The tests will reveal if a young brave is ready to take on the responsibilities of manhood, along with its privileges.

Throughout the day, the young men stand under the blistering rays of the sun. Of the sponsors, only Loco remains. The rest of the older warriors come and go, checking on their charges from time to time. Loco stands fast and seems determined to will his strength and courage into Massai's tired legs.

Finally, after many grueling hours, dusk brings relief from the sweltering heat. Still they stand, motionless and determined to pass the first of their tests. It will not be long until the cold night air will chill their bodies and make them wish for the sun to return.

Massai remembers his first night in the desert. He recalls how cold it was and how he shivered while Alchise seemed unaffected by the cold. Massai is determined he will do the same. Passing the tests is important. He will not disappoint Alchise or Loco. He wants Alchuni. He wants to prove to everyone, especially Alchuni and her father, Salto, the white blood in him does not make him weak. He is just as much a Chiricahua as any of them.

Standing in the dark, the young men hear the night sounds of owls and coyotes. They still stand, trying to ignore the aches in their legs and backs, and the emptiness in their bellies as the wood smoke from the village drifts on the night air bringing the aroma of evening meals.

To distract him from his hunger and exhaustion, Massai thinks of Alchuni and the small figurine she gave him for luck. It was with him, hanging from his breechcloth string. What did Tiana say? The beautiful Alchuni loves him and she will marry him. Warmth spreads throughout his body at the thought of her as his wife and suddenly the night chill is bearable.

After their evening meals, several of the sponsors return. They sit in a circle a few feet away and smoke their pipes. However, Loco stands alone. Massai can just make out the form of his uncle standing at the fringe of the darkness keeping watch over him, continuing to will Massai through the trial.

The air grows colder as the night wears on. Massai studies the moon, guessing from its position how many hours before the sun will peek over the eastern horizon bringing light and warmth. He imagines the sun's rays sinking into his cold joints, warming him.

He wonders how the others are doing. Even without looking, he knows Wolf still stands beside him. He can feel his presence and sense his determination, as sharp and keen as his own. Throughout the test, he hears occasional muffled moans up and down the line of youths, but none come from Wolf. None come from him, as he would rather die than show weakness. The months of living and training with Alchise changed him. The rebellious rich city boy from New York is gone. In his place is a young Chiricahua brave yearning to be a warrior.

Massai blinks. Toward the east, he can see a ray of light. At last, the sun peaks over the horizon. A new day has dawned. Massai withstood the night.

Loco's face slowly materializes as the darkness gives way to growing light. A smile crosses his face briefly then disappears. Only eight of the ten youths remain. Chato and Wolf are still standing. Tiana appears at her father's side with a steaming bowl of food. Loco takes the bowl from her and hands it to Massai.

"You will eat quickly then we go to the canyons to the west."

Massai wants to refuse the food and allow his exhausted body to sink to the ground. Loco stood all night the same as Massai. Knowing what Loco is doing for him, Massai obeys, takes the food, and eats quickly. It warms him and restores his energy. He barely gulps down the last bite when the old medicine man leads the youths to the outskirts of the village. Here the steep slopes of the canyons are visible. Here, they are informed, the run will take place.

"It does not matter who wins, only that you finish," Loco whispers to Massai before leaving him to join the other sponsors.

However, winning the race matters to Massai. He looks over at Chato. The Mescalero is glaring at him with hate as sharp as a skinning knife. Massai returns the look. Again, the young men line up. They get little rest and only enough time to eat. It is enough time for Massai's legs to loosen up.

Peponito stands before them, a water bag in his hand. Again, he chants to the four winds, then turns to face them. "If you lose the water from your mouth," he tells the youths with a face as hard as stone, "Slink off like a coyote and do not finish the race. Only those strong in body and spirit with the heart of the buffalo and the fight of the cougar will finish."

The old man steps forward and pours water into the first candidate's mouth. He continues down the line until each youth has a mouthful of water. Peponito points his staff to the west. There the runners can see several sponsors standing in the distance, each one posted along the way, far across the mesa. The last few are completely out of sight. The medicine man lowers his staff and the runners are off.

Massai runs easily behind Wolf. With each step, his legs come alive. Up ahead, Chato is in the lead, with only one youth close behind him. Massai knows it will be a long race, possibly all day. He is an experienced runner and knows to pace himself. Taking the lead so early will only use up valuable energy needed for the final push.

The first posted sponsor was further away than Massai thought. He judged it took them almost an hour to reach him. There are seven sponsors posted—seven hours or more of running. He ran almost that long when Alchise gave him this test back at the rancheria. Again, Massai is thankful for Alchise and his training discipline. However, he did not stand all day and night before he ran for Alchise. No matter, he will do it and he will win.

Unlike the first time Massai did this run, he thought little of the sweet tempting water in his mouth. This time he concerns himself with his fellow runners. He paces with the ones in front of him. He watches Chato's back, looking for the first signs of perspiration glistening on the Mescalero. Chato is too short-legged for long distance running. He has a barrel chest and will not have the speed or endurance when he needs it. Massai knows he has both the build and the stamina for such running. He competed in and won many races at school in the East. He feels as if he has been preparing for this race his entire life.

They pass the second sponsor and then the third, only four to go. Massai and Wolf move up two places. Now they run behind three others. Chato runs second.

The trail leads up, down, and then flattens out. Massai wants to let his feet fly on the flats but he holds back. Waiting and reserving his strength, as he knows he must. Wolf is starting to crowd the youth in front of him. Then there will be Chato to pass. Massai knows he will have to be careful as he goes around the Mescalero. He does not trust him.

Closing in on Chato, Massai notes the sweat running down his back. It is a sign of weariness. Wolf is still running smooth and steady. He will be Massai's biggest challenge. They pass the fourth sponsor and Wolf, with Massai on his heels, moves in behind Chato. Suddenly, the youth in front pulls up and falls to his knees in exhaustion. Massai looks into the fallen runner's face and sees pain and humiliation. Never, he tells himself. Never will he fall. He feels the water slosh in his mouth and now runs with even greater determination.

Now Chato is in the lead. The fifth sponsor is in sight. Wolf is pressing the Mescalero hard. Chato picks up his pace. Massai is impressed. He never would have guessed Chato would last this long, let alone have the ability to speed up. He reminds himself never underestimate an enemy.

Wolf matches Chato's speed and stays on his heels. Ahead is a long flat stretch, then another mountain. Massai decides he will take the lead on the upward trail into the mountain. Massai turns and looks quickly behind him. Six runners spread out nearly a half mile across the flat. The three leaders are pulling away.

The sixth sponsor is standing at the base of the mountain trail. The runners are still on the desert floor, but can see the steep trail ahead. If Massai is right, there will be one more sponsor ahead. Then a thought strikes him that makes him reconsider. Maybe the run isn't almost over. Maybe they will line up the sponsors again and the distance will be double. Then he remembers Chato's words in the village and Massai tightens his jaw and increases his determination. It does not matter what the distance, he will complete the test and he will win. He will pass Chato on the mountain trail ahead. He will make the Mescalero burst his lungs trying to catch him. He will make him pay.

Loco is the sixth sponsor. He watches the young men as they run past. Massai sees Loco give him an almost imperceptible nod of encouragement. As they start up the steep incline of the trail, Massai feels his legs start to burn. He pushes the feeling aside and keeps up his pace.

They crowd one another on the trail. Only a few feet separate them. Wolf makes a move and tries to pass Chato, only to be cut off on the narrow trail. Chato bumps Wolf hard with his elbow as Massai watches from behind. It is a foul. No one is permitted to touch another in the trials. No sponsor is there to see it. Anger rises in Massai. Looking ahead, he sees where the trail widens. With a sudden burst of speed, he bounds past Chato on the right, taking advantage of the Mescalero's preoccupation with Wolf. When Chato sees what happened, he becomes enraged and loses his stride, also allowing Wolf to slip by him.

Massai is now firmly in the lead with Wolf close behind. Bounding from boulder to boulder, he leaps over every obstacle on his way to the summit. The seventh sponsor waits at the top. Massai makes it over the crest and starts down to the flats, hoping this sponsor is the last. With a final burst of energy, he forgets about the pain in his legs and churns his legs for the finish.

Glancing over his shoulder, he sees only Wolf in pursuit. Massai's feet fly toward a lone figure in the distance. Then it dawns on him, the path of the race is taking them back to the village. Ahead Massai sees the tops of wickiups and then the old medicine man, Peponito. Villagers are gathering and yelling, cheering them to the finish. Did Massai hear his name? He cannot tell but he thought he did above the din. Blood pounds in his head, his feet pound in the dirt, and his heart pounds in his chest. Above it all, he hears the chants. Yes, the villagers are calling his name. His name and no other.

In a sudden rush of new found energy, Massai's legs pump like a well-oiled machine. At the finish, he stands before Peponito and the sponsors, including Loco. Massai looks at each one, his chest heaving, and waits. When Peponito gives him a nod, Massai spits the precious water at the medicine man's feet.

CHAPTER

NINE

Massai walks in circles until he regains his wind and his body cools down. Several times, he passes by Alchuni, Tiana, and a few other girls. His look seeks out Alchuni, and he stares briefly into her beautiful eyes, searching for some sign of approval. The maiden blushes and lowers her eyes. They both know she will be his.

Ponce soon falls in beside him as he walks. Laughing, he grabs Massai's arm. "Ah, brother, you beat the Mescalero."

Massai can only nod. He is still too tired to speak. Wolf, too, is exhausted and lies on the ground by the finish line. Several of the older men are lifting him to his feet. Chato is not in sight. Massai is not even certain Chato finished.

"Did Chato finish?" Massai asks Ponce, still panting.

Ponce nods. "Yes, he just now finished but you shamed him before the village and Alchuni."

"Is it finished?" Massai stops walking and controls his breathing. "Are the tests over?"

"Only this part, my friend. Now you will take your novice time in the mountains alone."

"When?"

"Tomorrow you go, but watch out for Chato," Ponce warns. "He will be in the mountains, too. It is forbidden to interfere or help a warrior during his novice time, but remember Chato hates you. He will not obey the laws."

Massai nods. He already saw Chato's disregard for laws on the mountain trail in the way he blocked Wolf. Massai looks at Ponce. "I thought Chato was your friend. Why do you warn me?"

"Chato rides with us, but he is the friend of no one. You are my friend, young Massai. This is why I tell you to be very careful. Chato is not to be trusted." Ponce grins and slaps Massai on the back before taking his leave.

Loco watches as Ponce walks away from Massai. He heard Ponce's warning about Chato and knows Ponce is right. Chato is friend to no one. He harbors the hate of the old bronco warriors who rode with Geronimo. Chato wants Alchuni for himself. Massai will do well to listen to Ponce in this regard.

Massai is pleased to see his uncle and greets him. "Ponce seems very happy today, uncle. You'd think it was he who just finished his trials."

Loco smiles. "There is much wagering on the run. Ponce bet many ponies on you. Now he is rich for one so young."

Massai looks in the direction Ponce went and shakes his head. "He had that much faith in a half-breed from the East?"

"No, nephew. He had that much faith in the nephew of Alchise."

Loco takes Massai back to his wickiup where the youth falls into a deep and well-earned sleep.

Alchuni watches with great excitement as Massai enters the village victorious. She holds back her impulse to run to him when he looks at her. She watches as Massai is led back to his wickiup by Loco and her heart yearns for him.

While Massai sleeps, Ponce comes to visit, but Loco will not let Massai be disturbed. Another comes also. She comes under the pretense of visiting Tiana but Massai is the one she longs to see. Catching Loco away from the wickiup, Tiana pulls Alchuni into the lodge for a peek at the sleeping warrior.

Gazing down into his peaceful face, Alchuni smiles. The small carving still dangles from his breechcloth. Both girls giggle softly as Alchuni runs her fingers lightly across Massai's cheek.

Loco sees the girls slip into the lodge. He grins, knowing Massai is missing much while he sleeps. Working beside the fire, his two wives smile to each other knowingly. They too were young once.

The morning mist hangs heavy over the village when Massai finally awakes and joins Loco beside the fire.

"Today you start your novice time," Loco said, puffing nervously on his pipe.

Massai watches as the smoke curls over his head. "Something bothers you, uncle?"

Nodding his head, Loco speaks only one word, "Chato."

"Chato?"

"I suspect that he may try to kill you."

"Because I beat him yesterday?"

Loco blows out a long puff of smoke before answering. "No, because the girl came here last night. He knows and is crazy with jealousy."

Massai's mouth falls open. "Alchuni was here?"

"Yes, in the wickiup. She saw you sleeping?"

"And no one woke me?"

Loco laughs. "She came to visit Tiana, but Chato thinks she came to see you."

Alchuni came to see Massai, not Tiana, and everyone in the village knows it. He pushes his embarrassment aside and contemplates his uncle's warning about Chato.

Massai trots easily beside Loco's horse. Loco is taking him away from the village. In less than an hour, he will be alone with only his wits to survive. Only a knife, some flint, a few snares and a fishing line will keep him from starving. Loco pulls his dun gelding to a stop. Below them lies the desert floor and beyond that, the mountains. Massai studies the broken country below him. Nothing moves. There is stillness as far as he can see.

"When Massai returns to the village, he will be a warrior," Loco said. "Go now. Let no one see you. Remember, you must be gone ten days."

"I will remember," Massai replies.

Loco turns the gelding back toward the village with only a nod good-bye. Stopping a few feet away, Loco turns back to look at Massai again.

"Watch for the Mescalero," Loco warns him. "It is wrong to harm him while he is on his novice journey. If you cannot avoid it, kill him, or he will kill you."

Massai studies Loco's stern face and sees he is serious. He is right, if Chato forces him, he will have to kill him. There can be no hesitation. Kill or be killed.

Watching Loco ride back toward the village, Massai turns and starts down the slope of the mesa to the desert's edge. The far off mountains are at least a day away. Casting one last glance back toward the village, Massai starts to the south as his novice journey begins.

The night's sleep did wonders for him. Except for the lingering ache in his legs, his strong young body fully recuperates. He actually finds himself looking forward to putting the survival skills Alchise taught him to work on his own. Ahead to the south, the mountains loom, reaching for the blue skies. They beckon to him.

There will be water in the higher mountains, he knows, but with no water pouch, he needs to stay near a stream or pool. Game will be there. Fish, too. His moccasins crunch softly in the desert sand as he treads lightly around the prickly pear and cactus thorns. Occasionally, a jackrabbit scampers from its hideaway then scurries from sight. Massai's sharp eyes take in his surroundings, his senses keen and alert.

From time to time, he thinks about Alchuni. Next time when he sees her, he will be a warrior. He promises himself, he will visit the wickiup of her father, Salto. Two weeks seems like an eternity.

A large desert tarantula makes a good target as Massai practices with his knife. His aim is close, but the blade split the ground an inch away, causing the black demon to jump sideways. Disappointed with himself, Massai retrieves the knife and returns it to its scabbard. Alchise taught him well, but he needs more practice and he will have it. Now he has almost two weeks to do nothing but hone his skills. A Gila monster eyed him suspiciously as Massai slipped past its resting place. One of the most dangerous of reptiles, the desert lizard fears nothing.

Massai travels steadily, sometimes even moving into a trot. When darkness comes, he is in a narrow canyon at the foothills with the mountains towering high above. He covers the distance in one day and is pleased with his progress. Finding an outcropping of rocks, he checks for snakes and scorpions then makes a dry camp for the night. He will find water in the morning.

From his vantage point, he can see back across the desert. If Chato comes, he will know it, for no one can reach the outcropping without dislodging noisy gravel. Fingering the sharp edge of the skinning knife, Massai knows he can kill the Mescalero if he has to.

Resting his head on a large sandstone, he studies the stars overhead. A coyote howls from one of the higher peaks, a lonely cry in a desolate land. Some would be afraid and lonely out here, but not Massai. Here, alone, he feels totally free. It is freedom in its purest form. Content, he drifts off to sleep.

Massai rises before dawn and continues his journey. He studies his back trail before moving away from his night camp. Chato is not allowed to have more weapons than the others, but he is not to be trusted. One thing Massai is certain of, Chato will come for him at some time. He cannot let his guard down. He will be ready.

He reaches the tall pines and cedars and now he has to find water. Loco told him of a brook and where to find it. He follows a smooth game trail that leads leisurely across the canyons, meandering back and forth, until he arrives on the banks of a small clear stream. It is just as Loco described.

Removing his moccasins, Massai wades into the cold water and submerges himself. The water is cold, much colder than the White river that runs beside the rancheria. The water is so clear and pure, he can see the rocky bottom. Brook trout swim casually back and forth, inviting an eager hand to pluck them out of the water. After a few clumsy attempts, Massai gives up the futile effort.

The mountains around him are beautiful. Red rock walls, with shades of gray and black, reach high above, taper down to smooth rock and gravel banks along the stream. Sycamore, willow, and pines line the banks, their green needles and leaves glimmering off the water. Birds sing from their lofty perches. The area is clean and unspoiled. Massai knows few men have passed through here.

Soon he will have to think about food, but for now, he is content to bask in the sunshine and listen to the sounds of crystal clear water cascading across the rocks below. Nature has its own voice.

A cougar, unaware of a human presence, slips down to the water's edge to drink. Flicking its tail, it crouches comfortably as it laps at the cool water. Both cat and man become aware of each other at the same time. Massai dives into the water and the cougar hisses as it bounds back to the safety of the trees. After a few moments, Massai cautiously emerges from the water. Quickly pulling on his moccasins, he looks to where the big cat disappears then vanishes into the tall pines in the opposite direction.

He will not light a fire tonight. A safe place will have to be found where Chato cannot surprise him with an arrow by firelight. Tomorrow he will have meat and a warm fire he promises his growling stomach. Several times during the night, he wakes. He learned to sleep light and to remain vigilant. Nearby an owl hoots then flaps its massive wings in pursuit of prey. An Apache warrior would consider this a bad omen but for whom? Surely, Massai thought, if he can hear the owl, Chato could too, if he is near. It will cause

Chato to worry. Massai smiles. Being raised in the white world does have its advantages.

The strange beliefs and superstitions of the Apache do not burden or scare him. Even Alchise is superstitious, and careful not to make the spirits angry. Men are the greatest cause of their own fears, Massai thought to himself. Yes, he will take the best of both worlds—white and Indian. He has the advantage over Chato.

Daybreak comes quickly. Birds sing in the fresh morning air. Several squirrels play in the trees around him. If he had a bow, he could try for one of them. He ponders whether he will ever master the bow like Alchise. So far, the skill eludes him. He saw his uncle hit a sage hen as it flushed, but he cannot even hit one sitting still. He studies the path back to the stream as he walks quietly among the pines. Cautiously, he picks his way down to the water's edge. So far, he sees nothing of Chato or the cougar, but still he is wary of both.

Not far from the water's edge, two fat cottontails hang limply in his snares. Quickly, he skins the rabbits and retrieves his traps. After washing the meat in the cold stream, he returns to his campsite. A fire will not matter now. As soon as he eats his fill, he will look for a better place to camp.

The meat revitalizes him, energizing his hungry body. Wrapping what is left of the rabbit in a skin, he starts up the canyon, following along the small stream. Large boulders block the water in places causing a cascade of water to fall in dozens of small waterfalls. Almost every pocket of deep water has fish in it. He knows he will not starve. Alchise was right that first day they met. An Apache will never starve. An Apache always knows where to find food in nature's land of plenty.

A soft wind stirs the trees and makes a whistling sound through the boughs and branches. He could live in this beautiful place forever. He no longer yearns for the easy life in a big city where tall buildings block out the sun. A place like this and Alchuni are all he needs. Walking along, paying close attention to the terrain, Massai finally finds what he was seeking. A narrow path leads to a hidden cave. Manzanita brush and thorn bushes hide the opening from the outside world.

Chato will not be able to detect his fire inside this cave. He will not be able to come through the thick brush without waking Massai. The cave is perfect. This will be his home until it is time to return to the village. Here he feels safe from the Mescalero.

There were signs that someone else used the cave, but it was long ago. An old campfire, its ashes still intact, lay in the middle of the cave. Perhaps it was Geronimo himself, when he was hiding from the soldiers. Small dry pieces of firewood are stacked against one wall. Spider webs and dust cover the woodpile.

Walking back down to the stream, Massai kneels and cups one hand. Dipping into the clear water, he drinks quickly, careful to keep his eyes on the nearby timberline. He no longer drank water like a white man, unguarded and sloppy. He learned to drink like an Apache—always on guard, always alert.

Cutting two slender shafts from the willow shoots along the stream, he quickly removes their leaves and moves back upstream. Rabbit signs are abundant in the thick briar patches that crop along the banks. Setting his snares, Massai gathers his poles and returns to the cave.

Sitting near the mouth of the cave, he goes to work with his sharp knife. First, he whittles the pole ends down to sharp points. Later, he will harden them over his fire and then he will have spears. Crude but effective weapons, if needed.

CHAPTER
TEN

C hato circles the village to the north. He wants everyone to see him leave in the opposite direction of Massai. Quickly gathering his bow and quiver of arrows from where he hid them days earlier, he swings wide of the village and heads south to pick up Massai's trail.

Never has Chato hated anyone as he hates the breed. Hate consumes him and hampers his reasoning. He will kill him, he thought, and no one would know. Many deadly things can happen to a man alone in the wild. Chato is so caught up in his hate for Massai; he is unaware that his every move is being watched.

Loco leaves Massai quickly so he can follow the bloodthirsty Mescalero. He sees Chato retrieve the bow and arrows and watches him turn back to the south. Loco is Massai's sponsor so he cannot go and warn Massai. It is not permitted. He knows any contact with Massai will break the training and would shame them both. Massai must complete his novice time uninterrupted. He must become a full warrior. Alchise entrusted the boy to him and he will not let his brother down but there is another way.

Quickly, Loco returns to the reservation and seeks out a well-made wickiup at the edge of the village. In front of it, a woman sews leather leggings. Dismounting, Loco kneels on one knee in front of the woman. He never comes to this wickiup. The woman is the daughter of the warrior who stays inside when he is at the village. She never married and Loco knows her father comes first. No horses in the pole corral behind the wickiup. No matter, the old warrior always hides them in the draw, out of sight.

"Kittohaya, I must talk with your father," he tells her.

The woman is pretty. Her smile shows a set of perfect white teeth, and her eyes twinkle in the morning sun. The buckskin dress she wears barely hides her well-rounded curves. What a waste of a fine woman, Loco thought.

"Why do you wish my father?" Kittohaya asks.

"The one who bears his name needs him."

Kittohaya's eyes flash. She knows of the young Massai and how he won the race. She also knows he was to start his novice time somewhere in the mountains.

"Why? What can my father do to help him?"

Loco quickly explains about Chato and the direction he was headed. He is sure the old warrior is listening from inside the wickiup.

"I will tell him when he returns from the south," the woman said when he is finished. Then she smiles.

Loco already has two wives, but this woman warms his heart. He knows she waits for another to ask. His brother, Alchise, has always been the only one Kittohaya holds in her heart. Even when they were young, she only had eyes for Alchise. Loco stands up and steps to the side of the horse. Looking one last time at Kittohaya, he mounts and rides away.

Alchise is older than Kittohaya by ten years, but she looks even younger. As a child, she followed Alchise like a puppy, and Alchise spent much time at the wickiup of her father. It was Kittohaya's father who had been Alchise's sponsor and teacher in the ways of war. They fought together under Cochise and then Geronimo. When Geronimo separated from Cochise, both warriors followed him into Mexico. Until Alchise quit fighting the whites, he and Kittohaya's father were inseparable. When Loco came of age to fight, he joined them in Mexico.

Loco remembers the night Kittohaya was born, even though he was just a young boy. They were camped in the Gila Mountains and it was a very cold night. After the birth, there was a big celebration and Loco was permitted to hold the newborn daughter of the great warrior, Massai. Now he cannot even speak to old Massai. Everyone knows he comes to the village from time to time to see his daughter, but no one speaks of it. Massai is still a fugitive. Most of the time, he stays in Mexico with the free ones who live in the Sierra Madres.

Loco knew Alchise still met with old Massai, far back in the mountains in their old hideaways. It saddens Loco to remember the old times and the warriors of Geronimo and Cochise. The Chiricahua were free then. Masters of their own land and destiny. Now, they are no more than fed cattle, waiting for death.

Inside her wickiup, pride fills the eyes of Kittohaya as she hands her father his rifle and belt of shells. Massai still has the vitality of his days with Goyathlay, who was better known as "Geronimo." Like Geronimo, Massai's spirit will live on after his body serves him no more.

Gray streaks in his hair but he is still straight in the back. The penetrating black eyes have a way of looking deep into the heart and reading a man's soul. A scar runs across the bridge of his nose and down one cheek, giving him the rugged look of a seasoned warrior. Kittohaya is his only remaining child. White soldiers killed three sons and one other daughter long ago. Massai fought hard, longer than many others, but in the end, it was not enough. The white soldiers covered the ground like locusts.

Old Massai knew how to hate. He knew how Goyathlay, old Geronimo, hated. Hate was not enough for Massai. When he escaped the white train in the East, he made his way home vowing revenge. He fought and killed many whites, but still they come. Finally, he quit killing, but he never surrendered, and he never became a reservation Indian. The white men thought him dead now and that was best. He was never seen by anyone except those deep in Mexico, his daughter, and his old friend Alchise.

Even some of the villagers now thought he was dead. Alive and strong, he is every inch a Chiricahua Apache. He listened when Loco spoke to Kittohaya, just as Loco knew he would. Old Massai wanted to call to his old friend, invite him into the Wickiup and embrace him but it is too dangerous for Loco.

Kittohaya walked with her father to his horse. Taking the rifle, he swings easily upon the back of his black gelding and looks at his daughter. "You should have married Loco," he tells her.

"You know I cannot do this," she replies, casting her eyes downward.

"He will never come for you daughter. He loves another, and while she lives he will wait."

"I, too, will wait, father."

Massai nods his head in understanding. He knows his daughter will wait for Alchise for the rest of her days. He then turns his horse into the breeze.

Chato has the advantage over Massai. He has weapons and a skin of

water. Traveling at a trot all day, he is determined to catch the half-breed
before he reaches the mountains. Studying Massai's tracks, he curses. Chato
is surprised Massai covers so much ground so fast and without water. Chato
knows Massai will find water in the mountains. It will do him no good,
Chato thought. He will catch up to the breed easily there. There are many
places to ambush an enemy in the high country.

A menacing smile crosses the Mescalero's face as he rubs his bow. He
will have Alchuni for himself when he returns from his novice time. She will
soon forget the breed. Alchuni will come to him. Salto will give her up for a
price and force her to marry him.

Old Massai studies both sets of prints as he follows the trail of the two
young warriors. Loco was right. The Mescalero follows young Massai, often
overlapping his prey's tracks. Old Massai will follow both and see if Chato
breaks the Chiricahua law governing his novice time. If so, then Chato will
die, as befitting one who dishonors his people's customs. Certainly he will
not be worthy of warrior status.

Young Massai sits cross-legged in front of the small fire that illuminates
the cave. One spear tip is already heat-hardened by the flame. Now he works
on the second. Two brook trout roast over the glowing embers. He will feast
tonight. Massai leans back against the smooth rock wall of the cave and stares
at the crackling fire.

He knows Chato is coming. He can sense it. Twenty years ago, a young
novice warrior would worry about white soldiers and the Apache scouts
hunting the bronco Apache. Now it is a single quarry, but the enemy is a
deadly Apache.

The Mescalero is dangerous and he has the advantage of surprise. Massai
will be ready as he slips quietly outside and sets his trap. The spear's deadly
point is spring loaded and awaits any trespasser that ventures up the small
trail. There will be no moon this night. Pitch-black darkness shrouds the
cave. Returning to his lair, Massai eats his fish and puts another notch on the
small stick he carries to keep track of the passing days. After eating, he
finishes the second spear and spreads the live embers of the fire for the night.
He will sleep light tonight with his new spear close at hand.

Waking, Massai instinctively grasps the spear next to him. The sun is
beginning to penetrate the cave's entrance. He pokes his head out. The spear
is in place, his trap undisturbed. Slipping carefully around his trap, Massai

walks to the water's edge and drinks his fill. This is the morning of the third day. If Chato is coming, it will be soon. Visiting his snares, he finds them torn apart, cut into small pieces. No animal did this. Chato was here and left his warning.

Just as Massai feels the hair on the back of his neck stand up, he hears a sound. He lunges to the side of the trail, just in time to avoid an arrow, which now pierces the ground where he was standing.

Massai runs to his cave, darting inside past his trap. All warrior candidates are required to be unarmed during their novice times except for their knife and what they can fashion for themselves. Chato had no time to make a bow and arrow, so he must have hidden them and picked them up along the trail. With these weapons, Chato has the advantage. Massai watches the trail. The Mescalero will not be foolish enough to come straight at him. He will wait. He knows eventually Massai has to eat and leave the safety of the cave.

Old Massai turns his gelding into a side canyon and blocks the entrance with dead limbs and brush. There is plenty of water and grass to last the horse for several days. He will follow the two young men on foot. With field glasses taken from a white army officer years before, old Massai spots Chato and watches him from a distance. He knows the Mescalero is a worthy opponent and he is armed, contrary to custom. Young Massai will have to be very cunning and skillful to outwit Chato.

Chato was not difficult to find. In his flight, he made no effort to cover his tracks. Old Massai's Winchester rifle covers Chato. The warrior's finger tightens slowly on the trigger and then relaxes. He will wait. He saw Chato release the arrow and caught a glimpse of young Massai's quick reaction, leaping out of harm's way. Massai is fast, like a cougar. Now he knows his enemy is armed. He watches as young Massai bounds up the small trail and into the cave. A cave he spent many nights inside over the years. Old Massai decides to wait and watch. He will see if this half-breed deserves his name.

Chato curses himself. The breed was an easy target, but he waited too long, relishing the moment, and Massai escaped. Now he is in his lair. He will have to wait for another opportunity. Chato knows to rush his enemy would be foolhardy. His bow will be useless at close quarters. No, Chato will wait. The breed will have to eat sometime. Chato is hungry himself, but he cannot hunt. Massai might escape while he is away then he will be the hunted instead of the hunter.

All day Massai watches from his cave but sees no sign of Chato. He knows he is out there, waiting. The fish satisfied his hunger, but that was last night. The remains of his rabbit are also long gone. Now his stomach is beginning to complain. He wonders how long he can stay alive without food. He remembers one of the stories from his short time in church. According to the white preachers, Jesus lived in the desert without food for forty days. Massai mulls the concept over and draw strength from it. There is only about a week left in the novice time.

Whippoorwills call to one another as shadows stretch across the bottom of the canyon. Young Massai continues to wait and watch. He is getting very hungry and thinks he might be able to fish at night. A deep pool is at the bottom of the trail. It will still be dangerous but at least the bow is no threat in the dark.

He watches all day and the Mescalero does not try to cross the water or approach the trail. There is little cover near the water except where the path to the cave begins. Taking his spear and a small piece of rancid rabbit meat he saved for bait, Massai leaves the cave as silently as possible. Checking the spear he had set as a trap, he reassures himself that Chato will not be able to enter the cave without setting it off. Every step Massai takes down the path, he stops and listens. Only the normal sounds of the night are heard on the soft night wind.

Pausing beside the path, Massai crouches and slides silently beneath a small log jam. He can fish from here without being detected. Flipping his baited hook into the water, Massai quickly feels a tug on the line and pulls a fat trout from the water. The fish flops a bit, and Massai fears the sound will alert Chato.

In short order, he catches another fish and starts back up the trail. Keeping his spear in front of him, young Massai feels his way back to the cave. Once inside, he relights the fire and begins roasting the trout. Sitting just inside the mouth of the cavern, he puts his back against the wall and waits. Massai knows the flickering flame can be seen from below. He wonders if Chato will be foolish enough to come for him.

From his own camp, old Massai grins. The young one is roasting fish inside the cave. He can smell it on the wind. He fished while Chato waits on the other side for him to come out. Now, with the smell of food, young Massai is baiting Chato as easily as he baited the fish. Old Massai is sure the young one will have a trap set for the Mescalero. If Chato takes the lure, he will walk right into his trap. Old Massai nods his head in approval. This is no scared white-eye from the East. Young Massai learned his training well.

Chato, too, smells the roasting fish and rage wells up within him. A twig snaps in his hands as he twists it. The breed's display of fearlessness taunts and infuriates him. He can see the flicker of flames on the cave's wall each time the fire flared from the dripping juice of the fish. Notching an arrow, Chato wades in the stream until he comes to the path leading to the cave. He has weapons. The breed, he is sure, has none. Creeping quietly, Chato moves up the path toward his prey. As the hate consumes him, Chato throws caution to the wind.

From within the cave, Massai hears the twang as the set limb sends the sharp spear hurling forward. A cry of pain follows then the sound of retreat. Bounding forward with his second spear ready, Massai hears splashing in the water below. Leaning down, he picks up the bloody spear and a bow. Smiling, he returns to the cave. Now he will be the hunter. Examining the bloodstained spear, he knows Chato is hurt. How badly, he does not know, but tomorrow he will examine the ground. The amount of blood will tell him more.

Old Massai hears the cry of anguish then the hurried retreat across the small stream. He knows Chato miscalculated and went after young Massai. His reward for his haste was injury and pain. The old warrior smiles in satisfaction. His namesake did well but what will the young one do now? He knows the rules of novice time. Will he follow and kill Chato, as was his right or will he complete his novice time in peace and reflection. The latter is the purpose of the time alone according to the laws of the Apache.

The old warrior wonders what his own decision would be in this situation. Would he kill his enemy or obey trial customs? He did both in his time, but now it is another's time and decision.

Old Massai follows the noise of Chato, who staggers clumsily through the brush. This one was foolish to begin with and now his anger with a man and hunger for a woman led him blindly into danger. After an hour, the warrior does not wait any longer to see if the young one will follow Chato. Chasing a man, even a wounded one, in the night can be a fatal mistake. When it is clear young Massai will stay in his cave for the night, old Massai is even more impressed. This means the young one is careful and patient, not giving to hot headedness or blind pursuit.

Chato is groaning and tripping over rocks in his haste as he scrambles down the canyon toward the flatland. He must not be hurt seriously, old Massai thought, or he would have holed up at least long enough to stop the bleeding. It is too dark to read any signs on the ground but there is no need. He only has to follow the sounds of the noisy Mescalero.

After about two miles, old Massai stops and turns back to his own small camp. Chato is in a hurry to leave the mountains. He is heading north.

That night, young Massai sleeps little. His trap worked. Chato was wounded and on the run without his weapon. He will rise with the sun to read the tracks left by his enemy. He will follow Chato to see where he headed. He already made up his mind that if Chato left the mountains, he would not follow but if he remains to fight, Massai will kill him.

In the morning, young Massai follows the blood trail that leads away from the mountains. Chato does not appear to be bleeding heavily, and Massai follows with caution. Soon, there is no more blood on the trail, but Chato's footprints are easy to follow. In his retreat, he did not attempt to cover them, making Massai wonder if he did it on purpose to lure his hunter. The trail continues to the north and Massai follows it until he becomes convinced Chato was intent on escape and no longer a threat.

Massai looks at the bow in his hand. This is better than the wound. The Mescalero broke the law of the Chiricahua, and Massai has his bow with his mark on it as proof. He does not need to go any further, so he returns to the mountains.

The old warrior takes no chances with his namesake. He follows and observes young Massai from a distance. Chato's bow is clearly visible in his hand. The old warrior figures Chato dropped it when he was first wounded. Now one has the bow and the other the arrows. Both are useless without the other. On this day, the one with the arrows was injured and in retreat. Old Massai is proud of the young warrior who carries his name. He defeated his enemy and he did it while respecting the laws of his people.

Massai returns to his cave and picks up the extra spear and his rabbit skins. Chato is gone but he might return. The cave is now known and no longer safe. If the Mescalero comes back, he will carry a rifle and he will be wary of traps. However, there is something else. Massai cannot shake the feeling that he is being watched. He knows it is not by the clumsy Mescalero. Feeling uneasy, Massai decides he will travel further into the canyons and find another hiding place.

This time Massai walks in the water or across the rock ledges that border the meandering stream. He will leave no traces for an enemy to follow, and he will make arrows for Chato's bow.

Many times during the afternoon, he circles high and watches the canyon floor behind him. Nothing moves. He seems to be alone but he still senses the presence of another. He listens intently but hears only the sounds of nature. Alchise made the restless Mason sit and listen to the wild sounds of nature around the cabin. He learned to identify the many birds and animals he heard and to imitate them. Now Massai is thankful that he learned so well, even though he fought against it early on.

At the end of the day, he seeks shelter for the night. He is physically and mentally exhausted. Dark clouds were forming all afternoon. Soon the rain will come. The shelter he selects will have to be high and dry, well above any possible flooding. Water rampaging down the canyon can carry boulders large enough to crush a man. The stream is peaceful and quiet now but with a hard rain, it will become a torrent, sweeping up everything in its path.

Several pieces of flint rest inside the rabbit skins. Now he needs feathers. Along the trail, he picks up several small willow shoots that can be fashioned into arrows. With a few strips of leather from his leggings, he will have what he needs to make arrows for Chato's bow. It begins to drizzle, causing Massai to rush in his effort to find suitable shelter. He passes a rock overhang but it is too close to the water's edge. Trotting faster, he finally spots what he is looking for—another cave.

Pulling himself over the lip of a flat rock that guards the cave, Massai enters the large cavern. Looking around, he sees signs that this cave, too, was once occupied. He finds ashes left from an earlier campfire, but unlike his first cave, this one was used recently. There is a small supply of firewood.

Fat raindrops are pelting the cave's entrance but the full storm has yet to come. Massai quickly returns to the stream to fish and is pleased when he quickly catches his dinner. There is no reason to catch more than he can eat. Fish spoil easily. On his way back, he will search for a feather. Thunder in the distance hastens him along.

Scanning the ground, he searches the cracks and crevices where a feather might be lodged by the winds that roar up the canyon. Finally, he spots several feathers and retrieves them. The feathers are stout and will provide adequate fletching for his arrows. Maybe with the bow and arrows he can kill one of the mountain goats that look down from their lofty domain high on the rocky ledges. His mouth waters with the thought of something other than fish and rabbit. He smiles as he thinks of the goatskin blanket he will fashion for Alchuni.

Safe inside his new cave, young Massai sits before the fire and chips a piece of flint with the back of his knife as the trout roasts. Outside the rain blankets the air, drowning out all sounds but the frequent and deafening clap of thunder. The stream below begins to roar as it swells from the downpour. Lightning flashes across the sky, filling the cave with bursts of bright light. Massai works on the arrows. He is dry and warm and soon his stomach will be full.

Two arrows lay before him. They are far from perfect but they are not bad considering what he has to work with. Strips of leather thong and rabbit hide hold the long, sharp pieces of flint in place on the notched willow shoot. Heated sap from sticky cedar boughs hold the feathers, which he ties on with thin strips of rabbit sinew. The arrows will only be good for one shot. Massai is not nearly as proficient with the bow as Alchise, but he practiced diligently and feels certain he can hit a target as large as a goat.

Soon the full fury of the storm is upon him. Water gushes in a solid torrent under the mouth of the cave. His thoughts drift to Alchuni. Is she thinking of him? Was she warm and safe? He closes his eyes and envisions her beauty and soon he is fast asleep.

The storm passes by the time Massai awakes. He steps to the edge of the cave and peeks out. The ominous dark storm clouds retreated to the east, leaving a smattering of white puffs across the peaceful blue sky. He takes a deep breath and inhales the sweet clean air that follows every storm. Below him, the stream rages with fury. Above him, water still dribbles down the crevices. He knows the high waters will subside almost as fast as they came. He only has to wait.

Massai notches his stick again. Today is his fifth day out. Time is going fast and soon he will return to the village. Today he has a challenge. He wants to hunt the mountain goats that live high above the canyons. Just one will be enough to feed him until his novice time is finished. As soon as the waters subside, he will set out.

Young Massai did not pursue the Mescalero and old Massai approves of his decision. The young one returned to the mountains when his enemy retreated. He will obey the laws of his people and honor Apache customs. It is good.

The old warrior is now free to return to his hideout in Mexico. He is no longer needed here. Young Massai will do well and the Apache Nation has a new warrior they can be proud of. Alchise taught this one well. He will bring honor to his people.

Chato progresses just as old Massai figured. His leg stiffens and he can only hobble around. The spear cut deep into the fleshy part of his thigh and tore through the muscle. He has to guard against infection or his mobility will be severely limited. Chato curses himself. He allowed his hatred for the breed to blind him and he carelessly blundered into the breed's trap. He studies his back trail and wonders if Massai would pursue him. If so, he will be helpless. He is wounded and weaponless. In his struggle to escape, he even lost his knife. He underestimated his enemy and now he might die for it.

Now he knows what the old men of the village meant about Chiricahua women. They are beautiful but can lead a man to his destruction. Alchuni will pay just as the breed will. She bewitched him. His hate for Massai and now Alchuni overwhelm Chato and he swears vengeance on them both. His eyes cloud over with pain, anger, and hate. They will pay with their blood for what they did to him.

CHAPTER

ELEVEN

Alchise and Loco are concerned as they sit before Nachita's wickiup. It was eleven days since Massai left the village. All the other novices returned. Chato came back with a deep cut in his leg, claiming injury from a fall, but both Alchise and Loco are skeptical. They are worried the Mescalero found Massai and killed him.

Both know old Massai was out to watch over the young one, but as of yet, neither return. Alchise looks toward the corral and his horse. He is tempted to go out looking for the young cub but to go out this soon will bring shame on Massai. They will give him more time.

Another concern crosses Alchise's mind that he does not share with Loco. It is possible young Massai still longs for his life in New York. Perhaps the young cub is still Mason Davis after all and used his novice time to escape his Indian heritage and return to the white world. Did Alchise misjudge him?

Late in the afternoon, Tiana emerges from the wickiup. She gazes out across the desert where something catches her eye. She puts down the pot she was carrying and uses both hands to shield her eyes from the low western sun. Something is moving far out in the chaparral. Something white and it looks like an animal. Tiana calls to her father. They are curious as both Alchise and Loco strain to see the distant figure. Suddenly Alchise yelps and slaps Loco on the back. Loco grins with relief. Even at that distance, both recognize the rambling trot of Massai. Quickly the two men sit back down and continue talking, pretending to ignore the approaching youth.

The rolled skin of a mountain goat hangs across Massai's left shoulder as he trots into the village. Looking neither left nor right, he travels past his uncles and stops in the center of the village. Several villagers watch as he breaks the bow he was carrying in two. He hangs it on the council lodge framework where all can see. All will soon know it is the bow of Chato.

Massai walks to Alchise and Loco. He removes the goat hide and presents it to Loco. "For you, uncle, a thank you gift for sponsoring me." Loco strokes the white fur. He looks up at Massai and motions for him to join them.

Alchise watches as the youth seats himself next to Loco. Something has changed. Massai barely acknowledges Alchise. He seems distant, almost arrogant, as though he scored a great victory. Alchise is curious about the hanging bow.

"It is good to see young cub again," Alchise said to Massai.

Massai smiles. "It is good to see you, my uncle."

Alchise nods at the goatskin Loco holds. "How did you catch the white goat?"

Massai lays a single arrow on the blanket at the feet of Alchise. Alchise picks it up and rolls it between his fingers. It is crude but sturdy. "And the bow?" He asks.

"I took it from the enemy who used it against me."

Loco and Alchise looks at each other but neither speak. Alchise passes the arrow to Loco, who eyed it. "Aye, bother. This looks like the ones we made when we were eight summers old."

Massai grins. He knows his uncles are teasing him. Although, it is true the arrow was roughly made. "I made two," he explains. "I had few tools to work with."

Both uncles grunt softly.

"I killed the goat with the first one," he tells them proudly.

Loco stands up and disappears inside the wickiup. Alchise looks proudly at the strapping youth. He has matured in the short period he was gone and it shows in his eyes. He seems older, quieter, and more somber.

"You have made me very proud," Alchise said to Massai. "I have heard how you won the race and proved your worthiness."

"Yes, but it was your teaching that made it possible." Massai looks into Alchise's eyes. "I am proud to be your nephew and proud to be a Chiricahua Apache."

Alchise reaches out and grasps Massai's strong arms with his own. Both are men and warriors now and a mutual respect of one man for another is born. The bond they share is stronger than the hardest oak.

Loco returns and hands Massai a beautiful silver trimmed bridle. "It is from the Mexican Grandee down in Sonora," he explains. "I took it many years ago. It is yours now."

Massai fingers the heavy silver bit and small bells that hang from it. "But, uncle, it is too beautiful to give away. I cannot take it."

"It is too heavy for my horses, so I give it to you. Take it," Loco insists.

Alchise reaches under his tunic and produces a bone handled hunting knife with a tooled leather scabbard. "I give you this," he said, handing the knife to Massai. "You will maybe give them to Salto when you go to his wickiup to visit Alchuni." Alchise smiles.

Massai smiles back. Somehow, his uncles know the goatskin was originally for Alchuni. It was only after coming into view of the village that Massai decided he would give it to Loco. Alchuni and her father, Salto, have been on his mind from the moment he saw the tops of the wickiups. A day did not pass in the mountains that he did not think of the visit he would pay them. His uncles probably realize that.

"Salto has many goatskins," Alchise said. "They are the hides of his father and brothers."

Loco snorts with laughter and Massai looks puzzled from one to the other.

"My brother insults his enemy," Loco explains, "yet presents to you the only gift Salto would accept for the favor of his daughter. Your uncle made a great sacrifice for you, Massai."

Before Massai can reply, Alchise turns his back, causing Loco to change the subject abruptly.

"Think carefully, Massai," Loco said. "Did you see anyone else besides the owner of the bow while you were in the mountains?"

Massai notices Loco's mood changes from lighthearted to serious.

"No," Massai answers. "I only heard the one who dropped the bow. I never saw him."

"But you know who it is?" Loco presses.

Massai nods. "I know."

"There was no one else?"

Massai thinks about it carefully. He remembers feeling as though he was being watched, but Loco and Alchise will probably laugh at him if he tells them. Instead, he shrugs.

Alchise takes note of the hesitation in the youth's eyes. "What is it?" He asks. "What do you not tell us?"

Massai draws a deep breath. "I felt many times that I was being watched. I circled and lain in wait, but never did I see anyone. Perhaps I was nervous after Chato barely missed me with the arrow."

"Chato!" Loco hisses. "I knew it."

Massai reveals more than he intended, but now he can hold nothing back. He tells his story, describing in detail everything that transpired from the first day until he returned to the village. When he was finished, both uncles were quiet.

After a long pause, Alchise speaks in a low voice. "You did well, young cub. Go now, visit others but stay away from Ponce," he warns. "Chato will be with him. We will leave in the morning."

Alchise knows Massai wants to find Alchuni, but it is not time for a formal visit with her father.

Loco, however, takes pity on him. "Tiana just left to pick berries with Alchuni and to tell her of your return," he tells him with a smile. "They are near the river."

Both men smile as Massai hurries off toward the river. They, too, were young once and both carry the weight of unrequited love in their hearts.

"Thank you, brother, for sending the old one to look after him," Alchise said after Massai left.

"You should go to his lodge and thank him yourself," Loco said.

Alchise nods. He knows his brother wants him to see Kittohaya, but he is also right about thanking old Massai himself.

"You're right, brother," he said looking into the fire. "Will you also go? After all, it is you who loves this woman."

"Yes, I have love for her but she is your woman. She will have no other."

"I have a woman," Alchise said still staring into the fire.

"You waste your life, brother," Loco said in exasperation. "The woman in your heart is married to a white-eye."

Many times the two spoke of this and always Loco becomes frustrated at Alchise's stubbornness.

"Besides, I already have two wives. You should take Kittohaya to your rancheria."

Rising to his feet, Alchise studies his younger brother. "You mean well, Loco, but this I cannot do."

"At least go to her and thank her for sending her father to help young Massai."

Alchise nods at this, then turns and starts for the far side of the village. Proud and straight as an arrow, he walks through the village oblivious to the admiring glances of the women and the respectful looks of the men. He is a living legend among the Apache people. Many said it was Alchise and old Massai who actually planned most of the fighting against the white-eye soldiers. Now it matters little but still the people remember.

Walking toward the large wickiup that sits by itself at the edge of the village, Alchise feels a lump in his throat. He swallows hard as he watches the woman named Kittohaya rise from her cooking fire.

Alchise approaches the woman slowly and stands before her. It has been over a year since he last saw her. She is a little older. They both are but her beauty has not diminished. Her large, dark, almond-shaped eyes stare steadily into his. She waits for him to speak.

For a long moment, they stand looking into each other's eyes. Without a single word, she turns and pulls aside the blanket that covers the doorway of the wickiup. Alchise enters first. She follows, letting the blanket fall back across the entrance.

Massai seeks Alchuni, but finds Ponce along the way. Ponce is alone and greets him warmly. He shows him the bridle and knife he received as gifts.

Will this be enough to bribe her father," Massai asks his friend.

Ponce laughs in his usual good-humored way. "Yes, but with Salto, they'll be just enough for you to visit her. Offer a couple of horses, too, and you might get the woman."

"What?"

"I make a joke, but I would keep the bridle and knife and find an uglier woman," Ponce advises.

Massai frowns and shakes his head. "My friend Ponce has no eye for anything beautiful. Look at the old, broken down nags you ride."

"Nags?" Ponce exclaims. He looks to his horse corral in mock dismay. In it are several fine mustangs. "Broken down?"

Both young men laugh aloud. They approach the corral and each one catches a horse and mounts. Riding through the village, they make sure to pass Salto's wickiup before turning toward the river.

"Did you see her?" Massai asks.

"No, but I was not looking for her," Ponce replies.

"Good. Then she is still picking berries." Massai urges his horse on.

Kicking their horses, they lope to the bank overlooking the wide river.

Below, several brown bodies in different stages of undress splash and play in the water. Massai studies the women briefly, looking for Alchuni or Tiana.

"Come," Ponce said as he kicks his horse and slides down the steep embankment.

Massai follows reluctantly, remembering the stern warning he received from Loco about watching the women at the river. Still, if Alchuni is here, he wants to find her. Sliding down the bank behind Ponce, Massai follows him back along the river to where the women bathe.

Alchuni is not among the bathers, so Massai has no further interest. Turning his horse in another direction, he only goes a few paces toward the berry patch when Alchuni, accompanied by Tiana, emerges from a thicket. They carry baskets filled with ripe, juicy berries. Greeting them, Massai is taken back by the frown on both girls' faces.

"Did you come to watch the women bathe again?" Alchuni asks.

Massai is surprised at first and then grins. "I came looking for you. I missed you."

Alchuni studies his handsome face then smiles. She is happy to see him and does not hide her feelings. She hands her basket to Tiana then as Massai reaches down for her, she grabs his arm and lets him pull her up behind him. Massai kicks and the horse springs into a gallop, disappearing up the embankment and beyond.

After riding hard for a few moments, Massai pulls the blowing horse to a stop. Reaching back, he swings the surprised girl back to the ground and then dismounts himself.

"And I thought Chato was forceful," Alchuni gasps as she steps away from the heaving horse.

"Did I hurt you," Massai asks.

"No," she said, eyeing his muscular build. She is pleasantly surprised at his strength. With one hand, he pulled her on to the horse as easily as if she were a child.

"Everyone saw and will be talking," she said.

Massai shrugs. "Let them talk."

"My father will beat me," she told him in earnest. "It is not allowed."

Massai bristles then softens. "I will see your father tonight," he tells her. "Come, we will walk back to the others. They will see there is nothing to their gossip."

Massai takes her arm and they walk beside the horse together.

"Do you wish me for your woman?" Alchuni asks him with downcast eyes.

Massai stops and looks at her for a moment. She is truly beautiful. "Yes," he said.

"For your first wife?"

"Alchuni asks many questions," he said. "Yes, for my… only wife."

The sparkling white teeth of the girl gleam as she smiles, then steps into his arms. Holding tightly to each other, they are only aware of the beating of their hearts. Neither see nor feel the presence of the warrior coming toward them. Only the sudden shriek of Ponce's warning alerts Massai.

Turning quickly, the couple sees Chato just a few feet away. In his hand is a hunting knife. It gleams in the sunlight. Ponce is afoot, running along the bank of the river toward them. Several of the girls run after him. Massai can see the dressing covering the wound the spear made in Chato's thigh. The Mescalero limps badly but he is still strong and dangerous. Holding up his hand, Massai stops the charging Ponce from interfering. This matter has to be settled between the two rivals.

"She's my woman," Chato snarls, motioning toward Alchuni. "She goes with me."

"She was never your woman," Massai said as he pulls his own knife and faces Chato.

Rage boils inside Massai. Chato was spoiling for a fight since the first time they met. Now he will get just that. None of the elders are here to stop it. Ponce will stay back. Now it will be settled once and for all.

Flipping his knife deftly in his hand, Massai feints at Chato's left side. Limping, the Mescalero turns to meet him. Massai knows he can easily kill Chato, but he would be killing a cripple. There is no glory in it, only shame, shame before Alchuni.

Twice more he lunges forward, making Chato fall off balance. Circling, he waits like a wolf after his prey. Chato gets to his feet, but his leg gave way as he tries to parry another thrust from Massai. Grabbing the Mescalero's wrist, Massai applies all the pressure his pent up fury could bring to bear on the man's arm. With a grunt, Chato drops his knife just as Massai delivers a solid blow to the temple. Slowly, Chato slumps to the ground at Massai's feet.

Massai holds Chato's long hair tightly wadded in his fist. "I will not kill you this time," he tells the Mescalero. "When you are well from your wound, if I find you near Alchuni, I will finish you." Then he pushes the near unconscious man backwards, mounts his horse and whips him hard, sending him lunging back up the embankment and away from the river. Alchuni and Ponce watch as he rides away.

Once at the village, Massai put the horse back into Ponce's corral, picks up his gifts, and trots back to Loco's wickiup. He wants to leave quickly, before Tiana has a chance to tell what happened. The meeting with Salto will have to wait for another time. He gathers his belongings and separates his grey from Loco's herd, then rides the short distance to Nachita's wickiup. Only the old warrior sits out front.

"Have you seen Alchise?" He asks Nachita.

Even with his failing eyesight, Nachita can see the serious look on Massai's face. Something has happened.

"He will return soon," he tells the young man.

"Tell him I will wait for him on the mesa, west of the village." Massai does not wait to explain before kicking the grey into a hard lope out of the village.

Massai feels he has to get away, out of the village. The wind in his face feels good as he gallops across the open floor of the valley. Somehow, he must stem the rage that is consuming him. He wants to kill Chato. He thirsts for the Mescalero's blood. Maybe he is a killer like the whites in the East thought he was.

CHAPTER

TWELVE

M assai hobbles his horse and makes camp on the lea side of a rock outcropping. Alchise will be able to find him. The glimmer of a fire will show for several miles. He is no longer concerned about Chato. He can ride but will not risk another confrontation until his leg heals. If needed, the Winchester rifle is just a step away against his blankets.

Two rabbits are roasting over a small fire when Alchise rides up. Hobbling his sorrel alongside the grey, Alchise squats beside the fire. The look on his face tells Massai he already knows about the fight. Handing Alchise a hind leg from one of the rabbits, Massai takes the other and sits down.

"Massai cooks good rabbit," Alchise said just before his strong teeth bite into the meat a second time. "How did you kill the rabbit?"

"On the way from the village with my bow." Massai beams with pride.

Alchise grunts. "This Alchise have to see."

Massai laughs. "Tomorrow, on the way home, I will show you. We will have rabbit again."

"Tomorrow we go to Fort Apache."

"Fort Apache?" Massai thinks about it while he chews. "I've heard my father speak of Fort Apache."

Alchise takes another piece of rabbit from the spit and stares reflectively at Massai. "Chief at fort send for Alchise. Wants me to come now."

"What for?"

"Not know. Maybe he wants horse." Alchise shrugs.

Not a word is mentioned about the fight or why Massai left the village so quickly. Massai knows Alchise will not ask. He will wait for the younger man to tell him if he wants to. It is not considered polite for one to meddle in the affairs of another. If Alchise does not approve of Massai's actions, he would have said something already.

"I did not ask for the fight," Massai said quietly. "Not in the canyon or in the village."

Alchise nods then rolls out his blanket and lies down beside the fire. "Someday, maybe, you have to kill Chato." The subject is closed. Massai knows there will be no more said about it. He understands now. If he kills Chato, Alchise will not disapprove. Rolling into his warm blanket, he pulls the rifle close. Chato is dangerous. As long as he lives, Massai will have to be cautious.

The two warriors look down on Fort Apache. They camped near the fort so they could enter early in the morning. Several buildings crop up around the fort's perimeter, making it look more like a small town than a fort. Alchise hangs several feathers in the sorrel's mane and tail. As they pass through the gates, under the watchful eyes of two sentries, the sorrel seems to come to life. His neck arches and his eyes spit fire as he prances proudly across the flat parade ground.

As proud as the horse is, Alchise sits even prouder. Head held high and shoulders straight, the warrior appears to be one with his horse.

Stopping in front of the fort's trading post, Alchise dismounts and looks up at Massai. "This is white man's place. Do not look at or speak to anyone."

Massai understands. He still remembers the whites from the train and the warning from the rancher, Luke Palmer. Alchise need not worry. Massai has nothing to say to the white world anymore.

Entering the trader's store, Massai's eyes sweep the heavily laden shelves that run the length of the building. He did not expect such a place at a fort. Anything one wants is stacked against or hung from the walls. Two clerks attend the people who roam back and forth, making a clomping sound with their hard sole boots. Massai looks down at his moccasins and smiles. He remembers how uncomfortable the city shoes were in the desert.

Alchise approaches a white haired man and stands silently until the man notices him. A white apron is tied around his waist and a pencil sticks out from behind his ear. Noticing Alchise, he stops what he was doing and pumps the warrior's hand.

"Alchise, my good friend!" The old store keeper smiles.

"It is good to see Garrett," Alchise said in English.

The storekeeper looks at Massai and smiles. "This must be the young Massai we've been hearing so much about." The man called Garrett eyed Massai up and down with open curiosity.

"I knew your pa, James Davis," Garrett said to Massai. "Good man."

Massai nods to him, but does not speak.

Smiling at the quiet young man, Garrett rubs his gray beard and turns back to Alchise. "So, what can I do for you today, old friend?"

"Need bullet for gun. Young Massai shoot 'em up quick maybe," Alchise tells Garrett.

Calling one of the young clerks, Garrett motions for him. "See that Alchise and young Massai here get anything they want."

Alchise holds up a hand to stop the clerk. "Alchise no bring Garrett yellow rocks this time," he said.

Garrett pauses, then smiles. "No matter, take anything you want."

Alchise lays the old scarred saddlebags on the counter and points at the shells. He did not lie. Massai shot many boxes of shells practicing with the Winchester. Wandering around the store, Massai picks up a beautiful red shawl. It would look good on Alchuni. If only he had money. Placing it back on the shelf, he reminds himself that it is of the white world he left behind. He proceeds past the rows of canned goods, then steps outside onto the front porch of the store.

A squad of soldiers marches by, sweating profusely in the early morning heat. The sergeant barks an order and the solders turn neatly, keeping in a perfect line. Across the parade ground, the ring of an anvil pierces the air. It is the sound of the post smithy shoeing a horse. Further down and on the other side of the post, several women do laundry. The fort is a bustling place. Massai will be glad to leave the fort and return to the peace and tranquility of the rancheria. They were gone from it a long time and he misses it.

"Well, well, well," a voice nearby said. "If it ain't my old traveling pardner, Massai."

Massai whirls around at the familiar voice that speaks his name. He already recognized the owner of the voice. The old scout, Macy, stands leaning against the adobe walls of the trading post.

"Would you look at this? He's a pure, bona fide Chiricahua warrior now, if I don't miss my guess." The old scout has his jaw stuffed full of tobacco, giving his face a lopsided look.

Macy pushes out from the wall and steps forward. He looks Massai over and spit a stream of tobacco juice onto the dusty parade ground. "Almost didn't recognize you, 'cept for your size," Macy said. "Hair's growed some and you're filled out a bit, too."

"What are you doing here?" Massai said to him in Apache.

Macy looks shocked. "Well, I'll be damned. Seems you've done gone and picked up the tongue, too. Old Alchise transformed you into in a right proper warrior." Macy looks around and grins. "I'll wager the proper folk around here are just jumping for joy right this minute."

Massai did not like Macy on the train and he does not like him any better now. He speaks in circles. It was difficult to figure out his meaning. It isn't so much what he said, as how he said it. The man makes Massai nervous.

"Alchise inside?" Macy asks in Apache, indicating the trading post.

Nodding, Massai answers the old scout's question without speaking. He watches as the buckskin-clad figure crosses the rough wood walkway without a sound and then disappears inside the store. Massai is about to turn back to the parade ground when Macy leans back out the door.

"By the way," he calls to Massai, switching to English. "Remember your old friend Bosworth? The one that saved your hide back on the train?"

Massai nods. "I remember."

"That card player, Slade Bonham, the one you called a cheat. Well, he done him in, right outside those gates there." Macy points toward the gates of the fort. Then, with a big grin, he tips his hat and disappears inside the store.

Massai's eyes widen. Bosworth is dead. The man was little more than a pig, but the thought of the fat man lying dead caught in Massai's chest. Bosworth probably saved his life back on the train. Massai feels responsible for the bad blood with Bonham.

Alchise exits the store and places the heavily laden saddlebags across the withers of the sorrel. Handing Massai a neatly wrapped bundle, he looks back at the store. Macy came out behind him and now stands with one leg propped against the outside wall. Swinging up on his horse, Alchise motions for Massai to follow without speaking. Massai feels the wrapped bundle and wonders what is inside. It is something soft and heavy.

"For your woman," Alchise tells him in Apache without turning around.

"The shawl? Thank you," Massai said. Alchise probably saw him looking at it and knew he wanted it for Alchuni. Alchise nods without looking at him.

The two riders make their way down the main street and stop in front of another building. Alchise dismounts and ground-hitches his horse.

Alchise indicates the package with the shawl. "If you don't catch wife with that, maybe you should go back East."

Massai smiles, Alchise seldom tried to make a joke, as that was Loco's position in the family. "You're probably right but it's expensive."

"No cost. Store man only want rocks for things Alchise need from him."

"Rocks?" Massai asks.

Alchise shrugs. "White man like yellow rocks. You see later."

Crossing the wide porch, the two warriors enter the post Orderly room. A gray-haired sergeant rises quickly from his desk when he sees the two Indians standing in the doorway. The man's hand went quickly to his side arm and then just as suddenly, the hand drops as he recognizes Alchise. "Damnation, Alchise, you scared the hell out of me!" The sergeant said.

Alchise nods and steps inside to let Massai come in and close the door.

"That is good, sergeant," Alchise said switching to English. "White-eye no need 'em hell in body. No good."

"You're probably right about that, old son." The soldier smiles, regains his composure, and sits back down behind his desk.

Massai is surprised. Twice in one day, Alchise made a joke. He seems to be at ease around these particular white-eyes. Massai studies the soldier and understands his initial jitters. The days of Geronimo still haunts the older settlers and soldiers. They would shoot an armed Apache on sight if they were startled or feel threatened.

"Alchise come see Nantan Bishop," Alchise tells the sergeant. "Him want Alchise come quick, maybe."

"I'll tell the Major you're here," the sergeant said. He disappears through another door and quickly returns.

With only a nod of his head, the sergeant ushers them into the adjoining room. A large man circles a well-worn wooden desk and grabs Alchise's arm. Massai can tell by the man's actions that he holds Alchise in very high regard. The Indian and the soldier shake hands.

"This has to be young Mason," the Major said as he turns to Massai. He takes a step back to study him, "Maybe I should call you, Massai."

"My name is Massai."

The Major smiles. "Last time I laid eyes on you, you were about this big." The Major holds out his hand about knee high and offers his hand to Massai.

Shaking the white man's hand, Massai can feel the great power in the huge fists of the older man, and he is impressed. He does not know why but he took a liking to the man, even if he is a white soldier.

"Come here, young man," the Major said, motioning Massai toward a side table. Sitting down on the far side of the table, the Major put his elbow on the table and motions for Massai to do likewise. "Ever arm wrestle?"

"Yes," Massai said.

He looks to Alchise, who smiles slightly and nods. Massai sits down at the table and takes the man's massive hand in his.

"Ready," the Major asks.

Massai nods.

Muscles bulge in both men's forearms as they put all of their power into the contest. Massai cannot move the huge arm an inch but his isn't moving either. Both men strain as they look into each other's eyes with fists clenched tightly. Neither will give, neither can press. Alchise nods his approval and several more moments pass. The Major is old, Massai thought. Surely, he will weaken soon but he does not. The muscles in Massai's arms burn from the wrist to the shoulder and he begins to wonder about his own endurance. Finally, the Major laughs, lets go and slaps Massai on the back in a good-natured way.

"He's pretty good," the Major said. "Pretty damn good. Davis did a hell of a job."

Alchise smiles knowingly then looks at Massai. "Nantan Bishop and Davis good friend. They both little chiefs when Geronimo chase us all over desert."

"I'll agree to that," Major Bishop said. "What he really means, we were both sergeants when Geronimo whipped our rumps twenty years ago."

"I thought Geronimo lost," Massai blurts without thinking.

"Maybe some see it that way, but I don't," Bishop replies. "We had a thousand soldiers, many Apache scouts, and half the Mexican army against his hundred or so warriors. No, son, I can't say we won."

Massai studies Bishop. He is different from Macy and the others. Bishop does not hold a grudge against the Apache. Major Bishop motions for them to take seats across from his desk. The chairs are straight backed and they remind Massai of the chairs in his father's parlor.

"We have a problem, old friend," Bishop said to Alchise, getting down to business.

He pulls a bundle of letters from his desk drawer and hands them across the desk to Alchise. Taking the letters, Alchise looks at them puzzled. He cannot read and Bishop knows it.

"They are complaints, Alchise," Bishop explains. "Many complaints! He smashes his huge fist down on the wooden desk so hard papers fly and Massai's body recoils. "You know what those papers are about so don't play the dumb Injun with me."

Massai tenses. He never saw a man so calm and friendly one moment and so angry and forceful the next. He wonders if he misjudged the man. Looking over at Alchise, Massai notices a hint of a smile tugging at the warrior's lips.

"Nantan Bishop should no get mad," Alchise said. "Bad for heart, maybe."

"Don't coddle me, damn it! I want these petty thefts and horse stealing stopped."

Alchise remains calm. "Why you no tell Calito. Him Chief of reservation. Chief of Chiricahua people."

The Major crams a cigar into his mouth and almost bit it in half. "Bullshit! He's just a figurehead that some pompous ass in Washington installed with the help of that idiot Indian agent, Gentry."

"Him still chief."

Bishop hands another paper to Massai then leans back in his chair. "Read that to your uncle, Mason."

Massai wants to correct the Major on his name, but thought better of it. Instead, he studies the official paper several minutes while the two older men wait. The Major is not joking. What Alchise fears most is about to happen. He reads the paper aloud. When he finishes, Alchise sits upright in his chair, his jaws clenched in barely contained anger.

Major Bishop leans forward and addresses Alchise. "The President of all the white-eyes signed this order, old friend. He is serious. If these complaints do not cease, the Army will move back onto the reservation."

"How much time before?" Alchise asks.

Bishop exhales with relief. He finally has the attention of Alchise. "I'll give you one month. If any more complaints come in, I'll have to act. Our illustrious leaders don't like their voters howling like mad wolves. Bad politics."

"You have Alchise's word. Stealing stop."

Bishop lights his cigar and leans back in his chair. "That's good enough for me. I'll stall the Army for one month."

Both Alchise and Major Bishop stand. Alchise takes the offered hand of the big man. Massai does not know if rage or worry crossed his uncle's face. Soldiers occupied the reservation for ten years after Geronimo was gone. Massai knows it was a very bad time for the Apache people.

"Let me see my rifle," Bishop said, holding out his hand for the Henry.

Massai is shocked when Alchise hands it over.

"Your uncle saved my life," Bishop explains to Massai. "I gave him this rifle in appreciation."

Massai is surprised. "You gave an Apache your gun?"

Bishop arches his eyebrows. "Not just any Apache, Mason, I gave a most trusted friend my gun."

Handing the Henry back, Major Bishop walks the two warriors to their horses. Massai wonders how the big man ever rode a horse to chase Geronimo. After mounting, they turn their horses and start back across the parade ground toward the gates. Massai notices the soldiers' eyes follow them as they pass.

Massai turns to look again at Major Bishop. "He's a big man," he said slipping back into the Apache language.

"He's good soldier. Good friend."

"I don't think he tried to beat me at arm wrestling."

Alchise smiles knowingly. "Cub grows wiser, I think."

They wheel their horses toward the post gates just as a buckboard passes beneath the catwalk. Even from a distance, Massai recognizes the blonde woman that visited the rancheria. The buckboard also holds a tall man and another blonde woman. She is the image of the first woman, only younger.

Massai guesses the younger woman to be the daughter of the woman he met. The man is probably Frasier, the woman's husband that she spoke of at the rancheria. Massai's eyes follow the buggy as it pulls up to the stables. Several riders rein in beside the buggy and sit slouched in their saddles. Massai watches their eyes stray to the Sutler's store and guesses why. He saw the whiskey bottles lined up behind the long bar. The men are probably thirsty and eager to remedy the situation.

Passing by the buggy on the way out of the fort, Massai looks into the eyes of the older woman. He half expects her to speak. When she didn't, his eyes move to the girl.

Massai is struck by the girl's beauty. In all his years in New York, he has never seen a young woman such as this. For a moment, he is mesmerized, unable to take his eyes from her. Honey blonde hair encircles an innocent flawless face on the brink of womanhood. She looks back at him with captivating crystal blue eyes. She holds his gaze like a jailer holds a prisoner.

Tearing his eyes from her, Massai forces himself to look away. He looks at the older woman and sees her glance at Alchise, then stares straight ahead, as though she did not know him. He is so entranced by the girl and puzzled by the woman. Massai does not see or hear the red-headed man bearing down on him until a solid blow from a rifle stock sends him crashing to the ground.

All eyes turn on the two Apaches as Alchise levels the Henry at the redheaded man.

"Red! What's gotten into you?" Yells the man in the wagon. Bounding out of the buggy, he rushes to where Massai is rising from the dusty ground.

"That son of a bitch was staring at Miss Audrey," the red-headed man growls. He is glaring at Massai, ready to strike him again.

The hard eyes of the rancher stare at the cowboy. "Watch your mouth, Red. Womenfolk are present."

"Sorry, boss, but I ain't gonna let no red heathen stare at a white woman like that."

"Was you staring, Injun?" The tall rancher asks Massai.

Massai gets to his feet and dusts himself off. He ignores the man's question and catches the reins of the grey. Glancing over at Alchise, he sees the Henry resting across the sorrel's withers. He also sees the hard look on Alchise's face.

"Fulton Frasier, that's enough!" The older woman yells. She climbs out of the wagon and stands clenching her fists tightly.

Frasier looks at his wife, then back at Massai. "A little lesson in manners won't hurt him none, Jean."

"No," the pretty girl protests. She steps beside her mother and glares at her father.

With a stern look, the rancher walks over to the women. Taking hold of each by an arm, he steers them toward the Sutler's store. Massai hears the hammer of the Henry pull back on full cock. Nerves strain and muscles tense. One move is all it will take to start a small war. The riders nervously stare at one another. They know Alchise does not bluff. He will kill some of them if they move toward the boy.

"Alchise let me see my rifle again." It was Major Bishop. He appears from behind the two Apaches and walk steadily toward Frasier's men. Alchise hesitates briefly and then hands the Henry into the Major's outstretched hand.

"Now yours, Mason," the Major said calmly.

Massai looks to Alchise, who nods. He turns the Winchester over to the Major.

"Now, gentlemen," Bishop said in a calm easy manner to the rancher and his men, "what did you have in mind?"

Frasier walks back to where the Major stands, leaving the women near the store porch. "We don't take kindly to Apache staring at our women," he said to Bishop.

"What is your intention, Mr. Frasier?" The question is hard as stone. Several soldiers gather around. They have no love for Apaches, but the Major is their commander.

"This is none of your concern, Major," Frasier growls, showing no sign of backing down. "But seeing as how you asked..." Frasier hesitates, looking hard at Massai. "We thought we might just whip his Apache ass."

Smiling, Bishop looks at each one of the riders. "All of you or just one?"

"Won't take but one," said the one called Red. He regained his nerve now that the Major has the Apache's rifles.

"Well now, cowboy, you're pretty big to be jumping on a boy." Major Bishop still has the smile on his lips, but there is ice in his voice.

"Give him up Bishop or I'll take him from you." Frasier spit at the feet of the Major. His voice is hard and menacing.

The smile leaves the Major's face as his big hand grabs a handful of the rancher's shirt. "Not on my post, Frasier. You're not taking anything."

"Wait," Massai said.

All eyes turn to Massai in surprise, all but Alchise.

"It's my fight," he said.

"Boy, that man is a half foot taller than you and fifty pounds heavier," Bishop said, still holding the front of Frasier's shirt.

Massai steps away from his horse. "It's my fight," he repeats.

"You keep him out of it," Red barks, pointing at Alchise.

Alchise did not move. He glances at Massai and studies the young warrior's face. Then with a nod, he pulls the sorrel and grey back a few feet.

"Take off your gun, Red," the Major orders.

Adding the six-gun to the two rifles he already held, the Major takes command of the situation. "Now, gentlemen, here are the rules. The first man to interfere, I'll personally shoot."

Red rushes Massai, throwing wicked punches with both hands. He knows if he can get the boy to the ground, his size will be an advantage. As he lunges toward the swift-footed Massai, he is met with thin air and a savage blow to his kidneys.

Falling to one knee, Red feels a searing pain knifing through his side. He gasps for breath. A solid kick to his face smashes his prominent nose and sends a gush of blood across his face. Wheezing through his mouth, the big man tries to rise again, but goes down under a heavy blow to the side of his head. Standing over the prone redhead, Massai glares at the other cowboys, daring another to step forward.

None of the ranch hands are cowards, but their biggest and best brawler was beaten so thoroughly and so easily that they are stunned into silence. An Apache, not yet a grown man, handily whipped the toughest fighter at the Frasier ranch.

Mounting the grey, Massai takes his Winchester from Bishop. He did not miss the Major's approving smile as he turns the grey in behind Alchise's sorrel. Passing through the gates of Fort Apache, he looks quickly back toward the store. Mrs. Frasier stands watching, her shoulders straight, her head held high. In spite of the hostile glares from the crowd of whites, he raises his hand and waves to her.

Jean Frasier returns the wave.

CHAPTER

THIRTEEN

Kicking their horses into a hard run, Alchise and Massai scatter dogs, chickens, and people in every direction. Heads turn as they leave the fort and disappear over a nearby hill. After the confines of the fort, it feels good as both men push their mounts to the limit. After awhile, Alchise pulls the heaving sorrel down to a walk and looks over at Massai beside him.

"I think cub grows up," he said.

Massai pauses before answering. "Now I know why trouble always followed me back east. At least I have a better idea."

Alchise nods. He understands what young Massai means. They are Indians in what is now a white man's world. It does not matter if you are in New York or Arizona, the whites fear and despise the red man.

"You fought well." Alchise looks over at Massai. "What cub do today, Alchise not teach."

Massai smiles, but it is a forced smile. "I had a lot of practice."

Alchise turns the horses back south toward the reservation. On the second day, late in the afternoon, Massai spots the first of the wickiups. Villagers suddenly come forth, greeting them with enthusiasm. Dozens of them, smiling and waving as he passes. Many whisper Massai's name.

"What's all this," Massai asks.

Alchise grunts. "They know of fight at fort."

"But how? It just happened."

"Apache at fort see fight. Come tell village."

Massai is surprised. "Then they must have ridden through the night."

Alchise smiles slightly. "They not soft like us, maybe."

Massai let out a laugh.

Hands grab at Massai's leggings as his grey follows the sorrel to Nachita's wickiup. The villagers now hold him in great esteem. Out of respect, no one follows them to the wickiup, but shies away when the two warriors dismount. Massai searches the crowd but Alchuni is not among them.

Loco stands waiting by the wickiup of Nachita. Tiana runs out quickly to take the reins and lead the horses to the corral. Her actions are more subdued than usual. She does not tease Massai or even smile at him.

Loco motions for them to sit. "I have not seen our people this excited since the last time Geronimo jumped the reservation." He smiles at Massai.

Nachita comes from the wickiup and sits beside Alchise. Looking over at Massai, he seems solemn. He studies the face of the young warrior for several minutes. No one spoke, waiting for the elder to speak first.

"My heart is proud for Massai," Nachita said with a sober voice. "But it saddens me. The Chiricahua people need no more trouble." He makes a motion with flattened hands.

"The young one did not start this trouble," Alchise tells his father.

Nachita shakes his gray head and looks again at Massai. "It does not matter. The white men will hate him now and seek revenge."

Alchise thinks about it. "Then I will take him to the rancheria, back to the White Mountains."

Nachita is not satisfied with that. "Do you not trade with the Frasier ranch? Do you not take them horses?"

Alchise nods. "You know this."

Nachita grunts softly and then turns to look Massai in the eyes. "You made an old man remember. Once we were a strong nation, a proud people but that time is past. Now we are a beaten race. Be careful young Massai. The white man will not forget what you have done but neither will our people. You have lifted our spirits."

Nachita rises and goes back inside the wickiup. The subject is closed and the fight will never be mentioned again at Nachita's wickiup.

"Go visit your friends. They wait for you," Alchise said softly. "I will speak with Loco alone."

Massai nods. He quickly gathers some items and leaves his two uncles with their thoughts.

Watching him disappear into the shadows, Loco shakes his head. "He is like another proud one I know."

Alchise nods. "Massai is right name for young cub."

"No, my brother, he reminds me of you when you were a young man. He has Massai's name but he is more like you. You were a chief, a general, a leader among our people. He will be the same."

"Then why you not show me more respect?" Alchise said.

Loco smiles, then both men return to their private thoughts.

Massai finds Ponce reclining in front of his wickiup. Wolf, Dosenay, Taglia, and two others in his pack sit in a circle around him. They are the Wild Ones, and those responsible for Major Bishop's problems at Fort Apache. They are young but they are men. In the east, they would still be considered boys. Here on the reservation, they passed their novice time. Warriors who rode with Cochise and Geronimo were young like these. At times, they can be as dangerous as rattlesnakes. Other times, they are like children, laughing and joking with one another. By Apache standards, they are ruthless and to be feared.

Jars holding tiswin lay at their feet, and Massai can tell they were feeling the effects of the mescal based drink. Ponce raises a hand in greeting as Massai approaches.

"Welcome my brother," he said. "Sit and drink with us."

Finding a place beside Wolf, Massai nods to them and sits down. Waving off the offered jar of tiswin, he studies the group. He has not seen Wolf since the day of the race.

"You ran well for a white-eye," Wolf said to him.

Massai chuckles at the compliment. "So did you, for an Injun."

"He fights well, too," said the fat, good-natured Dosenay. "I saw the red-headed white-eye fight. He is a mean one." He turns to Massai. "Why did you not scalp red-hair?"

Taglia spit into the small fire in the middle of the group and glares at Massai. "He is still a white-eye."

"I am Chiricahua Apache now. If Taglia wishes, he can use his knife and see what color my blood runs... or his own." Massai hisses the challenge through clenched teeth.

Bah!" Taglia stands and walks away.

Massai is well known now. No one, not even the elders, would challenge him and all the Wild Ones know it. They do not fear him but they will not take a chance with their lives by fighting him, unless they are forced to.

"Massai is Chiricahua. He is my brother." Ponce declares. He sits up and drunkenly gestures with a wide wave of his hand. "I will fight any who says different."

It grew darker as they talked, telling of long ago fights with the Mexicans or raiding with the Comanche to the east. All the stories they heard from their fathers and uncles.

"We tell old stories," Taglia said, rejoining the group. "I say we go south and raid. We will make our own stories."

Several voices ring out in agreement. Only Wolf and Massai said nothing. Ponce looks at his two most trusted friends.

"Neither of you have spoken," he said to them.

Wolf only shrugs. He would follow wherever Ponce leads.

Massai is not a follower. "If you raid, you will cause trouble for our people. Will not more trouble go bad for the Chiricahua?"

"Who will know?" The one called Bonito said.

"Maybe we should only raid the Mexicans across the border," Dosenay suggests.

Massai pulls himself to his feet. Looking around the fire at the young warriors, he shakes his head. He understands now, the Wild Ones do not raid for food or justice, they do so for sport. He cannot be part of it. Especially after what he learned at the fort. They care little that their actions cause consequences for them and their people.

"Why does Massai go so quickly?" Ponce asks.

"My friends make bad talk. I will not stay and listen," Massai said truthfully. "I do not wish to know your plans." He turns to leave.

"Would you tell others of our plans?" Ponce asks his friend.

Turning, Massai stares straight into the dark eyes of his friend. As he nods slowly, he sees Ponce's face harden.

"If Alchise asked me, I would tell. What you do is no good for our people. The white soldiers now threaten to occupy our reservation as in the past."

Taglia spits into the fire. "Leave us then. We will kill the white-eye if they come."

Massai came to Ponce hoping to get advice about approaching Salto. He should have asked Loco. Walking alone in the dark, he cannot even tell which wickiup belongs to Salto. An owl calls out across the river. Perhaps it is a bad sign, maybe he should go back and find Alchise and Loco. He stands, undecided and deep in thought. Turning back toward Loco's wickiup, he stops. His hand goes to the hilt of his hunting knife. A figure stands in the shadows a few feet away.

Tiana steps out of the darkness. "I will take you to Salto's wickiup."

"What are you doing here, Tiana?"

"I followed you and waited."

"All this time?"

"Yes," the girl replies.

Massai shakes his head. "But why? Your father will look for you."

Tiana comes closer, Massai sees worry in her eyes. "Alchuni is my friend. If you do not see Salto soon, he will give her to Chato."

"That's why I went to see Ponce. I wanted him to advise me about Salto."

"Bah," she said, "Ponce is bad blood. All the Wild Ones do is drink and talk of raids and stealing, like the Old Ones. What does he know of peace and love?"

Tiana was right. To raid the whites would be disastrous for the Apache people. This is a new time. Without peace, this Indian nation would perish.

"Will Loco be angry if you take me to Salto?" He asks.

She giggles, her warm, soft voice riding the gentle breeze that blows off the river. "He will not know."

"I thought young maidens are not supposed to be seen with men."

"You are my cousin." She smiles at him. "Now, if you will quit asking questions, I will show you to Salto's wickiup and hurry back to my father."

Tiana talks quietly as they walk through the darkness, giving Massai advice on what to say to Alchuni's father. Loco will give them both a severe lecture if he knew his only daughter was out here, even with Massai. She is a maiden and very pretty. She is also adventurous. Whoever marries Tiana will not find married life dull.

"There," she said, stopping in the darkness. Her slim finger, barely visible in the dark, pointing to a lone wickiup. One man sits beside the small cook fire smoking his pipe. "Salto sits before the fire."

Massai makes no move to advance toward the figure. Pushing him in the back, Tiana urges him to go. She smiles as Massai walks quietly to where the man sits. She knows he would rather be anywhere else than here, facing Alchuni's father.

Several minutes pass before Salto acknowledges Massai's presence.

Looking up at the young warrior through bloodshot eyes, Salto knows him immediately. Ponce is as tall as the young Massai, but Ponce is not nearly as muscular. He heard of the fight with Chato over his daughter. He also heard of the fight at Fort Apache. He was expecting the young nephew of his enemy.

"What do you want?" Salto asks in a gruff and hostile voice.

Massai steps forward and holds out the gifts he brought. He laid the bridle and knife at the feet of Salto. "I bring Salto gifts."

Salto eyed the beautiful silver work on both gifts and his gaze lingers approvingly on the knife. Salto was on the raid when Alchise took the knife from a dead Mexican. Salto tried to trade for it, but Alchise would not part with it. Now Alchise sends the knife with his nephew to offer as a gift. Salto knows it is a great sacrifice for Alchise. It speaks of his great love and respect for the young man before him.

"Why you bring me gifts?" Salto growls even though he knows the youth is there for Alchuni.

Many others came with gifts to ask Salto for the girl. They came until Chato killed over her and then the young men stopped coming. The Mescalero claimed her for his own and his claim goes unchallenged until now. Salto will not admit it, but he fears Chato and he fears for Alchuni.

Picking up the knife, he turns it over several times, studying its beautiful engraving. The knife brings up many memories for Salto. Looking up at the young warrior, he knows Massai will make a good husband for Alchuni. Much better than the threatening Mescalero. This one is strong and fearless, but with wisdom, much like the great warriors of his time.

"Sit. We will talk," Salto said, motioning for Massai to sit. "You know Alchise and I are enemies?"

"Yes, I know this, though I do not know why."

Salto nods his head slowly. "What I did was long ago. It shames me. I was young and cannot undo the wrong." Salto speaks squinting into the fire. "When I meet my ancestors, they will see the shame in my eyes."

Massai cannot ask the elder, but he yearns to know what Salto did. He can feel the man's humiliation as he speaks.

Salto shakes his head. "It is for Alchise to tell but he will not."

Massai nods. "I have not come to cause you shame, Salto."

"Then for what purpose do you come here?" He knows it is for Alchuni but the young man will have to say it.

"Alchuni," Massai said quietly. Then he clears his throat and speaks up, like a man and a warrior. "I have come for Alchuni."

Salto nods. "You must speak with Alchise first. Then, if you still want the daughter of Salto, you may visit my lodge."

Massai stands, knowing their talk was finished, at least for now. With a nod of understanding, he leaves the old warrior alone to gaze into his fire. Next to Salto is the ornate bridle. The beautiful knife he so admired never left his hand. The gifts were accepted. Massai feels relief.

Alchuni peeks out from the wickiup as Massai speaks with her father. Her eyes take in the rugged good looks of Massai and it warms her heart. The red headband and the blue tunic strapped with a heavy cartridge belt and hunting knife give him the wild look of the Old Ones. She has no idea what shame her father was talking about. Fear suddenly grips the girl. Did Alchise so despise Salto that he will forbid Massai from pursuing her?

Another pair of eyes also watch the two men sitting before the fire talking. These eyes burn in the darkness. Chato was crazy with jealousy and he plots his revenge. Alchuni is his. Massai will not take what is his and Salto will not live to give his daughter to another man.

Returning to Loco's wickiup, Massai is surprised to find his uncles still talking. Taking a seat opposite them, he sits quietly until they address him.

"Salto accept gift from nephew of enemy?" Alchise asks him finally.

"Yes."

The firelight reflects on the weathered face of Loco. "Ah, soon Alchise and Salto be relatives." He nods and smiles.

Massai looks at Alchise. "Salto said it is your place to tell me why you are enemies. He would not tell me but said he has great shame."

Alchise stares into the fire, lost in thought. It had been long ago but the day is still fresh in his mind. He remembers because he could never forget. His mind relives the memory and he begins to perspire. Beads of sweat form on his face as the memories flood back. The terrifying screams of the people and the thundering hooves of the armed riders. The roar of gunfire as the soldiers charged through the village, killing men, women, and children as if they were vermin.

He remembered the head of a small boy severed by the long knife of a soldier. He remembered calling for help as he tried to shield several women and children with his body. He was standing alone, out of arrows, armed only with a knife, as the soldiers advanced toward him. Slaughter was in their eyes. Frightened women and children cried out in fear as they clung to him.

The last thing Alchise remembered was a face looking down from the rocks above, then disappearing as soldiers opened fire. He shudders as he can still feel the bullets tearing into his flesh like hungry coyotes. The last thing he heard was the screams of death and pain that surrounded him. He remembered waking up with a heavy pressure on his chest. Pain wracked his body. Pushing the bodies of the dead from him, he tried to rise only to fall back into his own blood. Three bullets passed through his body. The soldiers left him for dead. Unable to stand, he dragged himself away from the carnage.

Nachita found him two days later, over a mile from the massacre. Only his hatred for one man kept him alive. With each painful inch of his journey home, he vowed death to that man, the one who fled, leaving the defenseless to die. Alchise still sees the face above him on the rocks and that face belongs to Salto.

Looking over at Massai, Alchise shakes himself from the horror of the memories. "It is finished," he tells him. "If you marry Alchuni, it is over. Salto will no longer be my enemy."

Massai notices the agony in his uncle's eyes as he spoke. Whatever happened between Alchise and Salto, it was clear that it had been horrible. Massai knows he can ask no more. Alchise was making a great sacrifice to set aside the past so he might have a future with Alchuni.

Rising, Alchise walks off into the darkness. Massai starts to follow but Loco holds his arm. "Leave him with his thoughts, young cub."

"It must have been very bad," Massai said to Loco.

"Yes," Loco said with a nod. "I was small. Alchise was a young man. We were at peace when the Mexican cavalry found us. Alchise... we lost everything. Our mother, two sisters... everything."

"Alchise blames Salto for this?"

"Salto ran off and left Alchise. Salto was not alone and many ran. The Mexicans were everywhere, shooting, and stabbing... it was a terrible thing to see. Alchise swore to kill Salto, but once he healed from his wounds, Cochise himself intervened on Salto's behalf. Alchise would not disobey his Chief, but he never forgave Salto."

"You lost everyone?" Massai asked.

Loco nods sadly. There was only me and Nachita left for Alchise. The rest were gone. The Mexicans killed many.

Massai can feel the anger knot in his stomach. "Salto is a coward," he said, spitting in anger.

Loco shakes his head. "Salto is not a coward. Neither is he a great warrior such as Alchise or Geronimo. There were too many soldiers. He could do nothing."

"But Alchise stayed." Massai was truly beginning to understand Alchise's anger toward Salto and now he too was becoming angry.

"Yes, Alchise stayed," Loco said looking into the eyes of his nephew. "He almost died with the others. Salto chose to fight another day."

Massai can hear the pounding of his own heart. Torn between rage and longing for the girl, he wonders if asking Alchise to forgive Salto was too high a price to pay for her.

Loco places a strong hand on Massai's shoulders. "A dead warrior cannot help his people. It is sometimes wiser to fight another day. Remember this, young Massai."

After a few moments, Alchise emerges from the dark and sits back down beside them. The memories are pushed aside and his mood changes. He smiles as Loco passes him the worn pipe and tobacco.

"Tonight we smoke," he said taking the pipe. "Tomorrow the village will honor Massai and those who passed their novice time and became warriors."

"Aiyee," Loco said with a grin. "We will dance and get drunk."

Massai smiles at Loco. Maybe he will dance but he is not about to touch the tiswin that will flow freely. The Indian agent, Gentry, made drinking tiswin illegal, but almost every warrior disobeyed him. The fiery liquid clouds the warriors' minds, making them surly and mean.

The pipe is handed back to Loco, who fills it with fresh tobacco. After lighting it, he takes several long pulls and hands it back to Alchise.

"Davis, he not smoke pipe," Alchise said, remembering how he tried to get the Chief of Scouts to smoke many times.

"No," Massai said, his voice taking on a sharp tone. "My father never did anything wrong."

Both old warriors sense the hostility in Massai's voice and change the subject to the earlier days of their people. Massai loves to hear the men's tales of times before all the trouble and death, and the stories of the great warriors. It is almost midnight when Loco decides it is time for bed. Massai and Alchise make their way toward Nachita's wickiup.

Just before they leave, Loco turns to Massai. "It was good Tiana showed you the lodge of Salto."

Massai turns in surprise at Loco's words, but Loco already ducked inside his wickiup. How did Loco know? Massai is learning there are few secrets on the reservation.

CHAPTER

FOURTEEN

M assai awakes early. Sleeping little during the night as even the slightest sounds seems to awaken him. Excited about the novice ceremony and the following festivities, anticipation keeps him awake late into the night. Wiping the sleep from his eyes, he notices a new set of deerskin leggings and moccasins beside his grass bed. Above his head hangs a bright red shirt. While he was sleeping, someone slipped in and left him new clothes.

His thoughts turn to Alchuni. She has not shown herself since his fight with Chato. She was not with the other villagers when he returned from the fort either. Suddenly, Massai is filled with uncertainty. Maybe she lost interest in him. Rising quickly, he steps outside into the crisp early morning air. Summer was almost gone and soon winter will be upon them.

Wood smoke hangs thick over the village. Women scurry about with baskets and utensils for cooking. There will be a feast tonight. The men are already slaughtering cattle to feed the entire village.

Alchise is not in sight. Walking to the corral, Massai sees the sorrel and the grey, but Alchise is nowhere to be found. He returns to the wickiup and takes a bowl of food Nachita's old squaw offers him. It is mostly ground corn cooked into a mush, but he has grown to like it. The old squaw watches him with a huge toothless grin as he scoops the mealy gruel with his fingers and starts to eat.

He eats mechanically and thinks about Alchuni. It will be a long time before the ceremonies begin. Maybe he can find her. He wants to know why she is avoiding him. The sound of a running horse takes his mind from the girl. Jumping to his feet, he leaps back, just as Ponce pulls his horse to a hard stop in front of Nachita's wickiup.

"Does Massai want to eat all day with the squaws or ride with Ponce?"

Massai looks up at the grinning Wild One. He sees no sign of the reckless drunk of the night before, only the cheerful face of his friend.

"I have not yet seen Alchise," he tells Ponce.

Ponce's white teeth flash. "I have seen your uncle. He says for you to ride with me."

Massai is skeptical. He knows Ponce will say almost anything to get his way. "Where did you see Alchise?" He asks.

"Never mind, but I did see him. I give you my word." Ponce hesitates then smiles again. "I don't think you should disturb him."

Massai grabs his bow and quiver and mounts the grey. On the way out of the village, they stop in front of Loco's wickiup where Massai leans down to whisper to Tiana. Her frown follows them as both young men race off on their horses, but her eyes follow Ponce. She could easily lose her heart to the strapping warrior if it was not for his reckless ways. She worries about Massai, wondering if he will join the Wild Ones or listen to Alchise.

The horses spray water high into the air as they splash across the river at full speed. The black horse Ponce rides is no match for the powerful grey. Massai has no trouble overtaking the smaller mustang.

As they thunder away from the village, dust and sagebrush fly in their wake. A covey of quail flushes in front of them, taking flight to escape the dangerous hooves. A desert fox, returning from his nightly hunt, crosses their path and quickly becomes their quarry. Dodging back and forth, the two youths make sport of trying to touch him with their bows. The fox reaches his burrow just as the grey bears down on him. He dives into his den just as the bow swats his furry hind end. Victorious, the two riders ride on whooping and shouting.

The warmth of the grey feels good on Massai's legs as he slows the horse to a walk. The heat does not touch the floor of the desert yet and the cool morning air sends a chill through his body. Little is said as the two young men enjoy their early morning jaunt and each other's company. Several wild horses and donkeys stampede away as human scent drifts toward them. The grey's nostrils flare and he tries to give chase, but Massai holds him in check.

Massai watches as Ponce notches an arrow deftly to his bow and sends the speeding missile toward an unseen target. Ponce rides forward and retrieves a still quivering jackrabbit, hoisting it up for Massai to see.

"Dinner," he announces.

"Supper tonight will be a feast," Massai protests.

Ponce laughs. "Tonight's feast is hours away, my friend. You'll be plenty hungry by then."

Riding to an outcropping of rocks, Ponce slides from his horse. A small, almost undetectable pool of water glimmers from underneath the smooth rocks.

"Massai fix fire, I fix 'em rabbit," Ponce said, mimicking the broken English and speech patterns of the Old Ones on the reservation.

Both youths sit cross-legged, waiting for the rabbit to cook. Despite his sparse breakfast, Massai is still hungry and the smell of the roasting rabbit makes his mouth water. He is enjoying the camaraderie of someone his own age, especially a free spirit like Ponce. The desert stretches as far as the eye can see in every direction. It flows like golden water to the mountains far in the distance.

"You should have been a squaw," Massai jokes after his first bite of rabbit. "You cook good rabbit."

Ponce laughs. "I prefer slabs from the rancher's cattle."

Massai remembered what Major Bishop said, and thought of the ranchers to the south. "We cannot eat a whole cow."

"Ah, but we could try." Ponce's eyes dance. "Dosenay could. We'll take him with us."

Massai takes another bite of rabbit and studies the face of his friend. He knows Ponce is baiting him to see what his answer will be. He thought again of the paper he read in the Major's office. Ponce is his friend, but Massai will not betray Alchise or the Chiricahua people to ride with the Wild Ones. He thought he made that clear the night before.

"I enjoyed the ride and the meal, my friend," he said to Ponce. "Now let us return to the village for the ceremony tonight."

He gathers the reins to the grey, mounts and starts off at a slow gait. Soon, Ponce catches up with him. The mood is quiet as they ride slowly back north toward the village. Ponce has his answer. Massai will not ride with his band. There will be no further discussion.

Stopping at the edge of the village, Ponce smiles and holds out his arm. "We are still friends?"

Massai takes the extended arm and smiles back. "Yes, Ponce, we are still friends.

Ponce whirls his black gelding toward his wickiup. "Then I will see you tonight, young Massai. You can watch me dance with all the maidens."

Alchise and Loco stand near the corral as Massai approaches. Both men are watching the activities near the large council fire that is being built. Tonight will be long remembered by the people of the village. Alchise thought back to his own novice ceremony. He, too, won the race, and Nachita presented him with a beautiful horse taken from the Mexicans.

Those were fine days, even great days. They were free to roam and raid. To hunt and fight. Now, Alchise thought, as he watches Massai approach, what is here to keep this new young warrior from joining the Wild Ones? He knows he, himself, might be tempted to ride with them if he were young again. A young man needs to feel alive and have challenges.

On the reservation, there is nothing to make their blood come alive except maybe a woman but only for a short time. Young Apache warriors need more. They need the excitement of the war trail. Alchise understands the young men who ride with Ponce. He understands Ponce. He also understands the Wild Ones but they must be stopped. Years ago, Ponce would have been a great warrior leader, but today he and his band are considered troublemakers and renegades.

The Major was not bluffing. If the raiding continues, the Army will move back onto the reservation. They will collect all guns and horses. There will be no hunting, little freedom, and stagnation with drunkenness. Alchise will not allow this.

Massai talks with his uncles several minutes then takes his new clothes and a sweet smelling soap the women of the tribe made and heads to the river. He rode hard and smelled of sweat and horses. Normally, that would not be bad, but this night is special. Several women smile as he passes but Massai ignores them. Alchuni is the only woman he yearns for. He will wait for her, if she still wants him.

Walking to a spot away from the main swimming place and out of sight, Massai strips and walks into the water. He lathers his muscular body then dives under, rinsing away the strong soap. As a child, he hated bathing. No matter how hard he scrubbed, his skin was still brown. Other children said he looked "dirty" and it made him feel self-conscious. Now he is accepted. He truly feels he belongs and he would lay down his life, if necessary, for the Chiricahua.

Several ducks float on the gentle current. Momentarily, Massai forgets about his past. He even forgets about Alchuni as he watches the ducks swim gracefully back and forth. Pulling himself from the water, Massai stretches out on a large boulder to dry in the sun. A rolling pebble startles him and he looks up to see Alchuni standing on the bank above him. Embarrassed, Massai bolts upright and quickly pulls a shirt over his nakedness.

"You fought for a white squaw at the fort!" She blurts out.

Massai can see her lip tremble as she flings the accusation at him. In her hands, she clutches something. It is the bridle and knife he gave Salto as gifts.

"It was because of the white woman, I fought," he replies. "Not for her."

Massai scrambles to his feet. Alchuni does not seem to notice or care that he is naked.

"They say she is very beautiful." She bristles and steps closer. "Is she?"

Massai saw what jealous women could do in New York. Here in the desert of Arizona, women are no different. Before him is a very angry, jealous woman holding a very sharp knife.

"She is just a woman," Massai said carefully.

Alchuni cocks one eyebrow. "You did not answer my question."

"Yes, she is beautiful, but not like you," he stammers. "Beautiful, I mean, but she is not nearly as beautiful as you are."

Alchuni snorts at his awkwardness. "When you fought over this beautiful woman, you shamed me in front of the village."

Still clutching his shirt in front of him, Massai stands exasperated. "I did not fight over her, Alchuni. I do not want her and I did not shame you."

"You do not want her?" She asks.

"No, I do not." He indicates the items in her hands. "If I wanted her, why would I bring gifts to your father? Why do you have those gifts with you now?"

Alchuni looks down at the items in her hands. "If you wanted the white woman, I would give them back to you." Her voice is sharp.

"No," he tells her softly. "I do not want them back." Stepping closer to her, he draws the beautiful maiden into his arms and kisses her.

Alchuni's hand went to her mouth as he released her. Turning, she looks to see if anyone is watching then goes into his arms again. Several kisses pass before Massai realizes he is still naked.

Alchuni laughs at Massai's embarrassment. Forcing her to turn from him, he quickly dresses in his new clothes.

Aware of his discomfort, they both laugh. As soon as Massai is dressed, their lips meet again.

It is almost sundown when they start back for the village. Massai can hear the rhythmic beat of the drums, as they get closer. Soon it will be time for the ceremony. It is an ancient ceremony to mark his passing from youth to manhood and to change his status to warrior. However, no ceremony can match the thrill of finally having Alchuni in his arms.

Kissing her one last time before they enter the village, Massai hangs back a few moments. He watches her as she makes her way alone toward her wickiup. Soon she will be going to their wickiup. Their wickiup, the thought warms his heart.

Alchise and Loco are already sitting around the large fire when Massai finds them. Pushing between his two uncles, he watches the dancers perform the ritual dances. Paint, feathers, and masks cover every dancer, making them almost unrecognizable. Massai is mesmerized. Since coming to live with Alchise, he has not seen an Apache ceremony. Now, he not only witnesses one, but he will take part in one. The ancient chants and throbbing drum beats are hypnotic. The colorful dancer's silhouette against the night sky in the glow of the sparkling firelight, never did he feel such exultation. He feels himself becoming one with the Old Ones of long ago. Once, they too went through a ceremony like this. Several warriors leap into the circle and join the dancing.

The steady throb of the drums reaches a crescendo and then with a shout everyone falls silent. Calito, Chief of the Chiricahua people, and the old medicine man, Peponito, step into the circle. Only the popping of the fire can be heard as everyone waits for their leaders to speak. Peponito sings the praises of the Chiricahua, of the warriors of the past, and for the new ones who just reached manhood. Massai studies the crowd looking for the young ones who failed the tests. He feels sorry for them. This night should have been a proud time for them. Now they have to wait until next year to try again.

The fire flashes, sending sparks high into the air. Beautifully, dressed women in colorful, beaded buckskin dresses stand to one side, away from the warriors. The firelight reflects off their shiny hair and glowing eyes. Calito raises his staff, the emblem of his status, and calls first for Massai, then Wolf and Chato, then Little Wing, Running Fox, and the others who finished the tests. Massai walks into the lighted circle and, one by one, the others join him. Gifts are brought forward and each man's name is called out loudly as he is presented with his gift. When Massai's name is called, the crowd whoops and hollers their approval until Calito quiets them. A highly polished bow and quiver of arrows are given to the winner of the race. Each novice receives his gift and then the dancing resumes. First, the maidens of the village dance and Alchuni is among them. Then the young warriors take their turn, each one trying to leap higher and yell louder than the others. Ponce, the tallest in the village, stands out as he leaps and twists high above the rest.

Almost every maiden's eyes turn toward the tall warrior as he dances. Massai remembers the words of Ponce earlier. He was right, he is going to dance with all the maidens tonight. Many of the maidens in the village show interest in the tall young warrior with the easy smile. If Massai did not know Ponce was the leader of the Wild Ones, he would never guess this gentle, good-natured youth leads the devastating raids on the white ranchers.

Massai watches Chato, too. He is the complete opposite of Ponce. His face is a mask of dark thoughts. The deep-set eyes flash fire every time Massai glances his way. It is easy to imagine Chato killing and plundering. He wears his anger and aggression as a heavy cloak. It is easy to see the hate and scorn is for everyone, including his own people and especially for Massai.

Massai watches Alchuni as she dances with the other maidens. Every time their eyes meet, she smiles boldly. Her feelings for the nephew of Alchise are no longer a secret in the village. Women always ask the men to dance, for it was the custom of the tribal dancing. Massai takes every opportunity to dance with the beautiful Alchuni. The rhythmic pounding of the drums match his own heartbeat when she moves close to him. Dancing to the Apache means something entirely different than waltzing means to the white man. This is very different and far more exciting and strenuous. It is not difficult, however, to follow the lead of Ponce is. Imitating his friend, Massai leaps and yelps with great excitement until he no longer follows but leads the dancing.

At sunrise, the old squaw rouses Massai from a deep sleep. His head aches and the drums of the night before still echo in his ears. The tiswin Ponce talked him into drinking gives his mouth a dry, sour taste. Alchise stands near, holding both his horse and Massai's. Groaning, Massai makes his way to the grey and forces himself atop the horse.

The jarring of his steed's stride as it plods behind Alchise and the sorrel sends waves of agony through his clouded brain. He worries he will pass out and fall off. Even the rocky ground looks more inviting than the back of the horse. His stomach is roiling. Each step causes it to lurch. Leaning over the grey's neck, he retches violently.

Massai wants to curse but a stern look from Alchise changes his mind. Where are they going so early and in such a hurry? Gritting teeth feel like fur to his sticky tongue, he plods on. He will endure the agony of his pounding head and sick stomach, but not without murderous thoughts for Ponce and his evil liquor. How much of the tiswin did he drink, he is not sure. He remembers stumbling and nearly falling into the fire, only to be rescued by Ponce and Wolf grabbing him by his hair. After which, they plied him with more drink.

He remembers the disgusted look he received from Alchuni. She turned away from him and walked back to her wickiup. Even Tiana scolded him before stalking off after her friend. If anyone else scolded him, he cannot remember. He only remembers more dancing and more tiswin. He remembers Alchise dancing and it surprised him. Alchise is not a young man, yet he moves almost as deftly as Ponce and that was his last memory. He did not even remember finding his own warm bed.

The beautiful morning was lost on Massai. He is in no mood to enjoy it. Both his head and stomach are relentless in their pain. In addition, Alchise does not speak a single word since pulling Massai from his bed. Two hours pass before Alchise looks back at him.

"Cub still sick?" He asks.

"I'll be alright," Massai mumbles in reply. Massai will not be the first drunk young warrior and he will not be the last.

Alchise nods to the west. "Good, you go there and look for horse tracks. Tracks with no shoes."

"How many?"

"Maybe six or seven." Alchise turns the sorrel left to the east of the trail.

"The Wild Ones?" Massai asks, but Alchise is already out of earshot.

Massai curses under his breath as he turns the grey. Ponce took them out after all. He was warned and was aware of the consequences. Massai almost pleaded with him not to raid the ranchers. Now they have Alchise on their trail. That is why the older warrior's face is so solemn. He wasn't upset with Massai for drinking. If Ponce raids another ranch, Major Bishop will hear of it and send in troops from the fort.

Massai groans as the grey starts pulling up a small rise leading to a high plateau. The ground is rough. Gravel and shale give way on the steep grade causing the grey to slip and slide. Just short of the summit, Massai dismounts and crawls over the top. Nothing for as far as he can see, there are no riders in sight.

Mounting again, he looks back down the hill. Alchise is still visible far to the east. Massai's head still aches causing him to nearly miss the tracks the grey just crossed. Reining the gelding back, he dismounts and kneels to study them. It was them, the Wild Ones. Massai knows the track of Ponce's black anywhere. The horse has a contracted right foot. It is smaller than the left and slightly deformed.

From the tracks, there appears to be six or seven horses traveling in a straight line to the southwest. Massai guesses they left the reservation as soon as the festivities ended. They are several hours ahead. They have plenty of time to raid before Alchise can catch up. Once the damage was done, it would be too late. The Army will be dispatched as soon as the Major finds out about it.

Forgetting his own misery, Massai kicks the grey hard, sending him back toward the valley. Alchise is not in sight. The thick brush and thickets can completely hide a man and horse. Sticking his fingers into his mouth, Massai let out a piercing whistle that breaks the stillness of the valley floor. Scanning the valley, Massai's sharp eyes finally spot a horse and rider as they come into view. Raising his rifle, Massai whirls the grey in circles.

Alchise sees Massai and sends the sorrel charging into a hard lope. Together they follow the trail. Hours pass. Inspecting the tracks, Massai can tell no animals or other desert life crossed the band's trail. They are catching up to the Wild Ones.

Alchise slows the horses to a walk. He does not want to risk getting too close. Soon it will be dark and then he will close in on the unsuspecting troublemakers. Alchise is like a wolf on a blood scent. His eyes and ears miss nothing. A bent blade of grass, a broken twig, a disturbed rock—they all have meaning.

Massai watches in amazement as his uncle sniffs the air, smelling for his prey. This was one of the many reasons people were in awe of Alchise. His instincts are uncanny. His movement is calculated and silent, like a stalking cougar. However, it is the look on the older man's face that shakes Massai. It is the shrouded look of death. Sensing Massai's hesitation, Alchise pulls the sorrel to a stop and looks over at his nephew.

"You do not wish to follow Ponce?" He asks in a flat tone.

"He is my friend."

Alchise nods in understanding. "Geronimo was mine, but the people come first. These young fools will cause great hardship for our people if they raid the white-eye."

"I know this, uncle, but he is still my friend."

"Why you not ride with friend then?"

Massai answers simply, "I ride with you." He studies Alchise's stoic face. "What if I rode with Ponce this morning?"

Alchise's face hardens and his eyes piercing. Massai wants to look away but he cannot.

"Then, I would be trailing you, young cub," Alchise said.

"Will you kill them, Ponce and the others?"

Alchise looks off in the distance, in the direction of the trail. "Not necessary if we stop them before they make trouble."

"What if you cannot?" Massai knows the answer before he asks the question, but he still has to ask.

"Then I will kill them." Through talking, Alchise kicks the sorrel forward.

Massai knows Alchise means what he says. He gave up much and made many enemies to protect the Chiricahua people. Massai finds himself torn between regret and respect.

For three days and nights, Alchise and Massai hold to the trail of the Wild Ones. Massai is curious about Alchise's tactics. They spotted the band many times, but each time Alchise slowed and allowed them to continue.

Ponce is foolish and he suspects nothing. There is no rear guard watching their back trail. His only focus is forward but behind him is the danger. Day after day, Alchise dogs them without the Wild Ones suspecting they are being followed. Evening comes on the fourth day and Alchise makes camp in an arroyo less than a mile from the Wild Ones.

Biting into the dried meat Alchise brought along, Massai looks at his uncle. "Why do we wait?" He asks.

Alchise leans back against a boulder with his Henry Repeater across his lap. "They go to the stronghold of Cochise, maybe."

"Cochise?"

Alchise nods, remembering the tall warrior that was once his chief. His novice time came when Cochise was the leader of the Chiricahua people. They were free then, masters of these mountains and valleys. They fought the Mexicans and almost always won. Then the white man came with many guns and soldiers. They were not like the Mexican army. The white cavalry were determined fighters, following the Apaches, hounding them relentlessly.

Cochise had many victories but he knew the white men were too plentiful. They were like leaves on a tree, pluck some off and more grow in their place. They overran the land of the Apache. Alchise remembered the day Cochise spoke before the council of elders, urging them to sign the peace treaty with the whites. His words made sense to the young, hot-blooded Alchise.

However Goyathlay, the one the Mexicans and whites called Geronimo, left Cochise. He and Alchise rode into the mountains of northern Mexico. There they raided back and forth on both sides of the Rio Grande.

Geronimo was a fierce fighter and leader, but Alchise watched the outnumbered warriors slaughtered by the well-armed soldiers. Finally, with Geronimo's second surrender to Crook, Alchise was finished. He would fight the whites no more. He did not fear for himself, only for the Chiricahua people. If Geronimo did not stop fighting, his people would be annihilated.

When Geronimo jumped the reservation and headed for Mexico, Alchise became a scout for the whites. Finally, it was over. Geronimo with all his warriors and their families were sent to Florida. Alchise would have been sent too, but his boss and friend, James Davis, warned him to stay away from the fort for awhile.

Alchise remembers his mixed feelings back then. He knows what must be in Massai's heart now. It is a hard lesson for the young one to learn, but no different from lessons other men had to learn before him.

Alchise remembered a time in his youth when a warrior's foot was wounded by a white man's bullet. The wound was not so bad at first, but because of his pride, the warrior refused treatment. When the foot turned black and began to smell of rot, the warrior and others of the tribe knew his fate. Alchise shudders at the memory of watching the warrior cut through his own leg at the knee. He bit down on a chuck of rawhide while doing it. When he was almost finished, he passed out. Nachita and the others had to finish the job. It seemed a foolish thing to the young Alchise, but his father explained it in a way that he never forgot. When a part of you is rotten, you must cut it away or the rest will die with it. Despite the pain and the loss, it was the only way to preserve the life of the wounded warrior. It was the following spring, almost eleven months later, when the warrior's wife gave birth to two sons, twins. With only one good leg, he lived to see two more of his children born into the world. It was a lesson Alchise never forgot.

So it was with Geronimo. He had to sacrifice his freedom so that his people might live.

Now the young hotheads ahead of them are causing the same trouble for their people. They will stop now or Alchise will stop them. Their lives mattered little to him. He watched many of their fathers die in battle. Soon the young rebels will join them, if that is their choice.

"Sleep now, Massai," Alchise tells him though it is still early evening. "Tonight we take their horses."

Massai watches as Alchise pulls a piece of jerky from the cloth bag. "Take their horses?" He asks.

"It is many days back to reservation. No horses out here for Ponce to steal. With no horses, they must walk back and be shamed in front of village. Maybe they learn."

Massai wonders what Ponce will do without his horse. Will he return to the reservation or walk on to the stronghold Alchise spoke of? He wonders what he would do.

To return to the village without horses would be a great humiliation and Ponce is too arrogant to suffer such shame. It would be a very long walk back to the reservation. Maybe that is what Ponce deserves. After all, he almost killed Massai with tiswin.

CHAPTER

FIFTEEN

Ponce and the Wild Ones camp near a large spring then travel slowly to the south. Massai's warnings are still fresh in the leader's mind. He deliberately passes far to the east of any ranches or homesteads. This will keep temptation out of Chato's path. He is getting harder and harder to control and Ponce wonders when he will challenge him for leadership of the Wild Ones.

They will steal horses, but it will be closer to the border this time, away from the reservation. The Major at Fort Apache will not know which reservation the raiders came from, or whether it is the work of Mexican bandits. The great Alchise will have no reason to interfere with them. Even though he also feels concern for the fate of his people, Ponce will do as he wished in the end. If Alchise meddles with the Wild Ones, he will end up dead. It is not what Ponce wants, but there might not be any other choice. Alchise is an Old One. His time has passed. The present belongs to the young warriors and they will fight anyone who rides against them.

Taglio and Dosenay bring down a large buck around sundown. Now it sizzles over the flames of their campfire. Ponce stands in the shadows of his camp listening to the whippoorwills and other sounds of the night. His eyes search the darkness but only the lonely vigil of a giant cactus stands watch with him in the evening gloom.

The tall frame of Ponce's silhouette by the fire is clearly seen by the eyes watching him from afar. Ponce thinks he is a great warrior, but in fact, he is little more than a spoiled child. Despite his friendship with Ponce, Massai feels his respect for him slipping away.

Alchise and Massai wait silently and they are patient. Time to act will come soon enough. Several times, Alchise has the sights of his Henry on the tall silhouette. He could have killed Ponce at any time. The young warrior and his band have no sense of danger, no instincts of caution. They are unaware that even the night calls they so readily accept as part of the night come from Alchise.

Good-natured bantering, directed mostly as Dosenay, goes on around the campfire below them. The roasting venison livens the spirits of Ponce's riders and they are in a celebratory mood. Tiswin passes back and forth. It was foolish of them and it disgusts Alchise. Massai is torn. It would have been fun to be around a campfire with his friends. The roasting meat makes his mouth water. Nevertheless, the camp below is the camp of raiders and their actions can bring disaster to their people. Massai remembers that and it strengthens his resolve to stop them.

"Soon it will be time," Alchise said, bringing Massai back to reality.

The horses are hobbled several yards from the camp. They should not be a problem unless Ponce places more than one sentry.

"I will take the horses," Massai whispers.

Alchise shakes his head. The Wild Ones were careless but they are still dangerous. Massai is new to this kind of warfare.

"When they sleep," Alchise replies. "Then you take horses. We will be patient until then." Alchise recalls his own first attempt at horse stealing. The white settler almost killed him and he carried a permanent scar from a bullet to remind him.

Massai is anxious. He waits to see if Ponce posts a guard and wonders who it will be. If it is Dosenay, he will be asleep in ten minutes. If it is Chato then it will be a different matter. He saw Chato stalking the camp like a caged animal. With so much nervous energy, Chato might volunteer to take watch.

After Dosenay and several others fall asleep, Wolf, Ponce and Chato remain sitting by the fire. Massai can hear them arguing but he cannot make out their words. Wolf said little, but Chato and Ponce are disagreeing about something. Massai knows Chato and suspects the Mescalero wants to raid white ranches. Whatever the argument is about, Ponce is obviously disagreeing with him. Massai feels a tug of sympathy for Ponce.

Two more hours pass before all is quiet and the camp is sound asleep.

Massai sees that in his cockiness maybe because of the tiswin, Ponce made a big mistake. A mistake not worthy of a warrior as he did not post a guard. Stripping himself of all weapons except his knife, Massai nods to Alchise then he crawls toward the now smoldering campfire.

A pinion tree provides cover as he lies surveying the sleeping forms. All are sleeping soundly. Alchise watches, the Henry cocked and ready. Massai creeps past the horses and into the camp. Alchise shakes his head. The young cub is actually crouching beside the fire, eating meat from the spit. Young Massai has the courage of his namesake and the reckless nerve only youth can provide.

After a few bites, Massai moves away from the camp without disturbing the sleepers. He was glad they had been drinking. It makes his mission much easier. Quietly, he moves to the horses and gathers them. He returns to Alchise towing seven horses and bearing a gift. Alchise wastes no time in wolfing down the still warm venison Massai offers him.

Morning finds Alchise, Massai, and the stolen horses safely out of range of the still sleeping camp.

"Massai will circle to the east and watch the Wild Ones?" Alchise orders.

Massai nods. "And you?"

"I will take the horses and continue. I will ride slowly so you can join later."

Massai feels honored as he is given the responsibility of watching the Wild Ones. It is a sign Alchise fully trusts him. Urging his horse forward, he kicks up a trail of dust as he rides back to monitor Ponce and the others. Alchise proudly watches him ride off. He knows the warriors of old would have approved of the young cub. He has proven himself many times in the past few weeks.

Ponce awakes with a start. Smoke still drifts from the dying campfire, but he senses something is not right. Still groggy from his sleep and the tiswin, he studies the sleeping forms around him. They are all there, even Chato. Some of the young men stir, but to Ponce it is too quiet.

Suddenly, he knows what it is, the horses. The usual sounds the mustangs make are missing and so are they. With a yelp, Ponce leaps over several bodies and runs to where the horses were tied. Tracks showed plainly in the trampled dirt. The horses were led away while they slept.

"Fools!" Ponce cries, waking everyone. "Our horses were stolen right from under our noses."

Chato is the first to his feet. "Why was no guard posted?" He asks. "This is your stupidity, Ponce," he yells into the face of their leader.

Looking at the tracks, Ponce walks around them, studying the ground. Tracks led to their fire, right into the heart of their camp and then to where the horses were tied. They could have been killed in their sleep. Ponce is both outraged and embarrassed. This was a serious lack of judgment on his part. Chato kneels and traces the tracks with his finger. Anger grows on his face like a gathering storm. He knows the tracks. He followed them enough in the mountains.

"It was the breed," he hisses, turning to Ponce. "The one you call your friend."

Several heads turn to watch Ponce's reaction. Ponce kneels beside Chato and looks closer at the tracks. "How do you know?" He asks.

"I know," Chato said as he rises. He looks out across the valley but sees nothing.

"We cannot catch him without horses," Wolf said.

Chato scowls at Ponce. "Our horses are gone! The great Ponce led us to this place where there are no ranches to get more."

Murmurs of agreement follow Chato's remark, but Ponce is not cowed by his rival.

"There are plenty of horses in Mexico," he tells them. "We are not far from there."

"I will go back to the village and I will kill the breed," Chato announces. "Who goes with me?"

Ponce studies the faces around him. "If we go back to the village on foot, they will scorn and laugh at us. It will be our shame."

"I go," repeats Chato.

From the nodding heads, Ponce can see that others agree with Chato.

"We will vote then," he tells the band.

Massai watches the valley from a mesa high above. If Ponce and his warriors return to the reservation, they will have to cross the valley or walk across many miles of desert.

He leans against a sandy bank and lets the morning sun warm him. He fights the urge to sleep. He had little sleep in three days and the thought of catching a few hours of uninterrupted rest beckon him. Soon the heat will overcome the morning chill, but for now, the air is soothing and the ground as inviting as a bed of straw. Massai forces himself to remain alert. He has to keep watch. He turns his eyes back toward the valley and the Wild Ones. Then he sees what he was waiting for.

There is a glint of a rifle barrel and the flash of a shirt. The Wild Ones are on the move. They are returning to the village on foot. Massai hunkers down and watches carefully. He has to determine how many are going back—all or just some of them. Alchise will want to know. Soon he sees them clearly and counts seven warriors, running in a slow easy gait, zigzagging through the sagebrush and thickets.

Gathering his reins, he takes one more long look at the running men, then mounts and gallops off after Alchise.

Ponce sees movement on the high mesa. None of the others look up, not even Chato. Ponce knows it is Massai watching them. Rage grips him as he squeezes the rifle with a death grip. Massai is supposed to be his friend but what friend would humiliate him like this? He thought of Alchise and curses him. If not for him, Massai would be riding with them.

Massai catches up with Alchise and the horses. "They're coming," he said.

"Good, now we go quickly to the village."

Alchise's words make Massai uneasy. Returning to the village will cause a deadly confrontation once the Wild Ones return.

All eyes of the villagers are on them as Alchise and Massai pass slowly through the reservation. Young children poke their heads from their wickiups and dogs bark their greetings as Alchise ties all seven horses to a stand of oaks near the center of the village. He made it clear that he wants all to see what happened to the Wild Ones. It will be a warning to anyone else tempted to ride with the young troublemakers. Some nod and smile at the humiliation that is about to be bestowed on the young renegades, but others just stare with dark faces at Alchise. Massai takes note of the mixed feelings of the people toward what Alchise did.

Corralling their horses, Alchise slides the pole gate into place and put his hand on Massai's shoulder. "We rest here tonight," he tells him. "Tomorrow we go back to rancheria."

Massai understands. The Wild Ones will not be able to reach the village afoot before the next evening or even the day after that. Alchise wants to be away from the village before they arrive. Alchise is not looking for a fight. He just wants them to stop raiding.

Tired, Massai wants to eat and sleep but his desire to see Alchuni is stronger. There will be no time in the morning and he has an obligation to fulfill. Finding Salto's wickiup, they invite him inside without hesitation. He is surprised to find that Salto is genuinely glad to see him.

Salto chews a piece of dried beef and offers another to Massai. He takes it with a polite nod and they both chew in silence for a few moments.

"You bring back many horses," Salto finally said, breaking the silence.

"Yes," Massai replies. He knows Salto recognizes the horses and to whom they belong.

"And their riders?" Salto asks.

"They walk back."

Salto nods and fingers the animal teeth in the necklace around his neck. "Alchise should have killed them," he said.

Massai frowns. "The horses?"

"The Wild Ones," Salto said in a stern voice. "They cause the people of the village much trouble. I, too, know of the paper from the Big White Chief. He should have left their blood on the desert floor. It would be better for all."

Massai studies the face before him. The lines of sadness and regret on Salto's face are deeply drawn as if they were traced by ashes from the fire.

"You probably know I have come to see Alchuni," Massai said, changing the subject.

"To take her to the rancheria of Alchise?" Salto asks.

Massai shakes his head. "Soon, but first we will be married by tribal customs. Tonight, I wish to talk to her. If it is her wish, then when I return to the village, this will be."

Salto smiles. "You make an old man happy but I am afraid Chato will come for her before then."

Massai frowns and leans close to Salto, looking him in the eye. "You would give her to Chato, even now?"

Salto shakes his head slightly. "Once maybe," he said, "Now he will have to kill Salto to take her. He is strong and it will not be difficult for him."

Massai understands. Salto is afraid that when Chato returns he will take Alchuni by force. Salto will die and maybe even Alchuni.

"If I have your consent," Massai tells Salto, "I will walk with Alchuni now. We will walk within the light of the fires for all to see."

Salto nods and both men stand in understanding. They are about to leave the wickiup when a figure stirs outside and suddenly Alchuni appears at the entrance. Massai's heart pounds at the sight of her graceful figure. He moves quickly to her side. They have her father's proper blessing. Massai takes her arm and gently guides her away from the wickiup.

Salto watches with pride as the two young ones stroll openly through the village. He knows his daughter has much love for this young courageous warrior. He also knows the old crones of the village will stare and cluck their evil tongues, but it does not matter. Let them talk. Soon Massai and Alchuni will be married and the wagging tongues will stop.

Alchuni ignores the prying eyes as she walks beside Massai. "You and Alchise return with the horses of the Wild Ones," she said softly.

"Yes."

"Will there be trouble?"

"They are still alive, if that's what you are truly asking." He turns to her. "There could be much trouble if we do not leave for the rancheria tomorrow. This is why I asked to see you tonight. I do not know when I will return but I will return for you."

Alchuni frowns. "When you do return and then what happens?"

"I will have Loco arrange with Peponito and Salto for our marriage. When I return, you will go back with me to the rancheria as my wife."

Alchuni stares into Massai's eyes a long time and he feels a pang of fear in his heart. She does not seem pleased with his plan.

"Are you not happy?" He asks.

She sighs. "Time will pass slowly for me until you return but I will wait for that day."

Massai's heart warms by her words and joy swells up within him. Mindful of the probing eyes on them, he resists the urge to take her into his arms. For now, the look they share will have to be enough for both of them.

Alchise and Massai ride into the yard of the rancheria. The little rooster seems genuinely happy to see them. Dipping his wings to the ground, he struts back and forth then throws out his chest and crows his noisy welcome.

Massai feeds the horses then tosses a few oats to the chickens that were scrambling to catch feed falling from the hungry horses' mouths. Standing with his arms across the top rails of the corral, the handsome youth listens to the river as it passes peacefully around the bend below. The tall pines make music as they sway in the breeze as their fresh smelling needles perfume the air. He turns toward the cozy cabin, happy to be home. He hopes Alchuni will find the rancheria as much of a paradise as he does.

The next morning, before daylight, Alchise and Massai head to the northwest. The sun barely peeks over the ridgeline when they splash their horses across the White River.

As he follows the steady trot of the sorrel ahead of him, Massai can tell Alchise is deep in thought. Steadily they climb toward a mesa, high above the valley floor. Looking down, the river resembles a small rope winding its way through the mountains. He wonders where they are going, but does not ask. Massai learned to respect Alchise when silent. When it is time, Alchise will tell him.

Massai smiles to himself. The old Mason Davis from New York was no more. Looking back at his days in the East, he now knows he was as much to blame as the whites for the trouble he experienced. He reacted to their taunts by fighting back but it was a never-ending battle. Here it is different. Here there is only Alchise. Alchise, Loco, and soon Alchuni, he finally found peace.

He is so engrossed in his thoughts, Massai almost cries out when Alchise suddenly disappears over the edge of the narrow trail they follow. For a second, he thought the sorrel lost its footing and plunged down the steep hillside. Leaning forward, he sighs with relief when he catches sight of Alchise's head below, still upright on his horse. Massai follows him down the hill, his heart thumping inside his chest as his horse lunges straight down, sliding on rocks and gravel. The horse finds sure footing again on an even smaller trail.

Once Massai is at the bottom, Alchise dismounts and climbs back to where they turned off the trail above. Massai watches as he erases all signs of their passing. Finishing with his task, Alchise remounts and starts down the smaller path. Massai holds onto his horse with a death grip as the grey follows the sorrel down a steep game trail that only a mountain goat can traverse with ease. The young man's muscled legs grip the grey's sides as he leans back, almost touching the horse's rump.

With one final slide, the horses level out onto the valley floor. Alchise slid from the sorrel and grins as Massai's legs buckle when he dismounts.

"Cub is praying to great spirit, maybe," he jokes.

Massai laughs with relief as he stretches and collects himself. He looks around in wide-eye wonder at the natural beauty that surrounds him. He thought the area around the rancheria was paradise, but this is even more spectacular. The small valley is a canvas of lush green trees and grassy meadows bisected by a clear meandering stream. Although the sun was high, the air is cooler and heat waves do not shimmer above the ground. A faint breeze moves through the trees. It smells fresh, moist, and earthy.

"I thought you had to die to be in a place like this," Massai said, his voice full of awe.

Alchise chuckles. "Back on trail, maybe cub thought he would die." Alchise watches the face of Massai and smiles. He remembers the first time Nachita brought him here. He was even younger than Massai.

"Few know of this place," he tells Massai. "Mostly the warriors with Geronimo." His voice is soft and reverent. "It is one spot left to Apache, white man not know about. Even on reservation, not many know. The Old Ones know of this place but are dead now or forget."

"Do Ponce and the Wild Ones know of it?"

Alchise shrugs. "Maybe, but maybe they only hear rumors. Stories from the Old Ones."

Alchise mounts his sorrel and starts toward the other end of the valley. Lush green grass brushes their moccasins as the horses follow the gurgling stream through the meadow. Massai reaches down and grabs a small handful of grass.

"A man would not need grain for his horse here," he said.

A covey of quail flushes in front of them. The valley appears to be abundant with wildlife.

"A man would not starve here either," he adds.

Alchise motions for him to pull the grey alongside before replying. His dark eyes wander over the peaceful valley. "Goyathlay hide here many times when white pony soldier chase him over the mountains. He was safe here."

"Was Geronimo really as bad as the whites say?"

Again, Alchise hesitates then nods his head. "Plenty bad," he said. "Mexican kill his family when he was just a young warrior. Turned his heart to stone. Make him go crazy, maybe."

Massai studies his uncle's face. "Was he your friend?"

"I tell you this before. Bad Apache have no friend, only trouble."

They ride on in silence until Alchise suddenly reins his horse. He points his forefinger at a grove of cottonwoods standing alongside the stream. "You born there."

"Here?" Massai's eyes widen.

Alchise nods.

Massai starts to ask more about his birth and about his mother. Why was she down here in this secret valley? Was Davis with her? Probably not, since this place is not known to whites. How did his father claim him and take him east? He has so many questions but knows Alchise will say no more.

Alchise eases his horse into the water. Massai follows and catches his breath. The water is as cold as the snow back East. They climb onto the opposite bank when a challenging snort comes from the trees. A blood-bay stallion charges into view and stamps his front foot. Several times, he squeals and rears onto his hind legs. Shaking his head and mane downward, he lays his ears back and fakes a charge at them.

"He's beautiful!" Massai whispers. The animal's bloodred coat ripples with sleek muscles and shows brilliant in the sunlight.

"Horse follow Alchise back from Sonora."

"You stole him in Mexico?" Massai's eyebrows arch.

Alchise shrugs. "Alchise leave Mexico. Horse follow."

Massai laughs at the thought. "I thought you were a peaceful Apache."

Alchise laughs also. "Mexicans have many horse. I just take one, this one."

Suddenly the big stallion bolts forward. "Here he comes!" Shouts Massai as he tries to turn his grey out of the horse's path.

Alchise's strong hand grabs the grey's bridle. "Be still. You scare horse."

"Me? He's the…"

Massai's words are cut off as the big bay whirls toward the two men in a charge then slides to a stop a few feet in front of them. Alchise laughs and then slaps his leather leggings. The stallion snorts then turns and lopes back to the tree line where the rest of his band is waiting.

"I didn't think he was going to stop," Massai said with relief.

"Horse just try to scare cub," Alchise said. "Apache and horse, brother. Horse no want to fight with brother."

"I thought you said the bear was brother to the Apache?"

Alchise smiles. "Apache big family. Many brothers."

Alchise makes his way to the same cottonwood trees he pointed out earlier and dismounts. Massai does the same. In a very small clearing among the trees, Massai sees signs of past fires and a small wickiup that was badly in need of repair. A shaky pole corral stands nearby.

The stallion and his mares follow the strangers at a safe distance but stop in the middle of the meadow. All ears are pointing toward the men. The mares, mostly bays and sorrels, some with colts at their sides, stand ready to flee at the first sign of danger. The stallion seems more curious than frightened. He was once gentle and broke, so he does not fear man as the mares do. They see few humans in the valley. Massai notices one older mare, a sorrel much like Alchise's sorrel. She moves slower but bosses the other mares and nudges them along. Massai guesses her to be the head mare.

Alchise stands and watches the horses with Massai. "That mare, the old sorrel," he said pointing. "She wife of stallion. Other mares all born here."

"Where are the other stallions," Massai asks.

"Males gelded when young. When old enough, I sell to white ranchers or Army." Alchise indicates his own beautiful horse. "Alchise's horse son of bay and old mare. One day maybe need new stallion for stronger colts."

"What will you do with the bay then?"

"Alchise honest Apache. Take horse back to Mexico. Maybe another one follow me here to this place."

Both men laugh causing the mares to back up slightly.

"The horses are beautiful, uncle."

"Yes, horses and valley both have much beauty."

"So, is this what you are supposed to bring to the trader at Fort Apache? To Garrett? Horses?"

Alchise shakes his head. "No. Horses for whites who chase cattle. Come. I show cub what Garrett wants."

He takes off going along the creek with Massai in tow. A hundred yards downstream, Alchise stops and ducks under a large rock outcropping. Standing aside, he points out the glittering rocks that twinkle like golden stars from the bottom of a small eddy.

"This is what Garrett wants," Alchise said pointing at the rocks. "White man crazy over yellow rocks. Kill for them."

Massai's eyes bulge as he kneels down and picks up a golden nugget. "This is gold!" He exclaims. "You're rich, Alchise!"

Alchise takes the nugget from Massai's hand and drops it back into the crystal clear water. It makes a noisy plop before settling to the shallow bottom of the creek.

"No, Massai. The yellow iron makes bad medicine. Brings much trouble."

"You can buy anything you want with it," Massai protests.

Alchise studies him with honest curiosity. "What I want with rocks? What I want, rocks not buy. Rocks white man's curse. Massai want, Massai take. Not for Alchise."

Massai looks at the gold nestled in the stream's gravel bed. Mason Davis would have hungered for those nuggets and the material wealth they could provide. He is no longer Mason Davis and has no desire to follow in his father's footsteps. He is now Massai, Apache warrior, and he is walking in the footsteps of a great Chiricahua warrior.

"No, uncle, I too have everything I want, at least almost."

Alchise smiles and nods his approval. "Soon you have wife, too. Then you have everything man need."

CHAPTER
SIXTEEN

It is after midnight when Ponce and the Wild Ones slip back into the village. They find their horses tied where Alchise left them. No one speaks as they lead them away to their individual wickiups. Shame is on the face of each young warrior and revenge is in their hearts but at least they were spared a public homecoming in the daylight.

Chato's face is a mask of hate. Alchuni and everyone else in the village will know of his disgrace. He cannot stay in the village until Alchise and Massai are dead. It is the only way Chato thinks he can regain his honor.

Ponce leads his black horse slowly toward his father's wickiup. Alchise and Massai outsmarted him and took his horses. Still, Geronimo lost many a horse and many warriors. Chato was wrong and he is a hotheaded fool. Ponce does not think Alchise and Massai should be hunted and killed for what they did. Ponce knows Alchise did it to protect the people on the reservation. As the leader of the Wild Ones, Ponce should shoulder the blame for the public humiliation. Deep in thought, Ponce does not notice the solitary figure that waits in the dark until he steps into his path. It is Calito, Chief of the Chiricahua.

"Your horses came back before you, Ponce," Calito said in a gruff low voice.

Ponce pulls the reins through clenched fingers, the leather burning against his skin. "Yes, Calito, they did."

"How does this happen," Calito presses. "Tell me. No one else will know."

"I am certain the whole village knows already," he hisses.

Calito shakes his head. "They only know Alchise brought the horses back."

Ponce is surprised and relates the story of the night raid on their horses to Calito. Finishing, he slaps the reins against his leg. Telling it makes it seem worse. Maybe Chato was right.

"What do you intend to do?" Calito asks.

"I do not know yet. Alchise is a devil. I do not fear him but I do not know how to fight him."

"Why did he take your horses?"

Ponce frowns. The old Chief is playing with him. "You ask questions you already know."

Calito grins in the darkness. Yes, he knows but he wants Ponce to say it. Saying it aloud will make the young warrior angry enough to thirst for revenge. Chato is the angry one but the Chief knows the others might not follow Chato. They will follow Ponce.

"What will you do?" The Chief asks again. "You lead the Wild Ones. To lose face is to lose everything."

Ponce feels his blood run hot. He heard the same words from Chato. He looks at Calito. "I will kill Alchise and then I will have his power and regain the people's respect."

"Alchise can easily kill you, all of you. He is, as you say, the devil."

Ponce draws a deep breath. "Then what should I do?"

Calito turns and indicates for Ponce to follow him. "Come to my wickiup. I have a plan."

In the wickiup, Calito and Ponce huddle close, speaking in low tones, until the sun rose. When Ponce returns to his own wickiup, his step is lighter and his shoulders a little straighter.

A few days later, the Wild Ones, with Ponce leading, quietly slips away from the reservation. Just outside the village, Ponce looks back and raises his rifle. "When I return, you will know the name of Ponce!"

Massai is sore and every move causes him to wince in pain. For almost a solid week, Alchise has him working with the young horses they caught and corralled. All the young males have to be gelded, those big enough to break need to be gentle, and halter broke for their trip to the Frasier Ranch.

Most of the geldings Alchise corralled are at least five years old. All are mud fat and ready for a fight. Alchise breaks them easily, speaking quietly and stroking them until they feel at ease. A few tremble uncontrollably at first but eventually give in to the reassuring gentle caresses.

There are a few continuing to resist no matter how much they work with them. They are the ones that cause most of Massai's grief. He tastes the sandy ground of the corral many times because of the free spirited ones.

After watching Massai hit the ground many times trying to break one particular horse, Alchise grins and said, "Maybe I give the mother of this one to the Mexicans as payment for the big bay."

"Maybe he gets his bad temper from the stallion." Massai banters back.

"No, bay stallion is gentle."

Massai laughs. He watched the old stallion squeal and paw the ground near the corral almost every day since they arrived. "I would not call him gentle."

"Cub not believe lion?" Alchise raises one eyebrow. "Come, I show you."

Happy to have a break, Massai watches as Alchise shoulders a plaited rawhide rope and whistles as he walks toward the stream. Within minutes, the big bay emerges from his herd and splashes across the water. A game of cat-and-mouse starts as Alchise tries to approach the stallion. For almost thirty minutes, Alchise talks quietly and eases around the skittish horse, each time closing the gap. Massai chuckles softly, sure the old stallion is too smart for the old warrior.

Suddenly, the grin falls from Massai's face. The rope in Alchise's hand snakes through the air and settles easily around the stallion's thick neck. The horse turns to bolt but the feel of the rope on his neck makes him stop resisting. The stallion still remembers how the rope can bite if he fights it.

Alchise pulls the stallion to him and then makes a hackamore of the rope. Curling the rest of the coils in his hand, he springs easily onto the huge back of the horse. Massai watches in amazement as Alchise sends the animal through his paces.

Even the sorrel and the grey they ride do not handle any better than the big bay. He whirls in circles, first one way and then the other. Backing up, loping in short, tight figure-eights, the old stud changes his lead perfectly. Massai is impressed but even more so when Alchise kicks the horse into a hard run down the valley floor and back. His tail and mane stand straight out. His ears are flat against his head with his neck stretched hard. Alchise leans over his withers and the horse goes faster than any horse Massai has ever seen.

As they pass Massai on the return, he can see the nostrils flaring, the soft brown eyes, and the beautiful hue of his blood-brown coat. The horse is enjoying the run as much as his rider. Alchise lets out a whoop of exhilaration. Massai feels the ground rumble as they pass him a second time. He wants to take his grey and chase after them, but he is certain his horse could never keep up with the stallion.

After many days, the chores are done in the valley. The horses are ready to trail to the rancheria and then on to Frasier's ranch. Massai wonders how they will ever be able to lead the horses up the steep rocky trail but knows Alchise did it many times before. He follows Alchise down the valley, ready to watch and learn.

High cliffs surround the small valley and seem to block their path, but Alchise continues riding straight toward them. A waterfall is ahead and Massai hears the roar of the falls long before he sees it.

Alchise dismounts and hands Massai several rawhide hackamores. "Put on horses. We lead now."

Looking at the waterfall and the sheer cliffs around and behind it, he is confused. "Lead where?"

"You see," Alchise said. "Just do."

Massai has been around Alchise long enough to know not to argue. They take only ten horses from the valley, but they are the best of the lot. There isn't a blemish on any one of them. They are all sorrels or bays, some with a spot of white or maybe a blaze, but most are solid.

Massai stands holding eight horses, plus his own grey, as Alchise approaches the waterfall. Riding his sorrel, Alchise takes the remaining two horses and disappears behind the sheet of falling water. Massai's mouth falls open. Alchise soon returns for two more horses. He continues until there are only four horses left. With Alchise leading two, Massai follows on his grey leading the last two. Hiding behind the roaring waterfall is a cavernous dark tunnel large enough for them to pass through. Light from the other end of the tunnel illuminates the wet sandy floor.

The first horses went through bunched up against a pole barricade at the mouth of the tunnel. Alchise quickly drops the poles and leads all the horses through. Once done, he goes back and removes any sign of their passing by brushing the ground and disguising the tunnel with branches. Massai looks back as they start their ascent up the high cliffs. Even from a short distance, the entrance to the tunnel is undetectable. The river that hides the cave comes from above. He realizes the Army must have run themselves ragged trying to find Geronimo and his braves.

Across the distant range of mountains, Alchise points out the tall pines that hide the rancheria on the White River. They will soon be home. Cactus and sagebrush quickly replace the lush green grass of the valley, Massai finds he misses the beautiful valley that was his birthplace.

Arriving back at the rancheria, Massai turns the horses into the corral. He walks to the cabin when the sound of galloping horses startles him. The thundering hooves bring Alchise quickly out of the cabin.

Recognizing the men as wranglers from the Frasier ranch, Alchise jacks a shell into the Henry. Seeing Alchise with his rifle, the riders quickly pull up their lathered horses.

The man in the lead, a bandy-legged wrangler speaks. "Mrs. Frasier sent us to fetch you quick." His words come out in short blasts of breath as he struggles to catch his wind. He looks down at Alchise and his uneasy eyes rest on the rifle.

"Why woman want?" Alchise asks, speaking to them in English.

"Reckon she'd be the one to tell you," the man wheezes. He spit a stream of tobacco on the ground beside his horse. "I was just told to come git ya and to be quick about it."

Alchise makes no move to comply. "You tell Alchise, why she want. Then we go, maybe."

Eyeing the rifle, another of the riders speaks up. "It's Miss Audrey. Someone took her from the ranch."

Alchise's face blanches at the words. Quickly, he orders Massai to gather their weapons and ready their horses. He tells the cowboys to bring the horses in the corral to the ranch. He and Massai will ride straight there ahead of them. At first the wranglers grumble, they do not take orders from Indians. However, their hesitation brings such a fierce look from Alchise that the leader turns to his men and orders them to round up the horses and that settles it. The two warriors mount their horses and set off at a hard run for Frasier's ranch.

After two hours of full, out riding, they reach the ranch. They find Jean Frasier sobbing on the front porch. She runs to Alchise as soon as he jumps from the sorrel. Her hair is messy and her face covered in dust stained tears. She is babbling incoherently. Massai hears the name Audrey several times.

Alchise grasps the woman's shoulders firmly and barks a command to settle down. Immediately she responds but continues sobbing quietly.

"Now, Tawano, tell what happen," Alchise said, speaking in English.

Jean Frasier looks wildly into Alchise's eyes. "They've taken her. They've taken Audrey. Please help me, my husband," she sobs.

Massai catches his breath. Did she call Alchise her husband or did he misunderstand? Maybe she meant they also took her husband, Fulton Frasier.

"Who take?" Demands Alchise.

"Apaches. Young ones."

"Show me."

A dark concerned look crosses Alchise's face. He and Massai follow her to the rear of the large ranch house.

Massai watches as Alchise searches the ground for tracks. He gets close to the ground, nose to dirt, reminding Massai of the bloodhounds used by the police back east to track escaped prisoners. Alchise traces a print with his finger and then motions for Massai to come forward. He points to the track and Massai looks at it carefully.

"Ponce," he said. He knew the twisted front print of Ponce's black anywhere.

"Go quickly," Alchise orders him in Apache, motioning to the southeast. "Look for trail. I will check this side of river. Go quick."

Massai looks to where Jean Frasier stands, twisting and turning her hands together nervously. He wants to say something to comfort her but does not know what.

"Go, Massai!" Alchise commands sharply.

As soon as Massai leaves, Alchise continues to look over the other tracks and then goes to the woman.

"I will find daughter, Tawano. I will kill who has done this thing."

Jean Frasier nods. She trembles and bites her lip as she locks her pleading eyes on his face.

"Where is your man and his riders?" He asks her.

Frasier took all the men but the ones I sent to you. He rode out this morning as soon as we discovered she was gone." She hesitates. "Be careful of him. He is full of hate for Apaches and now even more so."

Alchise understands what she is saying. "Has he no tracker?"

"He sent for a man named Macy."

Alchise stiffens. "Macy good tracker."

Jean Frasier starts to swoon but Alchise catches her. Helping her to a porch chair, he turns to go when she starts sobbing hysterically.

"Why? Why have they done this? It's like a nightmare. It's happening all over again," she wails. "Why? For God's sake, why?"

Alchise looks down at his feet and then places a comforting hand on her shoulder before stepping off the porch. He mounts his horse and remembers when the warriors brought her, Tawano, into the Apache stronghold many years ago.

"I go," he said with a flat voice, not betraying the anger and pain he feels on her behalf.

"Hurry, my husband," she said to him. "Take care of my… take care of Mason. Protect him from them."

Alchise's eyes flash at her. "Massai Chiricahua warrior now. Tawano no worry. Cub be okay."

CHAPTER

SEVENTEEN

Massai finds the trail of the Wild Ones as soon as he crosses the river. His sharp eyes easily pick up their tracks in the soft sandy banks. They ride to the west and they ride fast, their hooves biting deeply into the ground as they race along the river's edge. One horse carries double. The weight of an extra body caused the tracks to penetrate deeper into the ground. Studying the trail closely, Massai finds where the tracks of several shod horses intersect unshod ones.

"Frasier," Massai said to himself under his breath.

It seems the rancher is also hot on the trail of Ponce and his gang. Soon the trail will cool making it more difficult to read. The white men will lose ground and when they do, Massai does not want to blunder into them. To do so would be a fatal mistake. They might think he is one of the pack that took Audrey instead of someone trying to help.

Levering a shell into the Winchester, Massai fires a round into the air. He does not wait for Alchise. The warrior will hear the shot and follow. He wants to turn the grey horse loose and let him follow the trail at a run. However, with Frasier and his men ahead, he has to stop and study every canyon and ridge cautiously before crossing them. The men who ride with Frasier are seasoned riflemen and he does not want to give them a chance to test their marksmanship.

Studying the tracks, Massai is curious. Why did Ponce leave such an obvious trail? A child can follow the tracks. Somewhere ahead, Ponce will have to try to lose his pursuers. He has to. His horses' tracks are showing signs of losing speed. Are the Apache ponies exhausted after the hard ride to the white man's ranch? Is Ponce just being careless or is he careless for a reason?

Massai knows Frasier's horses are bigger, stronger, and fresher than the ponies of the Wild Ones. They are stock that Alchise sold to the ranch and they are also grain fed. The smaller horses will not stand a chance of outrunning them for long.

After a while, Massai pulls the grey up. He slides to the ground and studies the tracks carefully. Something about them changed. Ponce tricked Frasier. Along the way, he abandoned his horses. From the depth of the prints the Indian ponies made, Massai can tell only one warrior rode ahead trailing riderless horses. Frasier and his men followed the lone rider and the band of horses. It was apparent the rider and his horses were luring Frasier west, away from the Wild Ones and the girl. When Frasier catches up, the rider will turn the horses loose and return to Ponce and the others on foot. By then, Frasier will have lost their trail. Ponce probably assigned Wolf or Chato to such a task. The plan will work if Ponce and the others have extra horses hidden before taking the girl.

Holding the reins of his grey, Massai muses over this development. Which way would Ponce take his band? Will they go to the south, toward Cochise's stronghold and the Dragoon Mountains? It is also possible Ponce will gamble and turn north into the White Mountains.

Massai turns to the south and kicks his horse into a lope. He will angle east and south. He is sure the trail of the Wild Ones lies there. Ponce's only hope will be to reach the wilder and less settled country along the border. He might even be planning to cross into Mexico with his captive.

Why did they abduct the girl? This is much more serious than raiding ranches and stealing horses. If it was not for the hoof print of Ponce's horse among the others, Massai would have thought Chato overthrew Ponce as the leader. He knows Ponce would not ride with the Wild Ones if that happened. No, his friend Ponce is still leading the young renegades, of that he is certain.

As the grey trots easily across the hot Arizona desert, Massai tries to figure out the reason they took Audrey Frasier. The young warrior's sharp eyes search the scorching sand but finds no sign of the kidnappers. Uncertainly plagues his mind. Perhaps he misread the signs. His mind is in turmoil and several times, he starts to turn the grey back, only to reconsider and push the horse on. He will give it more time. If he does not find Ponce's trail soon, he will turn back and retrace his steps.

The pounding of hooves break Massai's concentration. Turning his horse toward a group of cactus, Massai dismounts and lies still, pressing himself against the ground behind a large Saguaro. He slows his breathing, making it easier to hear. Blinking sweat from his eyes, he tries to see through the sweltering heat waves that dance off the hot desert floor.

A rider circles ahead of him and raises his rifle. Massai grunts in relief. It is Alchise. He remounts the grey and rides toward him.

"Cub fall from horse again?" Alchise asks when Massai is close.

"I didn't know it was you." Massai surveys the landscape and turns back to his uncle. "I think Ponce and the others sent their horses on and then they set off on foot."

Alchise nods. "Cub do good."

"Did you find the trail?"

Alchise nods again. "Trail ahead. Ponce go south to place of Cochise."

Massai smiles. He guessed right but how did Alchise get ahead of him? The old warrior must have caught onto Ponce's trick sooner than he did.

"How far ahead are they?" Massai asks.

"Many hours, if they do not stop. The girl slows them. She cannot travel as Apache warrior."

He reaches into a sack and hands Massai a strip of jerky. He takes it gratefully.

"And Frasier?" Alchise asks.

"I think he still follows Ponce's horses to the west." Massai said, his mouth full of the dried meat. "I haven't seen any signs of the white men for awhile."

"Again, cub do good." In spite of the words of praise, Alchise's voice is laced with harshness. "Better whites go after horses. They are not good trackers but they are good fighters. If not careful, they will kill us. To them, Apache all the same. All bad."

Massai studies his uncle's face. He has never seen him so tense, so serious. The weathered dark face is set, cold, and hard. Massai can feel anger coming off Alchise as obvious as the heat waves that shimmer off the desert floor. He knows Alchise will not stop following Ponce until he finds him and the girl.

Just before they take off in the direction of Cochise's hiding place, Massai asks Alchise a question he already knows the answer to, but needs to ask anyway. "Uncle, what will happen to Ponce?"

Alchise looks out across the desert, then turns to look straight into Massai's eyes. "He is a dead man."

So far, Calito's plan has gone well. One of his most trusted braves rides in to report that Ponce has the white girl and was leading Alchise and Massai straight to certain death. Calito and several warriors lie hiding, waiting for their prey to pass below. All who wait with Calito hate Alchise, especially Calito. He is the Chief, but many of the people on the reservation revered and respected Alchise. Even many of the whites admired Alchise and treated him more like the Apache leader than Calito. More than once Alchise went against Calito's orders and humiliated him. It was easy to persuade Ponce that Alchise stood in his way of being a great leader of the Wild Ones. With Alchise gone, the people will know for sure that Calito is their leader. The young Massai, the half-breed, was like Alchise so he too must die.

Hoof beats sound in the canyon below. Calito clenches his teeth and picks up his rifle. Even though he is hiding and flanked by faithful warriors, he still sweats at the thought of confronting Alchise. He is a formidable enemy and one he fears. The spirits protect him and his skills are considerable. Calito knows in his heart that he can never take Alchise on his own. He also knows Alchise will be outraged by what the Wild Ones did. Calito steadies himself, counting on Alchise's rage to cloud his judgment to the point he will not become aware of the trap until it is too late.

Ponce and his band passes below. All but Ponce are unaware that Calito's eyes follow them. Many of the warriors with Calito quietly spit their contempt for the Wild Ones as they pass. They bring nothing but trouble to the people and now this. It would have been easier to take their lives but the shots would betray them and warn the one that follows. Their real quarry is Alchise.

Massai and Alchise pull up their horses and regard the tracks closer.

"The tracks are too easy to follow," Massai said.

"The cub is right. Ponce knows better. Maybe easy to follow for a reason. We must be careful."

They ride on with a heightened sense of awareness.

"Why are you so angry about the white girl?" Massai asks after a while. "Is it just because of the letter about the Army?"

"Someday, I will tell you. For now, we must find the girl."

Massai's guess was right. Chato was the one who led the horses west. Frasier's men follow him hard, tiring their horses in the effort. Passing a dry streambed, the wily Mescalero drops from his exhausted horse and sends it on its way without him. He watches as the horses follow his down the trail. Slipping behind a large rock, he hugs the ground and waits. Soon Frasier and his men pass.

With the white men safely following the horses, Chato rises and shakes the sand from his body. The white men are stupid. The squeak of their saddles, jingle of their spurs, and the labored breathing of their horses make it easy to track and watch them. Spitting in disgust, Chato turns north toward the reservation. He already rode forty miles or better, now he will run another twenty. A steady pace will bring him to the village under the cover of darkness.

Arriving before dawn, Chato finds the village still asleep. He squats beside the wickiup of Salto and listens. Nothing but the sounds of sleep come from inside the wickiup.

Slipping into Salto's corral, he quickly bridles a dun gelding and drops the reins. Chato rushes back to the wickiup. Alchuni is his woman and no one would or could stop him now. Pushing aside the leather entrance cover, boldly he steps inside and he is met by a startled voice.

"Who are you?"

Chato recognizes the voice of Salto, but ignores him. His eyes search the darkness for Alchuni until he hears her cry out. He steps over the old man and grabs her. She screams. Salto stands to protect his daughter but Chato knocks him down with one powerful blow. Grabbing the kicking and screaming girl by her long hair, Chato drags her over to the horse. He flings her over the dun's withers and mounts. Lashing the horse hard, he gallops out of the village, scattering dogs and cooking pots in their wake.

Alchise pulls the sorrel to a stop at the mouth of a rugged canyon. Steep cliffs border each wall. In the old days, they ambushed Mexican traders in this same canyon. It is not very big, but it is long and narrow. The perfect place for an ambush. Placing his warriors well, Cochise never lost a man or let one enemy escape from this place. It was aptly named the Canyon of the Dead.

"We must pass through here," Alchise tells Massai. "There is no other way."

Massai studies the canyon walls. The place is eerie. Hundreds of men could be concealed behind the boulders perched precariously around the canyon's rim. He can see where the trail widens further ahead and wants to kick his grey into a hard run until they clear the treacherous area.

Alchise holds the sorrel to an easy walk, trying to hug one wall of the canyon as closely as possible. Massai follows.

Stopping after a few feet, Alchise turns to Massai and whispers. "I go across here first. If someone waits for us, it will be here."

Massai nods and watches as Alchise moves the sorrel forward toward the spot where the canyon widens. When Alchise reaches midway, the walls of the canyon seem to explode with thunder. The warrior is lifted bodily from the sorrel and slammed to the ground.

Whipping the grey hard, Massai almost reaches Alchise when another volley of shots ring out. The grey shudders and collapses, throwing Massai across the body of the sorrel. Pulling himself behind the horse's carcass, he looks to where his grey kicks and screams, trying to get back onto his feet. Massai notices the horse's right foreleg is shattered and blood gushes from his side. Raising the Winchester, he places the crosshairs on the grey's broad forehead and pulls the trigger.

Ducking down behind the body of the dead sorrel, Massai feels the still warm body of the horse jerk as shot after shot is fired into it. A few bullets penetrate the carcass, barely missing him. The echo of the shots within the narrow steep canyon is deafening.

This cannot be Frasier and his men, Massai thought. They are too far behind, traveling in a different direction. He wonders if it might be another posse looking for the Frasier girl. Whoever they are, they must think that Alchise is dead, because they are now giving Massai the full attention of their rifles.

Looking to where Alchise is lying in a pool of blood, Massai can see the dark eyes of the fallen warrior staring back at him. Gripping his rifle in a crazed fury, Massai lets out a growl and is poised to leap up and charge the canyon wall. A familiar voice stops him.

"Cub be patient."

Alchise is alive, but Massai has no way of knowing how bad his injuries are. The sorrel is not big enough to shield them both, and the gunfire from above is too deadly for him to reach Alchise.

Flipping the Winchester over the Sorrel, Massai fires up at the canyon's rim. He fires quickly then lies flat as several rifles respond. There is a spray of blood and flesh as the bullets knock chunks of horsehide and flesh from the dead animal.

Shadows are already starting to creep across the small canyon, and

Massai knows with the approaching darkness, the ambushers will come down and finish their deadly work. Working his way along the dead sorrel, he spots a large boulder. It is big enough to shield both he and Alchise. He will use the coming darkness as a cover to move his uncle to a safer spot.

Looking over at Alchise, he whispers, "Uncle, as soon as the shadows come, I will move us behind the big rock."

Only a reassuring flip of an eyelid tells him the wounded warrior agrees.

Gathering up the Winchester and a belt of cartridges, Massai straps them to his body. When he moves, he will have to do it fast and the timing has to be perfect. Looking to where a water bag lay, Massai wipes his dry mouth. A drink will taste good and Alchise will need water. He will try for the water once he gets Alchise to safety.

Massai waits until the shadows in the canyon are long enough to give him the few seconds he needs. With the speed of a trained athlete, he lunges toward Alchise and grabs onto the warrior's cartridge belt. Massai drags his uncle to safety just as the attackers react and rain down a storm of bullets. The shots kick up the dirt and ricochet off the boulder, but Massai and Alchise are safe for the time being.

A quick check of Alchise's wounds reveals there are two and they are nasty, but neither are immediately life threatening. He tears a piece off his shirt and binds the wounds to stem the flow of blood. While he works, Massai thinks about the attack. He figures only three or four rifles were fired when he moved Alchise. He wonders if the others are already dropping down into the canyon to finish the job as darkness approaches.

Massai peers around the boulder and sees a movement high up in the rocks. He quickly fires several shots at the target. A scream sounds above the reverberations of the gunfire. A body clings momentarily from the lip of the ridge but then comes crashing down. It lands with a hard dull thud as it hits the canyon floor not far from Massai and Alchise.

He thought the attackers were white, so he is surprised to see the body lying nearby is Apache.

"Apache," Massai whispers to Alchise.

Alchise nods. He is not surprised. Either the Wild Ones are above them or others from the village are involved. Alchise knows he made many enemies over the years among his own people. Calito is one who comes to mind. Calito is chief and he can command other warriors to follow him.

"Be ready, Massai," Alchise said, struggling to speak. "They will come with the moon."

Massai knows they will come, but now he also knows he is fighting Apache warriors. He and Alchise will not leave the canyon alive unless he can manage to kill them all.

Checking the Winchester, Massai looks to where the Henry rests beside the sorrel. It will be needed. Alchise has two bandoleers of shells around his shoulders. Massai will wait. Maybe when there is more darkness, he can take the risk of reaching the rifle.

Another hour passes and only the buzz of blowflies on the dead horses can be heard.

Alchise slips into unconsciousness. Massai is able to stem the flow of blood from the two wounds, but he needs water to clean and bandage them properly. Massai's eyes scan the deepening shadows along the canyon wall. Their attackers will come, sneaking quietly across the sandy floor, but he does not know from which direction. His sweaty hands grip the Winchester tightly. They might come from both ends of the canyon.

He almost wishes they would rise up and come screaming into the narrow canyon. At least the waiting would be over. Massai draws a slow deep breath. Alchise is always trying to teach him patience. Now is the time he needs it most. From beside him, Alchise's ragged breathing sounds loud but he knows it is barely audible. Massai forces himself to remain calm and alert to the approach of his enemy.

If he loses control of his own emotions and fear takes over, they will both die. He thinks about the body of the dead warrior a few feet away. The man is old and gray-haired. Maybe all the attackers are seasoned warriors. Massai might be able to outrun an old warrior but he will not underestimate the experience of a hardened veteran fighter who is battle tested. If he was alone, he could try to outrun the attackers once it was dark but he is not alone and he will not run. He places a comforting hand on his uncle's shoulder. He will never abandon him, not even to save himself. He will wait, be patient, and he will be ready.

Up above a rock breaks loose and bangs its way down the steep face of the cliff. Someone is moving. Gunfire erupts and Massai jerks back, expecting the attack but none comes. Instead, the fighting is high above them. As the gun battle on the ridge above him rages, Massai stays alert and listens. He can hear shouts and groans as bullets find their mark.

Suddenly, a dark figure rushes his position and Massai has no time to swing around the Winchester. A bullet strikes the boulder beside his head and glances off into the dark causing granite chips to sting his face.

Instinctively, Massai pulls his knife and plunges it deep into the belly of the attacker standing over him. Another comes but he does not see Massai kneeling below, hiding by the body of his comrade. With lightning speed, Massai springs from the ground and buries his knife into the chest of the second man. He pushes it deep, twisting the knife and ripping it upward. His hand becomes wet and sticky with the flow of blood and the man groans. Face to face with his attacker, Massai sees it is Calito, Chief of the Chiricahua.

"Calito!" Massai gasps. He pulls his knife out and the Chief slides to the canyon floor. "But why?"

There is no response.

Looking out into the growing darkness, Massai waits with his gun and knife for more attackers. Above him, the battle is still raging and steady gunfire explodes. No more warriors come for Massai and Alchise.

Taking advantage of the distraction above, Massai quickly gathers the water bag and Alchise's rifle. He cannot carry everything and the wounded Alchise. Digging a shallow trench in the soft sand next to the boulder, Massai drops the Henry into it and kicks sand over it. He will keep the Winchester. They are not out of danger yet.

With the water bag and cartridge belts strapped across his shoulders, Massai heaves the wounded Alchise onto his back and picks up his rifle. Retreating the way they came, Massai reaches the end of the canyon quickly and looks for a hiding place. He does not know who is fighting Calito's warriors and whether they are friend or foe.

Struggling with his burden to a rock shelf that leads up the steep sides of the high canyon walls, Massai follows it a hundred yards before setting Alchise down. The wounds are bleeding again but he has no time to tend to them properly. Quickly he tightens the bandages, hoping to stop the bleeding. While doing so, he feels a hand on his leg and turns to find Alchise staring at him.

"There, young one."

Looking to where Alchise points, Massai sees a rock outcropping just ahead. He again shoulders the wounded man and struggles up the steep ledge. Straining for breath, he stops near where Alchise indicated.

"In there," Alchise gasps in a weak voice.

Massai's eyes strain in the darkness. Feeling his way, he suddenly feels the rock give way to a very narrow opening. It is a cave. Pushing his way inside, Massai eases the wounded Alchise onto the ground, then collapses beside him.

"Start fire," Alchise whispers. "Flint and wood against wall."

"But they will see it."

"No see. Cave hid well." His voice is weakening and Massai knows that without a fire, he will not be able to see well enough to tend the wounds.

Massai feels his way along the opposite side of the cave until his hand brushes against a small bag. Inside, he finds the flint and steel he needs and quickly has a small fire going. It lights the cave dimly but enough. He cleans and binds the wounds as best he can, Massai watches as Alchise slips in and out of consciousness. He then goes outside to erase any tracks he might have left. The cave is well hidden and he was lucky to find it, even with Alchise's help.

The firing of guns back in the canyon ceased. Peering cautiously through a gap in the rocks, Massai can make out the glow of a fire off in the darkness. Whoever won the battle is not afraid of being seen as they set up camp nearby.

Exhausted, Massai returns to the cave. He looks after Alchise, then props himself up against a wall near the mouth of the cave and drifts off into a fitful sleep.

CHAPTER

EIGHTEEN

Frasier looks over the riderless horses he has been following and his face hardens into barely controlled rage. Someone tricked him. Somewhere behind him, several miles back, the Indians left their horses and took Audrey with them. Where is Macy? He should have caught up to them by now. Without the old scout, Frasier is as good as blind in tracking the Indians.

The Apaches can be anywhere, heading in any direction, and now he is helpless to find them. He should have waited. He knew his wife sent for Alchise because she trusts the Indian. However, his hatred for the Apache and his own stubbornness overruled his good judgment. Now his daughter will suffer for his stupidity.

His only comfort is Alchise and his half-breed nephew might be out looking too, if Jean was able to persuade them. The incident at the Fort might convince the old warrior to keep his distance. Jean never spoke in detail of her captivity with the Apache. He senses there was a connection between her and the one called Alchise. He saw it whenever Alchise delivered horses to his ranch and he saw it at the fort. His jealousy causes him to have outright hatred for the warrior. As much as he despises Alchise, he loves his daughter more. He hopes Jean's bond with the Indian is enough to convince the wily old warrior to help.

Turning around, Frasier and his men follow their trail back to the east, hoping to meet up with Macy. His horses are exhausted but Frasier continues to push them hard.

Absently, he slaps the ends of his long reins hard against his chaps. The bay gelding he is riding is too spent to care. He just plods on in the direction he was pointed. They hear a horse coming hard before they see the rider. Frasier tenses as the horse and rider appear over a low crest. He relaxes, as he recognizes the lone rider as Buster, one of his ranch hands and the one he sent to find Macy.

"Caught sight of you from that high knoll over there," Buster said.

Frasier spurs his tired horse close to Buster. He stares hard at the man. "Where's Macy?"

"Started out alone and said for you to follow."

"Our horses are almost finished."

"Got you some new ones waiting." Buster tells him. "Macy's idea. Said you'd miss the trail and run your horses to death."

Frasier's eyes flash and Buster turns his head down to study the toe of his boot. "Sorry, boss, but those are Macy's words, not mine."

"Don't be sorry. The man was right." Frasier turns and motions to his men. "Let's go get those fresh horses."

Buster leads them to where they were hobbled. The horses grazed a short distance but were no trouble to round up. Changing their riggings quickly, Frasier's bunch charge out, following the trail Macy left for them. It is near sundown when they first hear the sound of gunfire ahead. Suddenly, Macy appears out of the sagebrush and rides toward Frasier.

"Big fight going on ahead," he mumbles through a big wad of tobacco stuffed in his cheek. "Mostly one-sided as far as I can tell."

"Who?" Frasier asks.

"Dunno." Macy shrugs. Removing his old beaten hat, he scratches his gray head. "Peers to be Apach from the sound of it. Don't rightly know who they're shooting at."

Frasier pulled his Winchester from its boot and nods to the scout to lead the way. "Let's go," he shouts to his men.

Macy leads the way and Frasier follows. They are Apache, just as Macy suspected. Frasier quickly moves his men into position. The Apaches were shooting down into the canyon. All their attention focused on whoever they have trapped down there. They have no idea they are in danger themselves. Refreshed with new horses and Macy's tracking ability, Frasier is ready to attack, hoping they are the ones who took Audrey.

The warriors, with their attention completely on Alchise and Massai, are taken by surprise when Frasier's men open fire on them. Ducking for cover, they are now under fire and the surprise attack leaves them suffering heavy casualties. The warriors eventually pull back and disappear into the desert, leaving their dead behind.

Frasier and Macy search the canyon floor for signs of the missing girl but find none. Both men see the two dead horses, and Macy recognizes Alchise's sorrel. He kneels on one knee and touches the dried blood where someone fell. He also sees the tracks where he was dragged to cover behind the boulder. There are three bodies. He checked all three. One, a few yards from the others, has a bullet hole in his chest. The other two were knifed. He recognizes Calito and one of the other warriors. Alchise is not among the dead. Macy guesses the young Massai is with Alchise and one of them was hit, while the other got them to safety.

Frasier frowns. "What do you think?"

Macy straightens up and points to the tracks leading back out of the canyon. "Two of them went that way. One carrying the other." Macy hesitates, then continues, "It's my guess the two they was shootin' at were old Alchise and the boy, the half-breed."

"Let's find them. They may know something about Audrey."

"Not tonight, it's getting dark and they will be too hard to follow, even wounded. We'll find them in the morning. They can't get far with one of them hurt."

"Tonight, Macy!" Fraser orders.

Macy steadies his eyes on Frasier. "It's too dark and I know Alchise. It's suicide to follow that Injun in the dark."

Frasier tenses, then turns away from the scout. Macy walks to the end of the canyon and peers off into the fading light. He saw where the two men, one carrying the other, left the soft sand and crossed onto the rocks. From the size of the prints, he guesses they belong Massai. If so, then Alchise was wounded. He leans forward and lightly touches a drop of blood left on the rocks and then he finds another. If Alchise was hit, he is bleeding badly. He knows he can probably track them a ways, but the approaching darkness causes him to not risk it. He also knows that somewhere out there, Massai is either helping Alchise or burying him, and Macy is not going to impose. Frasier wants information about his daughter, but Macy also knows that Frasier hates Alchise. Picking up a piece of dried sagebrush, Macy quickly wipes out all signs of the tracks.

"You owe me for this, old son," he said quietly under his breath.

Frasier is furious. He wants to find Alchise. He might know something about Audrey. Macy said one of the Indians was wounded badly and Frasier wants to know if it was Alchise. If so, he will be no help in finding Audrey. In his heart, he hopes it is Alchise. He wants him dead and out of the way. He wants to break the bond between the Apache warrior and Jean once and for all.

Frasier tries again with Macy. "One of them is bleeding and you still say you can't run them down?"

"They've disappeared," Macy lies. "Even blood can't be seen at night. You might as well get after them that got your gal."

Swearing, Frasier slams a foot into his stirrup and mounts. Turning, he looks down into Macy's face. "Lose another trail and I'll kill you!"

"Talk like that won't get 'er back," Macy said, looking Frasier in the eye. He knows the man is just blowing off steam from anger and frustration, but he is not going to be intimidated.

The next morning, Massai slips back into the canyon. Approaching with stealth, he slowly retraces his steps along the canyon wall. Puzzled, he sees where his footprints were erased. Other footprints headed in the opposite direction. Massai kneels close to the ground. There are two sets of new prints. One shows a white man's heavy boots and the other soft footwear, but not Apache. Massai figures the booted prints were of Frasier or one of his men and the other set probably those of the Indian scout, Macy. If it was Macy, why is he not following them? He is one of the few men who might have been able to find the cave. Massai wonders why the white scout deceived Frasier.

Retrieving the Henry, Massai quickly returns to the cave. He gives the now conscious Alchise a drink of water and tends his wounds. One was bad with signs of infection. In that case, it would mean death. The bullet tore a jagged hole when it exited Alchise's back. Pulling out his knife, Massai put the blade in the blue flame of the fire. He will burn the bad flesh out. He knew white doctors did this, and he heard Loco talk of it.

The bloodshot eyes of Alchise study the blade, as its tempered steel turns red. He suffered the bite of the hot knife before. It will hurt, but it is powerful medicine. It will stop him from dying. He is not yet ready to die. His day will come soon enough, but not until he returns the girl to Tawano.

Massai sees the muscles of Alchise's back contract as he places the red-hot blade against the torn flesh. Sickening vapors of burning flesh fill the cave, almost causing him to retch. Pain shoots from the eyes of the warrior, but he never utters a sound. Withdrawing the knife, Massai puts it back in the fire.

"I must burn the other side, uncle."

Painfully, Alchise turns on his side, exposing the bullet's point of entry. The hole is smaller than the exit wound. Massai clenches his own teeth as the hot knife again sends the stench of burning flesh up his nostrils. Heating water, he makes poultices out of Saguaro pulp and bandages the wounds with what was left of his hunting shirt.

The questioning eyes of Alchise rest on his face, and Massai knows his uncle needs some answers.

"The white men fought Calito's warriors," he tells him. "After we got away, someone covered our tracks. I think it was probably the white scout, Macy, who did it."

Alchise nods his head slowly. "Macy." He said the single word as if it alone explains everything.

"Why would Macy do this?" Massai asks. "On the train he acted as if he hated you."

"Macy not hate me," Alchise said in a weak voice, his words barely audible. "We not know why white-eyes do what they do. Maybe Great Spirit know."

Three days passed since the ambush in the canyon. Massai fusses over Alchise like a hen over chicks. When the fever came, Massai fought it with cool water from the dripping springs near the cave. When chills followed, Massai covered Alchise's trembling body with blankets recovered from their dead horses and stoked the fire higher. He snared a rabbit and made a broth for Alchise. Each night he keeps watch over his suffering uncle.

Daily, he checks the wounds for signs of rot. The chills and fever subside and Alchise's wounds begin to heal. Alchise wants to pursue the Wild Ones, but he is in no condition to travel. He orders Massai to go, but Massai will not leave him. Now, lying there in the warmth of the cave, words form in the old warrior's mind. Words about the girl and her mother but the words never reach his lips. The secret lived inside him too long and was buried too deep.

"I tell you one day," he mutters.

Massai opens his eyes. He was half asleep when he heard Alchise speak. "What will you tell me?" He asks.

Alchise draws a deep breath and exhales slowly but makes no reply. Massai closes his eyes and drifts off to sleep, leaving thoughts unspoken and questions unanswered.

CHAPTER

NINETEEN

Macy leads Frasier and his men away from the Canyon of the Dead at first light. The rancher still curses the old scout but follows him knowing full well Macy is his only chance of finding Audrey. Somewhere near the canyon, Alchise might be dead or dying. Maybe both of them were wounded. Alchise does not have Audrey. Frasier's desire to see him dead is not as strong as the need to find his daughter.

Frasier watches the same trail as the old scout but his eyes find little trace of the raiders. His hand tightens on his saddle horn. If the old fool loses the trail, he will surely kill him. He quickly casts this thought aside. His only hope lay with Macy.

Suddenly, Macy dismounts and studies the ground. "There they be," he announces with a grin.

Frasier's eyes strain to see what Macy is pointing at. The terrain is rocky. To him there does not appear to be any tracks, but Macy is sure he sees something.

"What is it, Macy?"

Macy picks up something and holds it up proudly. It is a small piece of leather hardly an inch long. "Broke off a moccasin, I reckon. Anyway, we've got 'em now. If'n they don't get to their horses pretty quick."

Frasier's thoughts went to his young helpless daughter. She is afoot being forced to march across the hot desert by a pack of bloodthirsty savages. She is healthy and strong, but the ordeal is difficult for even a hardened man. He looks at Macy and starts to say something but the scout cuts him off.

"She's alive."

"How do you know?"

Pulling his worn campaign hat off, Macy wipes the sweatband and replaces the hat back on his head. He looks away from Frasier. "'Cause we ain't found her body yet."

Frasier was a young man when Geronimo was on the warpath, but he still remembered. He remembers other things as well but there is no sense dwelling on it. There was no way of knowing what an Apache on a rampage would do. He does know Macy is right. Not finding Audrey's body means the girl is still alive.

Macy mounts and heads south, in the direction of Mexico. Frasier and his men follow.

Massai resets his rabbit snares when the sound of horse hooves echoes across the canyon. Slipping quietly behind a rock, he waits, the Winchester cocked and ready. An Apache warrior rides slowly into the canyon. He sits on his horse and studies the carnage in front of him—the two dead horses, three dead Apaches, one of which is Calito, his Chief. He looks up and surveys the ridges above. The lone rider is Salto, Alchuni's father.

Massai does not think Salto was part of the ambush, but still he keeps his Winchester trained on the shoulder blades of his uncle's enemy.

"Put down your rifle." The order comes from Massai in English then he remembers Salto only speaks Apache.

The warrior turns his horse around slowly, until his eyes rest on the gun aimed at him and upon the face of the young warrior who holds it.

"Put the rifle down," Massai said again in Apache.

Massai watches as Salto's rifle slips from his thick brown fingers and falls to the ground.

"Now dismount."

Sliding to the ground, Salto's eyes sweep his surroundings. "Where is Alchise?"

"Why do you ask for Alchise?"

Salto's face hardens, "I must join him."

"Join your enemy?"

"I need his help."

Massai studies Salto's face, looking for signs of treachery. "Why do you need his help now?"

"Chato has taken Alchuni from the village. He will join Ponce and the Wild Ones. I know Alchise follows them to return the white girl to her people."

Massai is shocked. "He took Alchuni?" Massai slowly drops the Winchester barrel. Chato has stolen Alchuni knowing he would follow. He intends to have both Alchuni and his revenge.

Salto watches as fire burns in the eyes of the young warrior facing him. "Chato heads south toward the Dragoon Mountains. I cannot catch him alone. I need Alchise."

"Come," said Massai. "I will take you to him."

Massai motions toward Salto's rifle. "Pick it up, but if you try anything I will kill you."

"I believe you."

Alchise is awake when Salto enters the cave with Massai behind him. Surprised to see his old enemy, he raises himself into a sitting position.

Looking at the leathery sad face of Salto, Alchise wonders if he, too, looks that old. They are about the same age. As young men, they raided the Mexicans to the south and the Comanche to the east. Maybe it was the white man's whiskey, the soft reservation life, or perhaps the guilt he carries. Whatever the reason, Salto ages beyond his years. Except for the bullet wounds he now suffers, Alchise feels as strong as he always has.

Massai squats beside Alchise, rifle resting easily across his knees.

Salto leans his rifle against the cave wall and then examines Alchise's wounds. "Massai has done well," he announces. "Your wounds are clean."

Alchise nods. "Why have you come?"

Salto sits before the fire with them. "I hoped to join you but now I must go on alone. You are not fit for travel."

"Chato took Alchuni from the reservation," Massai explains. "It was his tracks leading to the north."

Alchise shakes his head slowly. Now he knows. The Wild Ones will not return to the reservation. To take a woman from her people means banishment from the tribe. Chato can never go back.

Salto stands slowly and retrieves his rifle. "Your wounds are bad, Alchise, but they will heal. I must go now. I must find my daughter, even if I go alone."

"You must go with him, Massai," Alchise said. "The white girl must also be returned."

Massai's eyes flare. "The Mescalero has taken my woman. I do not care about the white girl." Then he looks at Alchise with concern. "I will go but not until you are stronger."

"Listen to me, Massai," Alchise said, leaning forward with difficulty. "As I put my people before my wife and friends, you will do the same with Alchuni. The white girl must be returned to her people first or the entire reservation will suffer. Then you can seek Alchuni."

Massai grips the Winchester, the veins standing out in his strong hands. "Who are my people, uncle? You talk of the white girl's people and of me saving my people on the reservation, but I am half-white, remember? I am torn between the two, just as I am torn between saving two women."

Salto kneels beside Massai. "You are Apache. You carry the name of the great Massai. Alchuni is my daughter, but Alchise is right. I let my people down once but not again. You must save the white girl or the Army will retake our lands. Many will fight and die."

"I cannot leave him, he is too weak."

Salto lays a worn hand on Massai's shoulder. "I am too old to help you, but if you will do this, I will look after Alchise until he is strong enough to follow."

Massai stares into the small fire with uncertainty.

"Salto will stay with me," Alchise said. "Our hopes go with you."

"Am I good enough to track and fight them on my own?" He looks at Alchise, seeking the truth.

"You are good enough," Alchise tells him. Turning to Salto, he said, "Salto will wait outside. I have words for Massai alone."

Salto nods and leaves the cave.

Massai leans close to Alchise. "What is it? What do you wish to tell me?"

Alchise raises himself slightly and Massai helps him. "I must tell you the truth. What you do is dangerous and you may not return. So you must know truth."

"I will return, uncle."

Alchise holds up a hand to silence him. "If Massai has choice, it must be the white girl you bring back. If you bring both, good, but the white girl must be safe."

"Why, is it because she is white or because of the Army?"

"Yes, because of the Army but it is also because she is your sister, the daughter of my wife."

Massai leans back against the wall of the cave, completely baffled. "My sister, but how can that be. I am half Apache."

"Massai, you are not the son of James Davis. You are my son and the son of Tawano, my wife. The white woman, Jean Frasier, is your mother."

Looking into the eyes of Alchise, Massai knows he is telling the truth. Alchise does not lie. Massai is speechless. Alchise is my father. Jean Frasier my mother. He realized long ago that something important was kept from him regarding his mother but not something like this.

"Your mother, Tawano, Mrs. Frasier, was my woman. She was captured by our people in a raid. When Geronimo surrendered, all white captives were returned to their families. Tawano fought to keep you, to take you with her, but I would not let her. The whites would have made you both outcasts among them, even more than you were made to feel like an outcast in the east." Alchise takes a long slow breath. "I took you from her and sent you to New York with Davis. I paid him with the yellow rocks to take you and raise you as his own."

"You gave us both up?"

Alchise slowly nods his head. Massai can tell he is exhausted and in great pain. "At the time, it was the only way I could give you and Tawano a new life, a fresh start."

Massai remembers the rancher on the train and the white men who rode for Frasier, even Frasier himself. He would have been treated much worse if Jean Frasier tried to keep and raise him. For doing so, his white mother would have been shunned and ostracized. He is in shock, but he understands what Alchise is saying and what he did. He finally understands how James Davis came into so much money and why he was distant as a father. The truth comes crashing in on him, shedding a bright light on the dark corners of his past at last.

He turns to Alchise. "I will bring the white girl, my sister, back." He hesitates and then lays his hand on Alchise's arm. "I will bring her back for you, my... my father."

Salto's bay gelding is old and not conditioned. It will not last long at the pace Massai is pushing him. Already his breath is labors and foam speckles his sides and neck. Still Massai urges him forward. Every mile the old horse covers will let him conserve his strength for the hardships to come.

Finally, the old horse can go no further. Massai slips off his sweaty back and straps on the small leather pouch containing water and a meager supply of food. Two bandoleers of shells for the Henry, Alchise's gun, boldly drapes over his shoulders.

Removing the braided hackamore, he pats the tired old gelding and sets off afoot southward across the rocky landscape. Feeling the wooden stock of the Henry snug in his grip is a constant reminder of Alchise. He is more familiar with the Winchester, but he expended most of his shells during the fight in the canyon. He left his rifle and its remaining shells back at the cave for Alchise.

Ahead, Macy leads Frasier and his men and they are closing the gap on the Wild Ones. On foot, hampered by the white girl, Ponce cannot travel as fast as those who pursue him. So far, the only thing slowing Macy down is the rocky terrain that makes tracking almost impossible. Still, from the tracks, Massai can tell the whites are closing in. If Ponce does not get horses soon, he will be doomed. Massai is surprised they did not hide some earlier.

Massai presses forward. Moving alone, he makes good time. Cautiously he scans every direction, checking every nook and cranny that can conceal a man. To stumble accidentally into the Frasier party would be fatal. He will circle the whites as soon as the sun goes down, providing they did not run Ponce to the ground first.

Massai wonders why Ponce does not abandon the girl. If he did, Frasier would give up the chase, and even if he didn't, the young Apaches can lose themselves in the hills. Surely, Ponce knows that Frasier follows. The dust cloud rising from the arid desert floor will betray the presence of the white men to the sharp-eyed Wild Ones. Maybe Ponce thought he could lose the bungling cowpokes. He has no way of knowing Frasier hired Macy. The old scout is on the trail like a bloodhound, sniffling out signs of Ponce and his men like no other white man could.

He also wonders if Ponce knows the white girl, Audrey, is his half sister. Maybe she was abducted for revenge.

Trotting slowly to the south, a film of sweat and dirt covers his copper skin. The shadows are beginning to lengthen. Soon it will be dark. He wonders how Alchise is and how he and Salto were getting along. Cautiously, Massai moves along, his ears straining for any sound that would warn him of the presence of Frasier's men.

As the shadows stretch and the light fades, Massai knows he will have to stop soon for the night. His nose catches a slight whiff of burning wood on the twilight breeze. The white men are close. Even with Macy, they cannot track Ponce and his men in the dark.

He wonders if Chato was bringing horses to the Wild Ones. With thoughts of Chato, comes the thought of Alchuni being dragged from her home. Massai grips the Henry tightly. So tight the veins in his hand stand out like night crawlers beneath his skin. He forces himself to relax. Anger and all-consuming hate for Chato will cloud his judgment, causing him to make fatal mistakes. He must remain calm and focus on what lies ahead. His mind races and the hair on the back of his neck stands up like prairie grass as he makes his approach. Then he sees them. Eight men, including Frasier, lying propped on their saddles. Tired horses stand hip shod with their heads lowered. Frasier's horses were spent. If Chato brings fresh horses, the rancher will fall behind and so will Massai. He has to circle these men and continue his pursuit of Ponce and the others.

Tomorrow will be the fifth day since the battle in the canyon. Massai is exhausted. He rode Salto's old horse almost to death. He trots at a steady pace to catch up to Frasier's party. He is also closing in on the Wild Ones. He cannot lose them now. The sun sets and darkness shrouds everything except the campfire of Frasier's men. Massai circles wide because he knows Macy will be watching somewhere ahead. The old scout is not with the others. He will be waiting, sitting quietly, listening, and watching.

Only the muffled sound of his moccasins can be heard as Massai leaves the smell of the campfire far behind. Maybe he already passed Macy, but he will still be cautious. Heading to the south, the miles fall behind him.

CHAPTER

TWENTY

Ponce stands alone in the dark, his ears straining for the sound of Chato bringing fresh horses. Behind him, the Wild Ones and the white girl crouch beside a small fire. He knows the whites are closing the gap, but there is no sign of Chato. He should have been waiting here at the rendezvous spot when they arrived. Calito promised to have horses ready for Chato to pick up and bring to them. Without the horses, they will not be able to escape Frasier's men.

Fingering his rifle nervously, Ponce listens intently to the sounds of the night. If the Mescalero does not come soon, he will leave the girl and escape into the mountains. He should not have let Calito talk him into taking the white girl. He should have taken his revenge on Alchise and been done with it. Turning toward the fire, he hears the distant sound of an approaching horse. He starts to smile but then realizes he hears only one horse.

Slipping quickly back to the fire, Ponce sends the Wild Ones for cover. Their rifles are ready as the rider gallops into their camp. It is Chato. He slides from the tired gelding and pulls a disheveled Alchuni from the back of the horse. She falls to the ground.

"Where are the horses you were supposed to bring?" Ponce asks Chato.

"There were none."

"You brought the girl. Why?" Ponce is angry. He does not need another woman to slow him down. He needs fresh horses.

Chato looks at him with defiance. "She is mine."

The Wild Ones emerge from their hiding places, but keep their distance from Chato and Ponce.

Ponce is livid, barely able to contain his rage. "You could not bring us horses but you bring us more trouble."

"She is my problem alone."

"No, Chato. Massai will follow us now. Alchuni is his woman. She is now the problem of all of us."

Chato laughs. "Has Ponce turned into an old woman? You know Massai and Alchise were killed in the canyon."

At this news, Alchuni lets out a low wail and buries her face in her hands. The men ignore her.

"You are stupid, Chato," Ponce tells him. "We do not know this. Now the whites are closing in on us. They have horses, we do not."

"The whites cannot catch us if we separate and meet at the stronghold."

"What about the white girl and Alchuni?"

Chato laughs again. Reaching down, he yanks Alchuni to her feet. "This woman is mine. You do as you like with the white girl. It was Calito's idea and your decision to take her. She is your problem, not mine."

Ponce looks around at the quiet but intent faces of his men. "We will do as Chato suggests. We will go to the stronghold, but the women will stay here."

Chato pushes Alchuni aside and faces Ponce. "She goes with me. She is my woman now."

Ponce faces Chato, raising his rifle, holding it across his chest. "I am still the leader here," he said.

The Mescalero scowls and turns to Alchuni. Ponce pulls his knife and goes to the white girl. Stooping down, he starts to cut the ropes that bind her hands.

Massai leaps sideways as the report of a rifle sounds to the south. At first, he thought he was the target but then realizes the shot was too far away. A lone coyote sends his anguish cry into the night as the echo of the gunshot fades. Frasier and his men are behind him but the shot came from up ahead. Massai wonders if Macy caught up with Ponce on his own, without his party. No, he thought, Macy is a scout not a fighter. He will wait and bring up the others before making a move. Cautiously, Massai runs toward the direction of the gunshot.

He has to hurry. Frasier and his men would have heard the shot as well, and could be on their way. Slipping silently through the chaparral and sagebrush, Massai crawls to the edge of a depression. Below, a small fire sends sparks of light shimmering into the darkness.

Two figures are beside the fire. His dark eyes can make out the blonde hair of the girl. The other has to be one of the Wild Ones. Rising from the ground, Massai steps forward. The blue eyes of Audrey Frasier open wide in fear at the sight of Massai. He ignores her and approaches the other figure slowly.

"Ponce!" Massai kneels beside his friend.

As his dark eyes open slowly, Ponce grimaces with pain.

"What has happened to you, my friend?"

"Massai," Ponce whispers with difficulty. "My eyes cannot see you well." He raises his head slightly. "The Mescalero."

"Chato!"

Ponce closes his eyes and opens them in response. "He has Alchuni. Shot me in back." He swallows. "White men close." Blood dribbles from Ponce's lips as he struggles to speak. "You must return the girl to her people." He coughs, choking on his own blood.

"Frasier is near. He will come and take her." Massai clutches Ponce's hand, gripping it, willing him to live.

"No, if the whites return her, the Army will still be hard on our people. You must return her, Massai. That is the only way."

"And you, my friend?"

"I was foolish. I listened to Calito. Now I die for it." He looks into Massai's eyes. "Alchise?"

"Wounded but he will live."

Ponce closes his eyes.

"What about Alchuni?" Massai asks. "Do I go back to the reservation and leave her in the hands of Chato?"

"Our people must come first."

Ponce is getting weaker. Massai tries to stop the blood from flowing but he cannot. The wound is too severe.

"Massai," Ponce whispers. "You must undo the wrong I have done. Promise me."

Massai looks into the eyes of his dying friend. "I promise."

"One more promise," Ponce said, extending a hand toward Massai's gun. "Do not let the whites find me alive."

Massai understands but his eyes widen in horror. "No, I cannot!"

"You are my friend. Do this for me." Ponce's voice is barely audible but his pleading eyes speak volumes.

Massai remembers his disbelief when Alchise told him of killing a friend. The friend was Ponce's father. It seemed such a long time ago, yet it is fresh in his mind as he kneels beside the dying Ponce.

It was over in an instant.

Quickly, Massai wraps Ponce's body in a blanket left behind by the Wild Ones. He goes to the frightened girl, picks her up, and carries her away to the safety of the thick chaparral. He gently puts her down and cuts her hands free.

"I am Massai," he tells her in English. "I will return you to your mother."

"And your mother, too," she said in a soft voice. Her eyes search his. "Brother."

Massai looks at her in shock. "You know?"

"Yes, Mother told me. She had to tell someone. It was our secret."

He shakes his head slowly. "I am now Massai, Chiricahua Apache."

"No, you are my brother, my mother's son. That's all that matters."

He studies Audrey. He thought she was just a pretty but weak white girl, but she shows strength. He stands. "Come, I will take you home."

"And Alchuni?"

"Massai's muscles tense. "I will come back for her."

"The one that shot your friend might kill her. He is vicious, like a rabid dog."

"You must come first. The Army will punish my people if you are not returned."

She brushes a strand of honey colored hair from her face. "Not if I come with you of my own free will."

Massai gathers his small bag and the Henry. "No. You are going home."

Audrey set her jaw. "No. Alchuni is yours. I will not go home while she is held by that madman."

Massai curses under his breath. "You cannot come with me," he tells her firmly.

"My mother kept up with your father for three years. I can keep up with you."

Looking at her, Massai knows she is not going to change her mind. He cannot carry her all the way back to Frasier's ranch. Without a word, he starts off to the south. She will just have to keep up.

CHAPTER
TWENTY-ONE

M acy waits patiently in the dark. He knows if Alchise is alive, he
will go after Audrey Frasier. If he is wounded, he will send the
boy. Macy is one of the few still alive who knows the truth about Alchise and
young Massai. He never spoke about it to anyone. To do so would mean
certain death at the hands of Alchise. Macy is no coward because a coward
could not have fought the Apache for so long and survived. However, Alchise
is another matter. He was the devil when stirred up.

If Alchise or Massai are following the Frasier party, he should have
caught up by now. Macy knows neither will approach the white men. Instead,
they will wait for the cover of darkness and circle around. Macy finds no
signs that another is in front of them except for the pack that took Audrey.
He also knows Alchise and Massai will immediately return the girl home,
providing they find her alive.

Now Macy waits, far away from the snoring and small talk of the white
wranglers. Good men, cowpokes and brawlers, but they were not soldiers and
not trained to fight Apaches. He hears a shot far off in the distance.
Mounting his horse, he heads off in that direction. Behind him, he hears
Frasier rousing his men. Macy hardly goes a mile when another shot rings
out. He knows Frasier is coming on hard behind him. He pulls up and waits
for them.

When the thundering hooves approach, he signals for the riders to reign in.

"What the hell's going on?" Frasier demands.

"Dunno," Macy said. "I waited so you fools wouldn't run them horses straight into a shootout." Macy points in the distance. "There's a small campfire just ahead. Spread your men out and we'll move in slowly."

The horsemen move in, surrounding the campfire where Ponce's wrapped body lay. Macy dismounts and pulls back the blanket.

"Who is it?" Frasier asks.

"One they called Ponce. The leader of the bunch that took your gal." Macy wipes tobacco dribble from the corner of his mouth. "Been shot once in the back and once in the head."

Frasier dismounts to take a look. "Who could have done it?"

"Hard to say." Macy checks the body again. "Probably one of his own."

Macy pokes around the camp. Daylight is starting to break enough for the old scout to read tracks in the sandy soil.

"Tell you this much," Macy said after a bit of pondering. "During the night another joined them. Rode up on horseback. Just one horse." He looks at the tracks again. "They left in the night. Most on foot but one on horseback. They'd be headin' south towards the Dragoons." Macy stands and looks off into the distance. "I figure your daughter is on the horse. Ain't none of her tracks mixed in with the bunch."

"You sure?" Frasier asks, snapping at him.

"Sure as I can be. She ain't here. Someone's riding the horse. Got to be her."

Macy stoops and notices another set of tracks. Ones he saw in the Canyon of the Dead. He guesses they belong to Massai. They lead off into the brush.

Macy and Frasier mount up. "Don't worry," Macy said to Frasier. "We'll catch 'em. They're still afoot."

Massai easily picks up Chato's trail, but now Audrey's tracks will be noticeable to Macy. He knows Frasier and his men will come hard and fast. Now he and Audrey are between the two groups. Five sets of tracks, plus those of the horse, lay plainly in the sand. The rider on the horse has to be Alchuni, but someone is missing. There should be six sets of tracks. Kneeling down, Massai recounts the tracks.

"What's wrong?" Audrey asks as she squats down beside him.

"One of the Wild Ones is not with this bunch."

"The leader, your friend, sent one of them to look for horses before the one you call Chato came with Alchuni."

Massai nods to himself. "Wolf must be the one that went and that's why Chato had the courage to shoot Ponce in the back. The others are afraid of Chato, but not Wolf. He would have stopped it or killed Chato in return."

Wolf will return soon, with or without horses. He does not know about Ponce. Massai looks back in the direction from where they came. Frasier must be only an hour or so behind.

He glances at the girl. "Come, we must go quickly."

Tired, dirty, and hungry, Audrey gamely sets out after Massai.

Dusk finds them entering the foothills of the mountains. Here, with the broken terrain and abundant foliage, it will be difficult for Frasier to spot them from afar. Audrey is exhausted but keeps moving. With her, Massai cannot gain on the Wild Ones, but at least he is keeping pace with them. Massai is impressed by her grit and determination.

They come upon a mountain spring. Massai lets the girl rest and they both drink deeply. He moves off and studies the trail again. It leads up the sandy pass that winds its way into Cochise's stronghold. If Chato stops for the night, Massai can catch him by dawn, providing Wolf does not return with horses.

Returning to the spring, he finds Audrey fast asleep. Quietly, he sits back against a large rock and places the Henry across his knees. They will rest for a while and then press on by moonlight. Tomorrow, they will find the Wild Ones and Alchuni.

Macy shakes his head in puzzlement at the tracks he surveys. He easily recognizes Massai's tracks, but now Audrey Frasier's tracks join them. Somewhere along the way, the two joined up together but instead of turning back, they move forward, following the trail of her abductors. What's more, Macy can tell the girl travels willingly with Massai, as there is no evidence he is forcing her.

He is thankful Frasier and his men cannot read signs well enough to know what is happening. The rancher is in enough rage without learning his little fair-haired girl is traveling with an Indian of her own free will. Sooner or later, the truth will come out, but Macy does not care to rush things. He is satisfied to let Massai catch up with the Wild Ones first. He wants to see what the young half-breed will do.

Frasier sent a messenger to the fort. By now there should be an Army patrol waiting for the Wild Ones near the Mexican border. There is no hurry now. The Frasier girl will most likely be safe with Massai. The young Apaches are boxed in which makes them even more dangerous. Macy is not about to rush into an ambush when help is so close.

Macy has a plan. He will track Massai and the girl slowly, stalling Frasier from closing in on them too quickly. He wants to give Massai time to make his move. Something about the way he is moving reminds Macy of the old days and tracking the great warriors such as old Massai and even Alchise himself. The days of the bronco Apache are gone now and the old scout truly misses them. Alchise trained the young Massai well and this might be Macy's last chance to track such a worthy opponent. He is in no rush. The girl is safe enough now that she is with her own brother. Macy wonders if Alchise told the boy anything yet and if young Massai knows Audrey Frasier is his sister.

Massai and Audrey stand at the outskirts of Cochise's stronghold surveying the gentle rolling hills that traverse the length of the canyons. Wild flowers and lush green grass cover the valley floor like a colorful quilt. Pinion trees, mountain cedar, pines, and chaparral dot the landscape.

Taking in the breathtaking natural beauty, Massai momentarily forgets his quarry. This is the home of the Chiricahua—his people. The air is as fresh and pure as new snow. He feels his blood race. No wonder the old Chief fought valiantly to hold onto these mountains and no wonder the white man fought just as hard to take them away.

"Massai." The voice of the girl brings him back to reality. "You were so lost in thought. What were you thinking?"

"You would not understand," he tells her sadly.

Kneeling, Massai studies the dusty tracks left by the fleeing Wild Ones. They still travel south making no effort to hide their trail. His dark eyes search out every rock outcropping and every possible hiding place. The ambush in the Canyon of the Dead is still fresh in his mind.

Turning, he looks to where the tired girl rests. "Can you go on?"

He barely hears her mumbled response before he begins moving into the stronghold. The Chiricahua people did not live in this place for many years, but the dilapidated remains of their wickiups still stand. These are the skeletal reminders that once a strong and proud people inhabited these mountains.

Audrey stops and kneels down in a cluster of multicolored wild flowers growing next to a clear little brook. "Isn't this a beautiful place, Massai?" She scoops the cool clear water with her hands and drips it down her neck and over her shoulders. It gives her relief from the heat, even if only for a brief moment.

Massai studies his half sister's face. "Almost as beautiful as you."

"A brother does not speak that way to his sister," she scolds in mock embarrassment.

"Well, I wouldn't know about that. You are the first sister I ever had. Sister or not, you are still beautiful."

Audrey smiles. "Thank you." A strong bond is already building between the two siblings. "Even though I'm tired, dirty, hungry, and frightened, this has been quite an exciting adventure." She looks off across the meadow. "I know now what my mother feels when her thoughts return to her time with the Apaches."

After scooping a handful of water into his parched mouth, Massai motions to the girl to follow him. "Come, we must hurry. It grows late and the trail is still warm."

CHAPTER
TWENTY-TWO

Following in Massai's footsteps, Audrey fords the stream where tracks of others are still fresh. Here the prints of the Wild Ones show plainly, where they climbed the bank.

"We are very close," Massai tells her. "No more than an hour behind them now." He kneels down to study the tracks and points them out to Audrey. "They are making no effort to cover their trail. Chato is either very stupid or he is gambling that Wolf will bring horses and he can make a quick getaway from those who track him."

He moves on, Audrey struggling to keep up. The sandy trail takes an upward turn so steep Massai has to reach back and offer his hand to the girl. She gratefully takes it. She is exhausted but determined to keep going. Near the top of the incline, Massai stops. He indicates to Audrey to rest while he goes forward to scout the trail. She readily takes the opportunity to relax against a nearby boulder.

Ahead, rugged cliffs stand on either side of the trail. It reminds Massai of the Canyon of the Dead where they were ambushed. He moves forward and spots a fork in the trail, but from where he stands he cannot tell which way the Wild Ones went. He motions to Audrey, who wearily gets to her feet and catches up with him.

Moving with caution, Massai enters the canyon. He clings to the side of the cliff to make it difficult for anyone above to see him. Silently, he indicates to Audrey to do the same. They are close to the area where the trails part when the sound, a clink of metal on rock, sends the two of them scurrying behind an uprooted tree.

Massai listens, another clink is followed by yet another and then several. It is the sound of horses' hooves on rock—shod horses. Someone is approaching from the north trail. Massai eases the hammer back on the Henry and waits. The canyon echoes from the scraping of hooves on granite.

Pushing Audrey out of sight, Massai tightens his grip on the Henry and sets his sights on the mouth of the canyon. White horsemen, no doubt, since Apaches rarely ride shod horses, unless they were stolen. He is calm, his hands steady, and his breathing easy. He is ready to kill if need be.

When the horses come into sight, there is only one rider. He drops from his mount and studies the ground. After looking along the south trail, he starts to remount the lead horse. Massai steps into view.

"Drop your rifle, my friend," Massai said to Wolf in Apache, pointing the Henry at his bare stomach. "Ponce is dead. Do not join him."

Quickly recovering from his surprise, Wolf squares his shoulders and studies Massai's face. "How did he die?"

"Chato."

"You lie," Wolf said, spitting out the words. "Chato was to bring horses. Only one horse passes this way. Ponce walks south."

"Look at the tracks again. Do you see the big footed track of Ponce among the others?"

Uncertainty crosses the young warrior's face. Keeping an eye on Massai, Wolf studies the ground again. This time closely. "Maybe Ponce rides the horse."

Massai shakes his head. "Alchuni rides. Chato took her from the village. Once more, I tell you, Ponce is dead. Chato killed him. Drop your rifle now!"

The movement comes as swift as a rattlesnake strike. Wolf throws himself sideways, firing as he dives for the ground. Echoes of the rifle blast reverberate up and down the canyon. Three of the five shots coming from the Henry catch the young warrior as he hits the ground. A final click sounds as the Henry's hammer lands on a bad cartridge and then all is quiet. Audrey emerges from her hiding place. Visibly shaken, she is relieved to see Massai unharmed and standing over Wolf.

"Is he dead?" She asks.

Massai steps back from Wolf's body. "Yes," he said simply. He cannot explain to Audrey, a white girl taken from her people, that Wolf, one of her captors, died a warrior's death, a brave death.

Stepping over Wolf's body, Massai motions toward the horses. "Hurry," he tells her. "We must leave here. The shots will bring others."

Massai helps Audrey up on one of the horses and then he mounts another. Before taking off, he cut the remaining horses free and spooks them in the direction from which they came.

"Aren't you going to bury him?" Audrey asks, looking at Wolf's body.

"There's no time." Massai glances one last time at his friend's body—the body of the second friend he had to kill.

Macy hears the distant gunfire. It comes from the direction of the stronghold. Pulling his tired gelding to a stop, he waits as Frasier draws close to him.

"Rifles?" Frasier asks.

Macy nods in confirmation. "Yep, one shot, then five quick 'uns. I reckon we're fixin' to find a body up ahead. Of that I'm pretty sure."

Kicking his horse forward, Macy makes way for the stronghold. No use tracking now. If the Wild Ones are heading for Mexico there is but one way—south. The gunfire confirms that someone is ahead of them. He wonders if Massai already came upon the band. He hopes it is not Massai and the girl they find dead.

Chato and the other Wild Ones also heard the shots as they echo from rim to rim in the canyon. Counting the shots same as Macy, Chato wonders if Wolf encountered the white men. If Wolf is dead, then there will be no horses coming to carry them into Mexico. They will have only their legs and the one horse to cover the hundred miles or so, that will bring them safely into the high country of the Sierra Madre Mountains.

Chato listened intently to the old men of the village speak of the Apache warriors still living wild and free in Mexico. Rumors mostly, old men's dreams, but if these free Apaches still exist, he will find them. He yearns to live the life of a bronco Apache with Alchuni warming his wickiup and giving him many children.

Ponce told him the Breed was still alive and now Chato believes it to be true. He hopes Massai is following him right now. He knows that as long as he has Alchuni, Massai will pursue him, better now than later. He looks up at Alchuni as she rides the horse. She looks miserable and exhausted, but still alluring. Chato smiles smugly. It does not matter to him that she loves another. It is he that has her. He will use her to lure the Breed into Mexico where he will kill him once and for all. This time, he will not fail.

Silently, the band of tired warriors follows Chato south toward Mexico. Along the way, Alchuni lets one of her moccasins fall from her foot. Dosenay sees it. He knows he should retrieve it but he does not. What does it matter? The Wild Ones are doomed. They are afoot and being followed by the white men and maybe even by Massai. He is not sure which one he fears more.

Later, Massai picks up the fallen moccasin and turns it over in his hands. It belongs to a woman, no doubt Alchuni. He places the moccasin in his leather pouch and remounts, kicking his horse forward.

Audrey studies Massai's face. "They are near, aren't they?"

Only a nod comes from the dark head in front of her. She knows his attention is on the trail. Every nerve in him is tense. She can see the finely carved muscles of his back tighten as he moves. Now on horseback, they can close the distance quickly but Massai knows he will have to be patient. It will be easy to run into an ambush if he is not careful.

The Mexican border has to be near. Massai has no knowledge of the area but Alchise told him that it is not too far from Cochise's stronghold. Crossing into Mexico will heighten their danger as the Mexican cavalry and bandits will be on the prowl. He still hopes to catch Chato before he enters Mexico. It does not matter because he will follow the Mescalero into hell if he has to.

His concern is for Audrey. He does not want her going into Mexico. Several times, he considers turning around and taking her home. He promised Alchise her safety would come first. Audrey is as strong willed as he is, and she insists on continuing.

He pushes his horse along the trail of the Wild Ones, stopping only to survey every possible ambush site. Several times, he leaves Audrey to hold the horses while he scouts ahead. Massai must be cautious but it is costing him precious time. Macy is behind him and most likely closing in. In fact, Massai is surprised the Frasier party has not caught up to them yet. He wonders if their horses are finally played out and the white men have to resort to following on foot.

He is lost in thought when the exchange of gunfire resounds down the canyon toward them. Massai vaults from his horse, grabs the girl, and tumbles them both to safety. The shots continue to ring out. He judges them to be near, maybe just a couple of hundred yards at most. Securing Audrey behind some large boulders, he gathers his horse and remounts.

"Wait here," he orders the girl. "If I don't return for you, just wait. Your father should be here soon."

"But I want to go…" she protests but Massai cuts her off.

"No," he orders, this time more sternly. "Stay here!"

CHAPTER TWENTY-THREE

The gunfire reaches a crescendo then fades just as Massai gets within range. A final salvo rings out and then the canyon walls are silent. Pulling the heaving horse to a stop, Massai looks down at the plump crumpled body of Dosenay sprawled across a pine log. Empty cartridges were scattered about and two dead white men lay nearby.

He finds Taglia and Bonito next. Their bodies are riddled with bullets, but from the white bodies sprawled nearby, Massai knows they too went down fighting. Chato and the Wild Ones walked into a trap but they fought hard. The small canyon is littered with dead men. Blowflies are already at work. He does not find Chato or Alchuni, bringing him both relief and concern.

A movement catches Massai's eye. Walking to a fallen white man, he rolls him over. It was the gunfighter from the train, the big man known as Slade Bonham. Pain riddled eyes flutter open and focuses on Massai.

"You," he said, recognizing Massai, speaking through blood specked foam that seeps from his mouth. "Came to kill… you." He struggles to speak.

"Did you see a girl?" Massai asks Bonham.

"Bury me," the dying man pleads in a barely audible voice. "Don't let the scavengers get me."

Massai slaps Bonham hard, sending a spray of blood across the sandy ground. "The girl, where is she?"

The man's senses seem to come back as he focuses on Massai. "I came to kill you, Breed." His words drip with hatred. "Kilt that fat son of a bitch you was with." The gunfighter's body trembles from a final spasm then slowly slumps back against the ground. Massai feels the man's last shudder as life passes from him.

Bonham is not one of Frasier's men. Massai does not recognize any of the other dead whites. They could have been part of a posse also on the hunt for the Wild Ones and to rescue Audrey.

Loabreno lies face down with blood covering his bullet ridden body. To Massai, the body seems small, almost childlike, as it lies motionless on the ground. He is about to turn away when he hears a whisper.

"Massai."

He turns back toward Loabreno to find the young warrior trying to lift his head.

"Massai," Loabreno said again, half groaning. He tries to lift his head and shoulders this time.

Massai drops to his knees beside Loabreno and cradles his head and shoulders in his arms. "What happened, Loabreno?"

"Chato. The young man swallows. "He hurried too much... trying to reach border. Run into white men. Many dead."

"Chato... where is Chato and Alchuni?

Coughing, Loabreno turns and looks into Massai's eyes. "Chato run away. Leave us to fight." He jerks as a bolt of pain shoots through his bullet riddled body. "Chato take Alchuni... Mexico."

Massai was wrong. This wasn't an ambush after all. The two parties accidentally crossed paths in the confines of the small canyon pass. In his haste, Chato did not take the precautions of having a forward scout. They never saw the gunfighters until it was too late. At such close quarters and with the panic of surprise, the fighting would have been fast and furious. Each side slaughtered the other.

Loabreno's dark eyes glaze over as his body goes limp in Massai's arms. Only one of the Wild Ones still lives—Chato. Easing the dead warrior to the ground, Massai whirls around at the sound of an approaching horse, the Henry ready to fire, only to find Audrey, wide-eyed with horror, walking her horse through the carnage.

"Are they all dead?"

Massai can only nod and his mouth cannot form words. They were his friends, his people. Now they are all dead. All except for Chato, the only Wild One who is not his friend. His hate for Chato fills his heart until he thought it would burst. It was Chato who led his friends to their deaths and it was Chato who took his woman.

His thoughts are interrupted by two shots in quick succession and the scream of the girl. Massai has no time to react as a bullet grazes his rib cage. He looks up to see Macy step from behind a boulder and collapse. From the corner of his eye, he catches another movement. He pushes Audrey down behind him and turns back to see a tall slim figure walk out of a nearby stand of timber with a smoking Winchester in his hands.

He is Apache. An old Apache. His long hair is streaked with gray and hangs straight down over broad shoulders. A red bandanna keeps the man's hair snug against a wide forehead. Massai watches him with a mixture of wonder and wariness. He has deep-set eyes and a hooked nose set into a weathered face, causing Massai to recall the bust of Caesar he saw once at school. An old scar ran across the length of one cheek. He looks like one of the legends of the Old Ones, come to life.

"I am Massai, Chiricahua Apache," the old man announces.

So this is the great Massai, the friend of Alchise. Here is the warrior who would not surrender, who escaped and returned from the east.

Massai finds his tongue. He addresses the old warrior in Apache. "This is why Alchise, my father, would speak your name, because you live."

Old Massai nods then walks over to Macy, who manages to sit and prop himself against a rock.

"Yes, I live but the scout Macy, he may not live."

Young Massai also approaches the scout. "How bad is it, Macy?" He asks the scout in English.

"Not good. Looks like old Massai finally finished me off." He grimaces in pain.

Young Massai kneels, opens the buckskin shirt, and looks closely. He closes it and looks into the eyes of the scout. "I'm sorry."

"Don't be. I'm long overdue. 'Sides, I tried my best to kill you and would've if the old one hadn't happened along."

"But why?" Massai does not understand. "You led Frasier away from Alchise and me back in the canyon."

Macy nods briefly. "Hand me my tobacco. It's in my shirt."

When Massai hesitates, Audrey comes over, reaches inside Macy's shirt pocket, and pulls out the plug of tobacco. She puts it to his lips. He takes a bite out of it and smiles.

"Thank ye, girl. A good chew is one of the few pleasures a man has out here. I reckon it's my last."

"Why?" Massai asks Macy again. "Why would you save me, only to try to kill me here?"

"The game was over, boy. I kill you and save the girl. I'm the hero. I saved your red skin back at the Canyon of the Dead in case I needed you to find the girl." He coughs then spits blood mixed with tobacco juice. "I knew either Alchise or you would go after her."

"Game?" Massai's strong hand clenches the front of the scout's shirt. "This is a game to you? All these men are dead. This is no game!" He let go of Macy's shirt, pushing him hard against the boulder.

Macy lets out a moan. His eyes close tight for a moment then he opens them again. "I'm already dead, boy. You can kill me faster but you can't kill me again."

A strong hand rests on Massai's shoulder. He looks up at the old warrior. Their eyes lock. "We must go. Soon the others come."

"You are Old Massai? My father's friend?"

The old one nods. "And you are my namesake."

"Do this for me," young Massai said. "Take this woman, my sister, and go to Alchise. He is with Salto, wounded in a cave back at the Canyon of the Dead. With you they will be safe."

The old warrior nods. "And you?"

"I will follow Chato to Mexico."

"Then take this, young one." The old warrior takes a beaded talisman from around his neck and places it over the younger man's head. "Now our people in the mountains will know you come from me."

"Thank you, my father's friend," Massai said to the older man. "Tell my father, I will see him in the place of the yellow rocks."

Without another word, the old warrior escorts Audrey toward her horse.

"No, Massai," Audrey protests. "I will go with you."

Young Massai goes to her and grabs her arms. He looks at her with serious eyes. "You will do as I ask. You will go with this man and find Alchise. You will stay with them until it is safe."

Fighting back tears, Audrey finally nods. She mounts her horse and follows the old warrior up a hidden passageway in the cliffs.

Massai turns to Macy. "You won't die just yet, Macy. So tell Frasier when he gets here to turn back. Tell him I'll be taking my sister back to his ranch myself."

"Be glad to tell him them exact words," the scout said through tobacco stained teeth. "Especially the part about Audrey being your sister."

Massai mounts his horse and stares down at Macy. "Sorry, Macy. I really am."

"Well now I've heard it all," Macy said with a half laugh. "A Chiricahua apologizing for the death of a white man. The old scout spit. "But then again, yer only half."

Without answering, Massai whirls his horse around and rides away from the canyon at a hard lope. There is no need to wipe out signs of old Massai and Audrey. If Macy lives long enough, he will give Frasier the message. If the rancher has any sense, he will return to his ranch and wait. Massai knows if Frasier finds the scout dead, he will press on. He also knows Frasier cannot track a buffalo in the snow. With Macy gone, the Frasier party will be unable to catch him.

Chato is not far and he is riding double. His horse is overburdened and cannot be pushed. Time is all Massai needs. With Audrey in safe hands, Massai will soon catch up to the fleeing Mescalero.

CHAPTER

TWENTY-FOUR

Chato flees the battle, leaving his warriors to die. Now he is alone, except for Alchuni, who despises him. No matter, he will find more young braves to follow him. There are always rebel Apaches willing to raid and steal under a leader such as him. He alone escaped the white-eyes in the canyon. Some will call him a coward, but those that could were dead. Only the woman knows what really happened. She is just a woman and she dare not speak ill of him lest he cut out her tongue.

A Chiricahua warrior must live. He must live to fight and kill more white-eyes. Smiling, he slips an arm around the slim waist of Alchuni and feels her stiffen at his touch. He scowls and tightens his hold. She will soon learn who is master. When they reach the wild country beyond the Mexican border, she will submit to him. If she will not, he will trade her. A woman this beautiful will bring much.

Still, Chato berates himself. The Old Ones would not have run blindly into the white gunmen as he did. However, the damage was done, there is no use thinking of it now. Soon he will be in Mexico. Never again will he set foot on a reservation. He will be free. Yanking Alchuni's hair, he forces her to look at him as he sneers and mocks her with his eyes. He feels her body shudder in fright then releases his grip on her hair. No words are spoken and none are needed.

Frasier rides cautiously into the canyon and finds Macy, still alive but near death. His men scatter to check the other bodies for life.

Frasier dismounts and kneels beside his scout. "You hurt bad?"

"Bad enough, I reckon." His words come between ragged breaths.

Pulling aside the scout's shirt, Frasier notes the wound and the large loss of blood. "Breed get you?"

"Maybe, maybe not."

"Audrey with him?"

Macy nods. "Yep." His chest rose slightly as he looks past Frasier. "Said to tell you... his sister... would be fine... just fine."

The rage Macy expected from the rancher does not come. Instead, he looks at the dying man in frustration. Without a scout, they are finished.

"Breed... tell you," Macy starts but never finishes. His chest falls for the last time. Frasier looks at the scout a moment then closes the dead man's eyes.

Frasier's men come at a hard run back down the sandy path in the canyon. "Looks like all hell broke loose here, Mr. Frasier."

Forgetting Macy, Frasier stands up and absently pulls his sweat stained Stetson from his head. He looks back down the canyon at the scattered bodies. The exhausted rancher slaps his leather chaps hard with his hat. "Yea, I reckon so."

"Boss," the man called Red said. "Them young heathens done killed Slade Bonham, too. Damndest thing I ever seen." Just a handful of 'em took on a whole band of gunslingers.

Frasier swears. "You weren't around when Geronimo rode or you wouldn't be saying that. Apaches are born killers." He looks at his men. "What about Audrey? Any sign of her?"

The men either shake their heads or look away. Finally, Buster speaks up. "Not a sign of her, Mr. Frasier."

Frasier swings astride his tired gelding. He takes a moment to look over his men. They are all about as exhausted as their horses.

"Swede," he calls.

A strapping young man with curly blond hair rides forward. "Yes, sir?"

"Head for Fort Apache. Tell Major Bishop what happened here and to come running. Then go to the ranch and tell my missus our daughter's alive and well and that we're going into Mexico to bring her back."

"Yes, sir," Swede answers and takes off.

"Red," Frasier calls out.

Red pushes his Grulla horse close to Frasier's mount. "Yeah, Boss?"

"You know the border. Know the small cantina next to the trading post?"

"I know it"

Frasier nods. He knows Red is familiar with the place. He keeps a woman there. "Your horse is the strongest and freshest. Go straight there and bring me back a Mex tracker named Joaquin."

Red tips his hat and starts to turn his horse.

"And Red?"

Red turns in his saddle. "Yeah, Boss?"

"There and back. Touch a bottle and I'll kill you. Understand?"

Without answering, Red spurs the Grulla cruelly and turns him south toward the Mexican border.

"You want to bury Macy, Boss?" Buster asks.

Frasier looks down at the body of the scout and scowls. "Leave him."

The old warrior and the girl watch from their vantage point on a high ridge and see a lone rider take off heading north. Soon another rider speeds off like the wind to the south, toward Mexico. The rest of the men also head toward Mexico following Massai's trail.

Old Massai scowls. As soon as he thought it safe, he unties the girl's hands and removes the bandana from her mouth. A precaution he took to prevent her from calling out and alerting her father. He did not know why the young one did not turn the girl over directly to her father, but he would not question his reasoning.

"Father goes to Mexico," he tells the girl in broken English.

"He still thinks I'm with Massai."

Old Massai nods. "Maybe Macy dead before tell father."

"You shouldn't have tied me up. We could have told my father. Now he'll try to kill Massai."

Again, the old warrior nods. "We help young one before we find Alchise."

"But how can we help him now?"

"I will send smoke to my people in the big mountains of Mexico." He motions for her to follow him. "Help get wood for fire."

Chato's tracks lead directly across the border. Massai follows, alert for danger as he crosses. The south pass into Mexico is covered with scrub brush, making it almost impossible to see for any distance. Dismounting,

Massai slips the hackamore from the horse and turns him back north.

Afoot he will leave less signs as he passes and he can travel with less chance of being spotted by unfriendly riders. Trotting steadily south, his muscles, tight from riding all day, spring to life. Somewhere not far ahead is the hated Mescalero and Alchuni. The thought of her warm smile spurs him on and calms his racing heart.

CHAPTER
TWENTY-FIVE

Frasier wearily gets to his feet and tosses the dregs of his morning coffee onto the small campfire. The sizzle and sputter of the coals mirror his fiery mood. Red was gone two days. Frasier was not known as a patient man on his good days but now he is in a black fury. He badly needs the Mexican tracker, Joaquin, and does not want to take his men into Mexico without him. Grabbing his saddle and gear, the tall rancher stalks to the picket line and starts saddling his horse.

A short freckle-faced man walks up to him. "Boss, you ain't planning on crossing into Mexico without us, are ya?"

Frasier shoots a look at the wrangler, one of his best, as he jams his Winchester into its boot. "My daughter's out there, Shorty."

"What about us, Boss? We're coming with you, ain't we?"

"You boys wait here for Red and the Mex tracker." Frasier mounts his gelding. "As soon as they arrive, you catch up with me as fast as you can."

"I don't know, Mr. Frasier." Shorty scratches his balding head. "There's bandits, rurales, injuns, and who knows what else over there. You best not go it alone."

"Sorry, Shorty, but I don't aim to lead my men into a massacre like we just saw. I'll head out alone and you men follow as soon as the new scout arrives."

As his men watch, Frasier disappears into the dense underbrush of northern Mexico.

"Damn fool, he should've at least taken a couple of us," Shorty said, kicking sand into the fire.

"We'd of been the fools if'n we went," said Buster, collapsing on his bedroll. "No siree, I'm sticking to American soil, gal or no gal."

Shorty bristles. "You ride for the brand, don't ya? Just like the rest of us."

Buster looks up at the other man. "Sure I ride for the brand but if he doesn't want us then he doesn't want us. You heard him."

"Yea, I heard him."

Chato walks with a spring in his step. He is in Mexico. The bronco Apaches will be close now. Looking up at the girl, he pulls her bodily from the horse and laughs as she crumpled to the ground.

Alchuni gasps as the air was knocked out of her. Tired and hungry, she cannot move from where she fell.

Grabbing the girl's hair, Chato pulls her head back. "You're mine now."

Alchuni gathers her strength. She spits at him and claws the hand that holds her. "I am Massai's woman. I will never be yours."

Releasing her, Chato laughs. "Massai, Massai," Chato mimics as the girl crawls away from him. "Soon the breed will be dead like Ponce and the rest."

He studies her. Even dirty and disheveled, she is beautiful. Her defiance only makes him want her more. The old men of village told stories of how the Old Ones had stolen their women. Well, didn't he do the same?

Rising to flee from him, Alchuni feels Chato's strong arms encircle her waist and drag her back to the sandy ground. She fights but she is no match for him as he tears at her cotton shirt.

"Massai," she screams again and again, as the Mescalero paws at her. "Massai!"

"The breed will not save you this time," Chato said, his hot breath against her neck.

Suddenly, Chato releases her and leaps to his feet. Five warriors encircle them. They appeared like apparitions, ghosts walking so silently neither Alchuni nor Chato heard them. They are Apache warriors the likes of which Chato had never seen before; solemn men, lean and hard, with unforgiving eyes. Although they are of his own people, Chato shrinks back.

They are the last of the bronco Apaches, the ones who fled to Mexico rather than submit to the white man's terms and live on a reservation. Chato only heard stories but now here he is face to face with the legends. Seconds seem like hours, as the warriors stand motionless except for their eyes, which first studies Chato and then darts to Alchuni.

A squat warrior breaks from the circle and approaches Alchuni. He continues to stare down at her as she crouches on the ground cringing before the fierce warriors.

"This your man?" The squat one asks her in words that are short and crisp.

Alchuni lifts her chin in defiance and spits a Chato's feet. "Massai is my husband to be, not this dog of a Mescalero."

All five laugh at the girl's insult. Courage is one thing the men understand and respect, even in a woman. This one has spirit and fire.

"You, Mescalero." The squat one addresses Chato. He seems to be the leader. "What do you and the woman do in our mountains?"

Chato's eyes search the faces of all five warriors, then rivet back to the leader. "I bring the woman and come here to live with my people, away from the reservation."

"She is your woman?"

Chato nods firmly. "Yes, she is my woman."

"She claims another will be her husband and calls you a dog."

"Do you always have to fight for her favor?" Another warrior asks. He is tall with a deep scar around his neck. The warriors laugh.

Chato's face burns in humiliation. The warriors seem hostile to him, while they side with the woman. He glances to where he carelessly dropped his Winchester when he attacked Alchuni. It is too far to reach quickly.

He looks around the circle of warriors and squares his shoulders. "I am Chato, Mescalero Apache, and I have come as a friend to my brothers in Mexico."

"We did not ask you here," the squat one said as he eyed Alchuni. "Maybe we take the woman and horse and leave Chato to the coyotes."

Chato swallows. He is no coward but the warriors were not like those on the reservation. There he and the Wild Ones were the ones to fear. Here he is alone. Here he is cowed.

He tries again. "You would deny a brother safety from the white-eyes?"

The warriors look back down the trail toward the north. "We see no white-eyes," the squat one said.

"One follows. A breed. All the others I killed and left for the buzzards. When he comes, I will kill him."

Seeing the warriors scanning the trail north gives Chato some of his courage back. He watches as they look at one another, conversing not with words but with their eyes. Soon the squat one barks an order and two of the younger warriors disappear without a sound.

"We will see if you speak the truth."

"He is coming," Chato replies as he stares after the two departing warriors.

The strong hands of the tall, scarred warrior pull Alchuni from the ground and sit her back on the tired gelding. Chato reaches for his rifle but another warrior takes it and motions him to follow. Alchuni cannot be sure but it seems the warrior leading her horse mouthed the word "Massai" before he turned from her. Did she really see it or was her tired and frightened mind playing tricks on her? Do the warriors know of her Massai? All her life she heard stories about the fierce Apache still living in Mexico. Now they are only too real.

Pulling at the leather straps that bound his food pouch, Massai knows it is empty. He will have to hunt soon. To go without food will weaken him and he has to be strong when he catches Chato. Kneeling beside a cold spring, he cups water in his hand and drinks while his eyes search the surrounding canyons. He is not far from the border. The village of the bronco Apache living here is near. Old Massai briefly described the area but he did not specify any landmarks.

Something catches his eye as he scoops another handful of water. Massai freezes. Something or someone is moving down the trail. Slipping cautiously up the slope, Massai positions himself behind a large cedar. Here he can overlook the trail yet remain unseen.

Two Apache warriors approach trotting easily, their eyes trained on the path ahead. Massai realizes they are backtracking Chato's trail. Their pace does not slow when they reach the place where Massai left the trail. He was lucky. If he was still on horseback, the warriors could have spotted his tracks.

Waiting until the warriors are out of sight, Massai slips back to the trail and continues south. Careful to watch his back trail, Massai picks up his pace, trying to put as much distance between him and the warriors. He knows that once they pick up his trail, they will not lose it.

Two hours later, he is studying the place where Chato pulled Alchuni from the horse. In the sand, Massai can see that a struggle took place. He also notices several new tracks. When the horse moved again, the new tracks followed. Massai becomes worried. Did the warriors he saw and some of their band come upon Chato and Alchuni and overtake them? It is possible they took Chato and his captive in to protect them. Massai knows either way he will have to be even more careful. He keeps to the horse tracks, following them wherever they might lead.

A hint of wood smoke drifts to Massai. He almost stumbles into the rancheria of the bronco Apache. From a small niche in the rocks, Massai can see the village. About two dozen wickiups were well concealed. Two sentries are posted on rocky ledges above. A few more feet would have brought him into their view.

He looks toward the fading sun. Soon he will be able to slip into the rancheria under the cover of darkness. For now, he will watch, making sure there are no other sentries.

Fulton Frasier shakes his head in rage. He is in the vast wilderness of the Sierra Madre and he is lost. It was foolish for him to set out for the border alone. Although he still feels right about his decision not to drag his men into Mexico without a scout. He does not need his men to do his killing for him. When he finally catches up with whoever kidnapped his daughter, he intends to kill him.

Once before, many years ago, he lost a woman to the Apache. He finally gotten her back, but the Army denied him the privilege of killing her abductors. Geronimo and his followers were sent east, out of reach of his avenging hands. Rumors were that Alchise was involved, but both Major Bishop, Sergeant Bishop back then, and James Davis, the Chief of Scouts, assured him there was no truth to the rumors.

This time it will be different. He will have his revenge and never again will any man, red or white, attack his family. He never got over the loss of his wife and the helplessness of not being able to avenge it. Now he means to kill. He will kill for Audrey, and now, finally, he will kill for Jean. He is lost in his murderous thoughts when a heavy slug from a high-powered rifle slams into him, knocking him from his saddle. He lands face down in the sandy soil.

Hot fire sears his side as he feels something wet and sticky flow against his skin. The sound of clinking metal approaches. He knows the sound. It is the almost musical sound of silver spurs. Frasier reaches slowly for his pistol but only finds an empty holster. His searching eyes find his pistol in the sand an arm's length away.

"Try gringo," a voice above him said. "The pistolo, she is no so far

away." Frasier turns his head and looks up at the huge sombrero shading the face that looks down on him. "Try, Señor Frasier, it is your last chance."

The voice is familiar to Frasier but he cannot place it. Focusing his eyes to peer under the sombrero, he sees the dark sneering face of a Mexican staring down at him. His white teeth flash as he glares at the helpless rancher.

"Joaquin?"

"Si, Señor Frasier. It is I, Joaquin. You send for me, no? I come pronto."

Frasier groans and tries to sit up. "You bastard, why did you shoot me?"

A faint sigh of sadness escapes the Mexican's mouth. "Ah, Señor, I will tell you but Joaquin no think you like hear this thing."

"Tell me, damn you." Frasier clutches the wound in his gut.

"No matter, this will be last thing you hear, anyway."

Frasier watches the Mexican pull a large skinning knife from its sheath. He raises himself up onto his knees.

"You remember, Señor Frasier, when I worked for you last? Your gringo foreman, Red, he beat Joaquin badly for talking to Señorita Audrey. Now I am told she is in Mexico. Now she will be Joaquin's woman. You think of this Señor before you die."

Frasier swears and tries to lunge at the man but only succeeds in falling back to the ground. "Damn your hide to hell."

"Hell, maybe but the pretty Señorita will make it heaven for a while. You should thank me, Señor. It is I, Joaquin who will rescue her from the Apache devils." An evil laugh erupts from the man as he steps on the reaching hand of Frasier.

"Where's Red now?"

"Ah, Señor Red, Joaquin does not think he will work for you no more." A red mop of hair falls at the rancher's side. "Too bad. Red, him no need hair no more, I think."

Frasier turns on his side and tries to draw back as the Mexican steps toward him, the blade shining in the sunlight. He cannot leave Audrey alone to suffer at the hands of this devil. Frasier did not even know about the beating. He thought Joaquin just up and quit without a word. At least that was what Red and the men said.

He looks up at the crazy Mexican. "I'll pay you anything, Joaquin. Just stay away from her."

Joaquin laughs as he raises the knife in a high arch. The laugh is high pitch and shrill. "Soon, Señor Frasier, I will have payment enough. Think of Joaquin's hands on her as you die."

The sneer on Joaquin's face freezes as two arrows penetrate deeply into his broad back, buckling him at his knees. He pitches forward, dead before he hit the ground.

Frasier sees two Apache warriors advancing on him and knows he will die next.

CHAPTER
TWENTY-SIX

Massai waits patiently as the sun slowly fades in the western sky. Villagers sit around the now visible campfires. He counted only two sentries but has concern there might be others yet unseen. He will have to enter the village and rescue Alchuni before sunup. His only opportunity will be under the cover of darkness, but even then, his chance of success is slim. If he fails, they will both die.

Silently, he moves forward as a cool breeze chills him to the bone. Not only is he cold but his body is tired and hungry. He thinks of Alchuni in one of the nearby wickiups, possibly still held captive by Chato, and it strengthens his resolve.

A shrill whistle from one of the sentries causes Massai to duck behind a small brush pile. He holds his breath as two horses trot past. Massai can tell one horse is a pale color but he cannot make out the riders. He slips forward, covering most of the distance to the rancheria while attention is on the new arrivals.

Crawling under the dense limbs of a cedar at the edge of the village, Massai watches as they ease a body to the ground from one of the horses. Several warriors gather around the still form. With the fires of the wickiups illuminating the village with dim light, Massai is able to see the body is a white man. His eyes strain to see who it is. A lump catches in Massai's throat as he realizes the body on the ground is that of Frasier. Was there another fight and are his men dead? Did Macy live long enough to tell Frasier about Audrey? Unanswered questions race through Massai's mind while he watches from his hiding place. He knows Frasier must be alive or the warriors would not have brought him back to the village.

In a snap decision, Massai makes a bold move. He jumps to his feet and briskly walks toward the group surrounding Frasier. The warriors are unaware of his presence until a sharp whistle snaps their attention away from Frasier and toward the fast approaching unknown warrior. Immediately, several rifles point toward Massai, causing him to stop in his tracks.

A squat warrior with white paint splashed across his nose approaches him and eyes the talisman around his neck. "Are you the one the girl calls Massai?"

"I am Massai."

The squat warrior nods in acknowledgment. "She said you would come. I am Otoe, Chief of this rancheria. We were expecting you."

"You knew I was in the mountains?"

Otoe nods. "We knew. Old Massai sent us smoke to tell of your coming."

Massai lets out a brief sigh of relief. At least they let him come in on his own. To be found hiding would have been a disgrace. "And the girl?" He asks.

Otoe points to a wickiup. "There, resting."

"Did the Mescalero hurt her?"

"No, she is not hurt, only tired. She is a fighter."

As much as he wants to go to Alchuni, Massai knows he must attend to Frasier first. He is Audrey's father and his mother's husband. He studies the faces of the other warriors. "Is the white-eye dead?"

"Soon he will be," Otoe answers.

Massai moves close to Frasier and kneels by him to feel for a pulse.

"I'm alive," Frasier said, his voice barely audible. He opens his eyes and looks at Massai, recognizing him.

"Why are you here?" Massai asks him in English. He can see Frasier is in considerable pain.

"Audrey," Frasier chokes. "Where is she?"

Massai is surprised. "Audrey? Didn't Macy tell you?"

Frasier closes his eyes.

"I sent her to safety, to Alchise, after the fight in the canyon. He will bring her home. I told Macy to send you back to your ranch."

Frasier shakes his head slightly. "Macy is dead. He said nothing." He closes his eyes again then opens them and locks them onto Massai's eyes. "You swear she is safe."

"Yes, Audrey is safe." He grasps Frasier's hand and grips it as he speaks. "Now we must get you out of here."

"You killed a white man. You cannot go back. The Army will hunt you."

Massai said nothing. Instead, he stands and walks back to Otoe. "I have come here to kill a man," he said to Otoe, switching to Apache. "First I ask you to fix this man's wound. He did not come here to harm you. He was wronged."

"And the man you have come to kill?" Otoe asks.

"The Mescalero dog that stole my woman from her village. It is my right to ask for his blood."

Otoe glances toward the wickiup, which holds Alchuni. "You will kill a man for stealing a squaw."

"Not just for stealing my woman but for killing my brother Ponce, leader of the Wild Ones, and for leading many strong young warriors to their deaths then deserting them like the coward he is."

"But we do not know this to be true."

Massai rises to his full height. "If you think I lie, ask the woman."

Otoe studies the solemn young face in the fire's glow and knows he speaks the truth. "Why do you wish to save this white-eye?"

"He is my sister's father."

Confusion covers the face of the squat leader. "I do not understand."

"She and I have the same mother, but my father is Alchise."

The old medicine man chants steadily through the night as he works on Frasier's wound. As dawn breaks, he stares across the wickiup at Massai, who stayed by the rancher's side all night. The old man smiles a toothless grin at Massai.

"I married Alchise and Tawano many moons ago. We were free, wild as buffalo. You were born in the hidden valley, I remember well. You screamed much, scare horses, keep warriors and Geronimo awake." The old man chuckles.

Massai blinks at him in the dimness of the wickiup. "You were there?"

The medicine man nods. "Warriors want scalp of small Massai, but other Massai was so proud Alchise name you Massai, he said he'd kill any who harmed you." The old man chuckles again and turns his attention back to Frasier.

"You were with Geronimo?"

The old man tosses his head toward the door. "Otoe, too. Many here with Geronimo. Many there in hidden valley when you born."

Frasier moans.

"Will the white-eye live, old one?" Massai asks.

The shaggy gray head nods. "Yes, he live. You sleep now."

"Thank you," Massai said.

"No thank me, young Massai." The medicine man looks down at the white man. "He thank you. If not your friend, I not save."

Massai nods in understanding and stands to go.

As soon as he leaves the wickiup, he steps into the path of Chato. The two were about to fight until several warriors intervene, holding them apart.

"Eii-ya." The stout arm of Otoe falls between the two enemies, stopping them. Otoe looks into Chato's eyes. "Massai demands the blood rite," he tells him. "Will you fight?"

Chato hesitates. He has no choice, either fight or lose face. He will kill the breed and Alchuni will be his. He will have the respect of the warriors. "I will fight."

Otoe nods at each of them. "When the sun is high, you will fight to the death."

Shrugging loose from the warriors holding him, Massai spots Alchuni in the company of some of the other women. He starts toward her but Otoe stops him.

"If you kill the Mescalero, then she will be yours. Until then, she belongs to no one." Massai looks at Alchuni, then at Otoe. "Come," Otoe said. "We will talk."

Nodding at Alchuni, Massai follows the squat chief into the dark interior of his wickiup. Otoe's wickiup is larger than most. As Chief of the rancheria, his responsibility is to take in visitors or care for anyone losing their home or possessions. Massai sits cross-legged across from Otoe.

These people are poor and the wickiup shows it. Thin blankets cover the walls, and the eating and cooking utensils they possess are old and battered. Only the weapons to hunt and make war with are in good condition. Bows, knives, and levered rifles stand neatly stacked near the opening of the wickiup, readily available at a moment's notice.

As Massai looks around the Chief's wickiup, his eyes meet Otoe. "Yes, my young friend," Otoe said, "we are poor but we are free. We do not wear the metal tags of the white man. Nor do we drink his poison."

Massai understands. He watched Ponce, Wolf, Dosenay, and the other Wild Ones throw their lives away because of the white man's restrictions and free-flowing alcohol.

"Sometimes," Otoe continues, "when the young cry for food or the Mexicans come and raid and kill, I think maybe better if we go north and surrender to the white-eyes. Then maybe grow fat and lazy and live in peace at the place they call San Carlos."

Massai can only listen and nod as Otoe speaks. The sadness in the Chief's voice is thick enough to touch. He tries to understand. Until coming to live with Alchise, Massai always lived in luxury. He never had to hide, run, or go hungry. Even life with Alchise, though not luxurious, is a life without want.

Thinking back to his days with Davis, he was ashamed. It was not James Davis' fault. He tried his best to keep the young J. Mason Davis in check, but the task proved too great. Here in Otoe's village are people who truly suffered. He had known Otoe only a short time, but already he feels the pain the man carries for his people.

"You are the young one who carries the name of Massai," Otoe said, "but you are from the white world. You lived among them. I ask you now because your heart is good toward the Apache people. I need your advice. I believe you have wisdom far beyond your years."

Massai hesitates. What can he say? Who is he to advise this great warrior? He is just a spoiled half-breed who was rejected by the white man's world. Now, people's lives are at stake.

"I am not the one to give you advice, Otoe." Massai shakes his head slowly. "I am just learning about life. You should seek out Alchise or the old Massai for such matters."

Otoe nods sadly. "The old warrior says we should stay here. Alchise offers no advice. I not know what is good for our people. Once we were many. We fought bravely against the whites and the Mexicans. Slowly, our numbers have fallen. Some slipped back to the reservation. Now we are few here, only about thirty families. We are hunted like animals and we starve. We cannot defend our women and children against our enemies." Otoe shakes his head in despair.

"I cannot tell you what to do but Alchise is a friend to the chief of the white-eyes at the fort. If you wish, I will talk with Major Bishop. He seems like a fair man."

Otoe looks puzzled. "You say, young Massai, that a white Army man is fair?"

"This one is. He does not hate the Apache."

"And the agent, who runs the reservation, is he fair?"

Massai shrugs. "This I cannot say. I have not met him."

Otoe looks deeply into Massai's eyes. "If the Mescalero does not kill you then maybe you will talk for us."

Massai smiles. "He will not kill me but I ask, Otoe, why did you not let us fight till the sun is high?"

The Chief smiles. "You had much anger, my young friend. Not good to fight with anger. Now you are calm, more careful. You will fight smarter."

Massai smiles back. "Thank you. You are a wise chief."

Otoe nods his acknowledgement of the compliment. He took a liking to this young warrior. "I have fought many times over a woman. Some were worth it, some not. However, this is for sure, if you die, you will never know."

Massai laughs. It is the first time he laughed in many days. It relaxes him and he feels ready for whatever will come.

Alchuni steps from her wickiup and looks up at the sky. The sun is high and it is time. Pulling herself straight, she walks though the village toward the throng of warriors gathering at the far side. Chato is standing alone, off to one side.

Alchuni approaches Chato with her eyes blazing. "I, Alchuni, daughter of Salto, have come to watch you die." She spits at his feet and turns to join the other women.

The hate dripping from her words humiliates Chato. He can feel the villagers' eyes on him. Anger blazes in his heart. He will kill the breed and he will possess Alchuni. He does not care that she hates him. Once she is his, she will pay for his humiliation.

Otoe and Massai, standing nearby, also hear Alchuni's words. Otoe nudges Massai, "This one will make you a good wife."

Holding two knives high in the air, the old medicine man turns to the four corners of the earth chanting in each direction. Then reaching down, he grabs a handful of earth and tosses it into the air.

Across the way, Chato flexes the muscles in his arms and sneers, "I am not wounded this time, breed. Soon you will be dead and I will have the woman."

Otoe leans in behind Massai and whispers, "Be calm, my friend. Remember, fight smart, not with anger."

Each man holds a razor sharp skinning knife. Their eyes lock. The sun meets its zenith and the medicine man raises his war club. "Ya!" It commences.

Both warriors circle warily. Warriors, women, children, everyone in the village watch as the two battling warriors feign and parry. Alchuni catches her breath. No one supports Chato but they respect him as a fighter. Alchise taught Massai well, but the Mescalero is more experienced in knife combat. He is aggressive, while Massai is content to parry and move away from the darting knife of Chato.

Chato makes a lunge. His blade flashes in the sun and blood trickles down the arm of Massai. Massai backs up a few steps and reconsiders his opponent a moment. He remembers Otoe's words. He decides that to fight smart, speed is more important than strength. With knives, a slow or awkward move can bring sudden death. Sweat is running down his chest and arms. Chato lunges quickly again, this time leaving a red stain across Massai's chest.

Chato grins. He easily avoids Massai's blade. Onlookers quietly watch. They know Massai is in trouble and Alchuni turns away in tears. Otoe stands as a statute, his face a mask, his eyes missing nothing.

Again, Chato's knife slashes out and again it connects with flesh. "I will cut you into small pieces for the buzzards, breed," he taunts.

Several times, Massai tries to hit Chato but the lightning speed of his opponent's knife keeps him at bay. The Mescalero is crafty. He will take his time and wear Massai down, which each cut draining his blood and weakening him.

Chato lunges again. This time Massai falls to the sandy ground and kicks the legs out from under the Mescalero. Rolling with the quickness of a cat, Chato springs to his feet causing Massai's knife to bite the ground where Chato fell.

"You are too slow, breed," Chato taunts.

The sun beats down on the two warriors as they cautiously circle each other. Chato repeatedly lunges, taking the offensive, while Massai retreats to avoid the blade's razor sharp edge. Massai feigns another kick. When Chato dodges it, Massai catches him with a powerful forearm, sending the Mescalero reeling to the ground. Before he can recover, Massai's blade finds Chato's left shoulder. Massai finally draws Chato's blood.

The villagers shout their encouragement. Chato makes his first mistake. Both men taste the hot steel. Frantically, Chato attacks, slashing and stabbing at Massai, who can only retreat from the maniacal onslaught. On one big thrust, Massai makes a desperate grab for Chato's wrist and clamps an iron grip around it.

"Now who's too slow?" He yells into Chato's face. Taught muscles bunch in Massai's shoulders and forearms as he twists the wrist behind his opponent's back until Chato screams in pain.

Massai drops his knife and uses his other hand to grab Chato's throat. Loosening his grip on Chato's wrist, he clamps onto his inner thigh and picks the struggling Mescalero up over his head. In one last display of massive strength, Massai slams him down across his extended knee. The sound of snapping bones is drowned out by a scream of agony and one last guttural gasp from Chato's crushed throat. Dropping the dead man, Massai steps back. Blood covers his body from his oozing wounds.

The villagers are silent, standing in awe of the strength of the young warrior and the spectacle of death they just witnessed.

Alchuni breaks from the crowd and runs to him. The villagers cheer as she leads her victorious warrior away from the battlefield to a small stream that borders the village. There she cleans his wounds.

Massai and Alchuni sit across from each other before the small fire in front of Otoe's wickiup. Massai's wounds are now covered with salve from the old medicine man. There will be scars, physical memories tying him to Chato and the Wild Ones forever.

Frasier's injury is clean and no infection. The big rancher is strong and he will recover quickly. Soon they will head north to the border and the fate that awaits them. Two Apache scouts from San Carlos brought word that Major Bishop is camped on the border and waiting for Massai to cross. If he does not, Bishop threatens to pursue him into Mexico.

Three days passed since his fight with Chato. Massai's wounds are beginning to heal and Frasier is getting stronger. Otoe arranges for the old medicine man to perform a traditional Apache marriage for Massai and the young maiden, Alchuni. The young half-breed from the east has grown to manhood. He is a full Chiricahua warrior and now a husband.

CHAPTER

TWENTY-SEVEN

Frasier rests easily on the travois they made for him. Looking over to where Massai stiffly walks from the wickiup, he smiles. The old hatred was gone. He understands the people he had always hated, but now because of one young man, he also comes to respect the Apaches. This young man rescued his daughter and now saved his life. Frasier is a changed man.

Otoe watches with concern as Massai nears. "My friend walks like a turtle. Slower maybe."

Massai groans as he looks up at the back of the gelding. It will be painful to mount the tall horse. Looking down at Frasier resting on the travois, he smiles. "Maybe, I'll ride with you," he said in English.

The rancher grins. "You would be welcome." He did not see the fight with Chato, but he heard about it from Alchuni.

Massai is not surprised at the friendliness in the man's voice. For three days, they spent much time together. They came to know what is in each other's hearts. Concerned about Massai's safety, Frasier counsels him to remain with Otoe until he talks to Bishop so he can straighten things out. Massai is more concerned about Alchise and Audrey. He needs to know they are well. He intends to finish what he set out to do.

Massai mounts his horse gritting his teeth, holding back any moans of pain. Once settled and ready to ride, he looks down into Otoe's upraised eyes and extends his arm. "We will meet again, my friend."

Otoe nods. "My warriors will see you safely to the border then wait for Major Bishop's words."

With Alchuni mounted behind him and the travois in the rear, Massai turns his new bay gelding, a wedding gift from Otoe, toward the trail that leads into the passes.

"Wait," calls Frasier when the travois is alongside Otoe.

When the horse halted, Frasier holds out his hand to Otoe. "I have never been a friend of the Apache," he tells the Chief. "We have had our differences but all that has changed. You saved my life. If Major Bishop will not allow your people on the reservation, come to my ranch. It is large. I will welcome you. All of you."

Otoe understands some of his words but not all. He looks to Massai, who translates for him into Apache.

"Will this not cause you trouble?" Otoe asks in Apache, which Massai translates.

"We will work it out." After hearing Frasier's last words, Otoe takes the offered hand and they shake.

The trail to the border is as Massai remembers it. Otoe's warriors ride front and back to protect them from Mexican soldiers and banditos. Frasier winces but refuses to complain when the trail got bumpy.

Jean and Audrey occupy his thoughts and he is eager to get home. Nearing the border, Otoe's warriors hold them up and scout the trail leading to American soil. Massai sits the bay gelding and listens. A gentle breeze blows through the cedars alongside the trail as a hawk swoops down. Turning, he looks back at the mountains. It seems peaceful but he knows a lot of blood was shed on both sides of the border.

Returning as silently as they left, Otoe's warriors return with news that Major Bishop and his men were waiting just on the other side of the border.

"Good," Massai tells them. "We will go but I will send word back from Bishop."

The dragging travois bounces softly on the trail as it passes to the north and draws near to the Army camp. Massai stops the bay and studies the row of white tents that line the trail. They are spotted. Soldiers take position with their arms ready. Apache scouts sit their horses expectantly. They saw the destruction behind them in the canyons, now they want to see the young warrior, Massai, who is fast becoming a legend among the Chiricahua.

Massai gives Alchuni a reassuring look and kicks his horse forward. He is nervous but does not want it to show. He was raised with whites but now he is more Indian than he ever was white.

He can make out the large frame of Major Bishop standing at the front of his men. All eyes are on him, waiting for him.

CHAPTER

TWENTY-EIGHT

Mounted scouts and foot soldiers surround them quickly as they cross the border. A soldier snatches the Henry from Massai's hand and several rifles aim toward him. The Apache scouts remain apart, observing the young warrior with respect. A corporal approaches and jerks Massai bodily from the gelding causing Alchuni to fall to the ground.

"Hold up!" Yells Frasier, raising himself up on the travois. "Can't you see the boy's hurt bad?"

"Boy, hell," the corporal snaps. "He killed the scout Macy and a dozen others a few miles from here."

Major Bishop approaches. He holds out a hand and helps Alchuni to her feet. "That'll be all," he said to the corporal, dismissing him.

"Yes, Sir." The corporal let go of Massai and retreats.

"Let me have his rifle," Bishop said to the soldier who took it. The Henry passes into the Major's huge hand. "Massai, come with me. You men bring Mr. Frasier and the girl to my tent."

Massai turns to Alchuni and gives her a reassuring look. From behind her, he spots a woman coming from one of the tents. It is Jean Frasier, Tawano, his mother. She rushes to where the soldiers were helping her husband from the travois.

"Let me be," Frasier said, shoving the helping hands of the soldiers away.

He turns to Massai. "Massai, come here and give your stepfather a helping hand."

"Yes, sir," Massai said, and went to the rancher. Slipping one of Frasier's arms over his shoulder, he helps him hobble to the Major's tent. Alchuni rushes to Frasier's other side and wraps her arm around his waist to help. Jean Frasier and Bishop look on in surprise then join them inside. Once there, they lower Frasier into a chair and make him comfortable.

Bishop shakes his head in amazement. "Well, I see you two have become real chummy since I last saw you."

"Wait a minute, Major," interrupts Frasier. "I'm sure you have questions, but I haven't laid eyes on my wife or heard anything about my daughter since all this started."

Jean Frasier wraps her arms lovingly around the rancher and kisses him warmly. Smiling, she looks into his face. "Audrey's fine. She is home at the ranch now."

At the news of his daughter's safe return, tears begin to form at the corner of Frasier's eyes, but he blinks them back. "Good." He reaches up and strokes his wife's face tenderly. "Now, woman, greet your son and his new wife."

Again, both the Major and Mrs. Frasier are at a loss for words. Jean Frasier looks at Massai and then back at her husband. Frasier nods at her gently. "Yes, Jean, I know."

Jean Frasier turns to Massai, but hesitates, almost afraid to say or do anything. Massai steps forward, close to her, and she breaks down, taking him into her arms. She holds him a long time, crying as she did so. Massai, too, fights back tears as he embraces his mother for the first time.

Jean then turns to Alchuni and holds out her hands in welcome and Alchuni takes them. Speaking in Apache, she welcomes Alchuni as a daughter.

"English, Jean. Speak English so I can understand," Frasier said to her.

"But Alchuni doesn't speak English," Jean protests.

Alchuni steps forward and stands beside the rancher's chair. "I speak good English. Agency woman teach."

Massai's jaw drops. He had no idea Alchuni could speak English.

"Well since you all speak both English and Apache, guess I'll have to learn some Apache." Frasier smiles at everyone.

Major Bishop watches Frasier during the reunion of mother and son, looking for any sign of resentment but he sees none. Frasier truly seems a changed man. He picks up a cigar box and offers a cigar to both Frasier and Massai. Massai declines but both the Major and Frasier light up.

The Major summons his surgeon and watches as the doctor removes the bandages the old medicine man had applied. Examining the wound, the doctor looks over his spectacles at Frasier. "Who treated you, sir?"

"Reckon I was too weak to see."

"What's the matter, Mr. Nelson?" Bishop asks the surgeon.

"Nothing, Major, but someone did a fine piece of work on Mr. Frasier. I was just wondering what was put on the wound."

Bishop snorts through his nose. "Probably Apache salve. I've had it used on me many a time."

"Whatever it was, it did a good job." The surgeon addresses Frasier. "You're going to be right as rain in no time, sir."

"I'm glad Mr. Frasier is going to live. At least long enough to hang with Mr. Davis here." This time the Major is not smiling.

"What are the charges, Major?" Frasier asks. Massai stands quietly, waiting.

"Will murder do, sir?"

Jean Frasier stiffens. "Who did they kill, Major?"

"Take your pick. We buried bodies all the way from the Canyon of the Dead to the border."

Frasier's face hardens. "Neither I nor Massai killed anyone."

"I did." All eyes turn to Massai. "I killed the one called Wolf. He gave me no choice."

The Major takes several quick puffs from his cigar. "And who else?"

"No one on this side of the border, Major."

"And in Mexico, how many?"

Frasier starts to speak but Massai raises a hand to stop him. "One, the Mescalero called Chato. It was a fair fight."

Major Bishop looks at Massai thoughtfully. "I know you killed the warrior called Wolf back in the canyon." The Major removes the cigar from his mouth. "Because that Henry was once was my rifle, remember? I know how big a hole it'll put in a man." He replaces the cigar and speaks with it clenched between his teeth. "We figured out the Wild Ones and Bonham's bunch surprised each other and pretty much wiped one another out." Bishop looks directly at Massai. "What about the one called Ponce? He was shot twice, different rifles, yet someone took the time to cover him. I understand Ponce was your friend, son."

Massai understands the Major knows the Henry killed Ponce but he remains silent.

"Who killed Macy?"

Massai shrugs.

"Macy was dying when I reached him, Major," Frasier answers.

"You're lying, both of you!" The Major explodes as veins bulge in his neck.

"Lying, Major?" Frasier challenges. "My daughter was abducted by the Apaches who died in those canyons. No jury in Arizona will convict me of anything?"

Major Bishop studies Frasier a long time while puffing steadily on his cigar. "You're probably right about that, Frasier, but young Massai here is still under my jurisdiction."

"I'll vouch for him, Major."

"Do tell. Your riders gave me a different story. They say you set out to kill him."

Frasier swears. "Hell, my men are liquored up half the time and you know it."

Bishop pulls up a chair and sits down behind the makeshift desk in his tent. "We'll see."

He knows Frasier, guilty or not, will never be convicted under the circumstances. The girl was returned unharmed by Alchise, though Bishop is not clear how she came into his custody. The fight in the second canyon eliminated two of his problems, the gang that rode with Bonham and the Wild Ones. Massai killed two Apaches, two of the Wild Ones, but the Major has no problem with killing renegades who kidnapped a white girl. Macy is the only dead man he is not sure about, but the scout has enemies throughout the area. Finally, no one seems to be screaming for justice on behalf of any of the dead.

The Major scratches his head and smokes his cigar while he continues to think about everything. Young Massai probably saved the lives of both the rancher and his daughter. He should be considered a hero, not a murderer.

Massai approaches the Major's desk. "Major, I have some friends across the border that would like to turn themselves in and come to the reservation."

The Major looks up. "Friends, Massai? You mean bronco Apaches that have been killing and raiding for years below the border?"

Frasier rises up slightly from his chair. "You pompous old goat. Massai said friends and that's what they are. They saved my life."

"You mean they want to get the hell out of Mexico where they're getting killed off one by one." He turns to Frasier on the verge of a rage. "Sir, I'll thank you not to refer to me as an old goat. I'm in charge here, not you!"

"Alright, you old jackass."

"Well now, that's more like it." The two men grin at each other and an understanding passes between them.

The Major looks thoughtfully at Massai. "Okay, Massai, bring them in. I would like to see these friends of yours."

"Major," the young warrior said, pleased that the tension broke between Frasier and the Major. "They are as you say but now they seek peace and a life on the reservation."

Bishop gets up and motions to Massai to follow him outside. Turning the Henry over in his big hands, he sets it down casually against the tent wall.

"Frasier's right, Massai. No court in the land will convict him of killing an Apache. They haven't forgotten Geronimo, nor are they likely to for a long time. However, you are another matter. Macy's dead and I reckon I know who killed him but that won't do you any good." Bishop looks to where Alchuni sits quietly. "She's a good one. I think Bishop will be a good name for a boy, don't you, Massai?"

Massai nods and smiles. "A fine name, Major."

I need to get Alchise's rifle back to him but I don't know how, especially if you go to the stockade."

"It is a problem."

"Well, I'd better send a runner for your friends across the river."

"Otoe is the Chief. He's waiting for your decision."

The Major mulls the name over in his mind. "Otoe, I have heard that name before."

"He is a good man, Major. You can trust him."

"I hope so, Massai. I just got rid of one problem with the deaths of the Wild Ones. I don't need another." The Major looks across the land toward the border. "Guess I'd better send that runner." He looks at the rifle leaning against the tent. "Sure wish I could get that rifle back to Alchise."

Massai watches as the big man strolls casually toward the Apache scouts, taking his soldiers with him. Losing no time, Massai picks up the Henry and enters the tent. He motions to Alchuni. "Come, we must go quickly."

Before he leaves, he faces Frasier. No words are spoken. A mutual respect had grown between the men that needs no words. After a strong handshake, Massai heads for the door.

Jean Frasier follows them outside and hugs them both.

"Tell your father," she tells Massai, her eyes moist. "Tell him thank you."

Massai quickly unhitches the travois and helps Alchuni up on the big bay. Massai mounts gingerly behind her. He looks down at Jean Frasier. "I have never known you as my mother but I would like to. Soon, I will visit the Frasier ranch."

Jean Frasier watches as the young couple quietly slips out of the Army camp.

CHAPTER
TWENTY-NINE

S teadily, they ride to the north but without urgency. There is no hurry. Massai's wounds are healing and they are happy to be spending time alone.

They ride into the small canyon where the shootout between the Wild Ones and the Bonham gang occurred. Massai and Alchuni come across many graves with makeshift markers where Major Bishop and his men buried the dead. Massai spots a silver concho belt hanging from a cross that marks one grave. The belt was worn by Slade Bonham, the man who killed Bosworth. He remembers when he met Bonham on the train. It was less than a year ago but seems a lifetime ago to Massai. So much happened in such a short time and he went through so many changes. The train was from a different lifetime.

So many died in this canyon, friend and foe alike. Massai studies each grave. Some do not bear crosses but have sticks with feathers attached to them with bits of leather. They are probably the graves of the Wild Ones. Bishop gave each one a proper burial, the white and the Apache treated equally in the end.

With one final glance around the canyon, Massai turns his back on it forever. This was the destiny of these men, but not his. His destiny lay ahead, still to be determined. Leaving the canyon behind, he and Alchuni ride toward the White River.

Four days of easy riding finds them close to Alchise's rancheria. Massai knows he will not be there. The warrior will be waiting for his son in the secret valley. Old Massai would have given Alchise his message.

Something moves near the bank of the river. Pushing Alchuni forward, closer to the neck of the horse, Massai shoulders the Henry and waits. A lone figure rides out from a stand of pines and waves. Massai recognizes the proud erect rider coming toward them and lowers his rifle.

"Massai," he calls in greeting.

The old warrior pulls up beside them. He studies the healing scars on Massai's body and the girl with him and nods his head. He knows their meaning.

"Aye, young one, it is good to see you."

"And you."

"Your father waits for you and your woman."

"Is he well?"

Old Massai nods. "He is well. My daughter, Kittohaya, cares for him." Old Massai greets Alchuni. "Salto, too, is well and has returned to the village." Alchuni smiles with happiness at the news.

Massai is pleased. "It is good. I am happy for them and Kittohaya is a good woman."

Old Massai comes closer and looks into the young man's eyes as he speaks. "Your mother, Tawano, is a good woman, too, Massai, but she is white and she is married to another. She can never be the wife of Alchise again." Massai nods. "Your mother cares for you as much as she does your half sister, but you live the life of an Apache. You are in different worlds."

"I understand," Massai said, holding his head up.

The old warrior watches him and knows the young man does understand. "When you are well," he tells him, "I will come again and we will hunt the cougar. Alchise says you can kill a cougar and a deer with one arrow. This I would like to see."

Massai smiles. "Where do you go?"

"Back into the mountains."

Massai looks at the old warrior. "They have come in, the bronco Apaches. Otoe speaks with Nantan Bishop."

"Then I will visit others."

"There are more?" Massai is surprised.

The old warrior and friend of Geronimo laughs and kicks his horse into a hard lope. Massai and Alchuni hear the cry of a great Chiricahua Apache as he rides out of sight.

"Come," Massai said to Alchuni. "We will be home before dark if we hurry." He turns the bay onto the path that leads to the valley and to Alchise, his father.

Once in the valley, Massai is pleased to see Alchuni is as enchanted by its beauty as he was on his first visit. Perhaps their children will be born here, as he was.

They stop near the small stream and dismount. Massai smiles as he watches Alchise emerge from the rebuilt wickiup. A sturdy, handsome woman comes out after him. Together they walk across the meadow toward the young couple. Alchise is moving slowly but he looks well. His head, as always, held high.

Far out across the lush green meadow, a blur of chestnut catches Massai's eye and he hears the thundering hooves of the stallion as he races the wind.

Massai takes Alchuni's hand. They are home.

THE END

CPSIA information can be obtained at www.ICGtesting.com
Printed in the USA
BVOW09s1028040515

398845BV00026B/344/P